THE
LYING
WOODS

THE
LYING
WOODS

ASHLEY ELSTON

HYPERION

LOS ANGELES NEW YORK

First Edition, November 2018
10 9 8 7 6 5 4 3 2
FAC-020093-18362
Printed in the United States of America

Text is set in Adobe Garamond Pro, Arial Narrow, Avenir/Monotype;
Accolade Serial; Flyerfonts Filler/House Industries
Designed by Maria Elias

Library of Congress Cataloging-in-Publication Data
Names: Elston, Ashley, author.
Title: The Lying Woods / Ashley Elston.
Description: First edition. • Los Angeles ; New York : Hyperion, 2018. • Summary: Owen Foster
is pulled from his elite New Orleans boarding school when his father's assets are seized and,
back in his small town, begins to piece together his father's past despite mounting danger.
Identifiers: LCCN 2017058435 • ISBN 9781368014786 (hardcover)
Subjects: • CYAC: Mystery and detective stories. • Fathers and sons—Fiction. • Secrets—
Fiction. • Embezzlement—Fiction. • Family life—Louisiana—Fiction. • Louisiana—Fiction.
Classification: LCC PZ7.E5295 Pre 2018 • DDC [Fic]—dc23
LC record available at https://lccn.loc.gov/2017058435

Reinforced binding

Visit www.hyperionteens.com

For Miller, Ross, and Archer

Excerpt from the diary of Leonard Trudeau:

Step one—Cleaning the orchard

Just before the pecans are ready to fall, it is imperative to first clean the ground beneath each and every tree. The old limbs and leaves should be removed along with any other clutter that may have accumulated in the last year. This is the best way to prepare for the harvest, giving the next crop of pecans a clean space in which to land.

1

I wake to a Post-it note stuck to my forehead. Yanking it off, it takes a few seconds before I'm alert enough to focus on the words.

PAYBACK'S A BITCH

Lunging out of the bed, my legs get twisted up in my blanket and I end up on the floor. Face-first.

What did he do?

In the never-ending prank war with Jack Cooper, I struck last when I replaced the photograph he took for Fine Art Appreciation with one from last month's *Playboy*. Mr. Wheeler gave him five Penance Halls and I've been looking over my shoulder ever since.

Jack's side of the room is empty. The drapes are pulled back and his bed is made but his MacBook is gone as well as his lacrosse gear.

What did he do?

Crossing the room, I stand on the chair against the wall and lean forward so I can open the door without being in front of it. The residence building is the newest on the grounds, but it's still old by most standards. The heavy wooden door looks like it could withstand any assault, but all you need is a wire coat hanger and the antique lock springs open. Every night, we wedge this chair under the handle so we can sleep without fear of what the other guys will do to us, but it won't protect me from Jack, who sleeps five feet away.

I push the door open but nothing swings down and hits me . . . no water comes pouring in . . . nothing.

No way I'm going to the showers; that's what he expects me to do. I throw on my uniform, do a quick search through my backpack to make sure he didn't stick anything in there, and then head toward the main building, grabbing my phone on the way out. I overslept so no time for breakfast. But that's okay. Maybe he was planning on getting me back there.

I find my friends just as I'm heading into Hunter Hall, but Jack isn't with them.

"What's up, O?" Ray asks, while he finishes off a croissant. Ray is a giant guy who's a genius on the lacrosse field but also made baking cool here at Sutton's, and most mornings his creations are the first to go. The way he feels about breakfast pastries is what he's most known for. Well, that and the ever-changing designs cut into the fade of his black hair. Right now it's a wave pattern in support of Tulane and the upcoming football game against Southern Mississippi. He even dyed the tips of his twists green. "What's on your face?" he asks.

My hand flies to my cheek. I didn't look in a mirror—did Jack draw something on me? A dick or a set of boobs? Turning, I catch my reflection in the glass case that holds all the athletic and academic trophies our school has won.

It's only a smear of toothpaste.

I rub my cheek until it feels raw. "Have y'all seen Jack?" I ask.

They all start mumbling as they look around and are surprised he's not with the group.

"He was just here," Sai adds.

Shit, this is going to be bad.

First hour is trig on the second floor of the main building. I only have a few classes with Jack and this isn't one of them, so I'm going to have to wait him out and pray it's nothing too humiliating.

My first thought when I see the headmaster motion for me to join him in the hall a few minutes after class starts is . . . This is it.

"Owen Foster, a word, please."

I take a deep breath and prepare myself for the worst. I'm halfway across the room when he holds up a hand, stopping me. "You may want to grab your things."

It's bad if I'm not coming back to class. I'm going to kill Jack.

I pass my friends on the way back to my desk and try to ignore their quiet jabs.

"Porn or pot?" Ray asks.

Sai leans back. "Or maybe they know you had that girl in your room the other night . . . what was her name?"

With my back to my teacher and the headmaster, I flip them off and whisper, "Tell Jack I'm going to kick his ass."

The walk down the main hallway to Dr. Winston's office is quiet except for the soft echo from our shoes when we hit the small sections of polished dark wood floors that peek between the islands of thick rugs. This building that houses the classrooms looks more like the interior of someone's home than a high school, and it was the main selling point for my parents when they dropped me off here at the beginning of middle school.

My mind runs through all of the things Jack could have done to get me back while I follow Dr. Winston into his office. But of all the things I'm prepared for, seeing my mother is not one of them.

I quickly scan the room for my dad, but it's empty except for her.

Jack's dead if he set me up for something so bad they called my parents. Dr. Winston motions for me to have a seat next to Mom in one of the empty chairs in front of his desk, but I can't move.

One look at Mom stops me cold. We both have the same out-of-control curly brown hair; normally hers is pulled back and tamed, but today it looks as wild as mine does. Her skin is pale even though we also share the perpetually tanned look and the dark circles under her eyes are new. And even though she's always been petite, it looks like she's lost weight. It's only been a few weeks since I've seen her, but she looks rough.

This isn't about something Jack did.

"What's wrong?" I ask still rooted in my spot just inside the office.

Is something wrong with Dad? Why is she here alone on a Tuesday morning looking like she's about to fall apart?

Dr. Winston puts a hand on my shoulder, nudging me toward the empty chair. I shake him off. "Just tell me. I can see it's bad. What is it?"

Mom sits up straighter and squares her shoulders as if she needs to physically prepare for this conversation. "Owen, please sit down."

I drop down in the seat hoping the second I do she'll spill it.

"What is wrong?" I ask, spitting out each word.

"This is about your dad," Mom starts but I interrupt her.

"Is he dead? Sick?" I hate this. I hate the sadness radiating off her. I hate how Dr. Winston won't look me in the eye. "Just say it. I can't stand this."

"He's not dead or sick," Dr. Winston answers. "But it is serious."

Mom takes a deep breath and then slowly exhales, stalling for every second.

"Your dad . . . has done something terrible. I got wind of it several weeks ago but just recently found out how bad it is. And he left. He left us to deal with what he's done."

My mind races. "What did he do?"

Mom gnaws on her bottom lip, not answering me or looking at me anymore. Seconds tick by and still nothing from her.

"What did he do?" I ask again.

"It's complicated. Very complicated. I don't even know where to start. . . ." Mom looks at Dr. Winston, her eyes pleading for help. Mom is always rock-solid, so it freaks me out to see her struggling with whatever it is she's trying to tell me.

"Owen, let me see if I can help your mother explain." Dr. Winston perches on the edge of his desk, arms crossed over his chest. He looks at Mom and asks quietly, "May I?"

She nods, then stares at him, emotionless.

Yeah. This is bad.

But instead of telling me what's going on, he asks me a question. "What do you know about your father's company?"

I lean back in my chair, frustrated. This is a stupid question. "They frack wells for oil and gas drilling."

"And business has been good over the last ten years," he adds. There's something about his tone that doesn't sit right. It makes me feel defensive although I have no idea where this is going.

"Yeah, you could say that," I answer.

Dad's business, Louisiana Frac, *has* done well over the last several years. A new natural gas shale was discovered and that discovery changed everything. Changed our town, changed the people in it. Changed Dad's company.

"You understand that stock options were offered to employees in exchange for the cash your dad needed so he could buy more equipment and hire more people?" Dr. Winston moves around his desk and sits in his chair, steepling his fingers in front of him.

I'm nodding along, trying to anticipate where he's going, but it's like my mind is stuck and I can't think past his next word.

Louisiana Frac went from being a small business to one of the biggest employers of our town. The men and women who have worked there for years, who worked there under my grandfather, now own a small part of the company. Everyone knows this. It's what brought our town back to life.

Mom won't look at me. She won't join the conversation. And I can't help but feel irritated that Dr. Winston is drawing this out.

"I know all of this. I just need you to tell me what Dad did," I say.

Dr. Winston's hands drop to his lap and he sits up a little straighter. "I'm trying to put this in context so you understand just how badly your father devastated your town. There are over two hundred people employed by Louisiana Frac . . . who own stock with Louisiana Frac."

Devastated my town? I'm out of the chair and pacing in a tight circle in front of his desk, silently begging for him to get to the point.

Dr. Winston rubs a hand across his mouth. "But your father has deceived the employees who worked so hard and invested so much to help build that company."

I'm shaking my head.

"Even though the company was making more money than it ever had, your father didn't manage it well. Not at all. In fact, it's more than that. There are accusations of embezzlement, hiding debt, nonpayment to suppliers, and environmental complaints."

I stop in front of his desk and say, "I don't believe my dad would do that."

Dr. Winston tilts his head to the side. "Well, there are several government agencies that believe he did. Your dad has disappeared and so has all of the money—the money from the bank accounts, the money from the employees' pensions, every last cent. It's estimated your dad ran off with millions. And not only have the employees lost their retirement money and are out of a job, they're also left holding stock in a company that is completely worthless. As of right now, Louisiana Frac is closed for business."

I wait for the rest of it. The part where all of this makes sense. "You're telling me that millions of dollars are gone and no one knows where it is and you think my dad did something wrong."

Dr. Winston leans forward in his chair and looks at me like I'm stupid. Or deaf. "Have you not been paying attention to what I've been saying?"

"Someone does know where it is," Mom says in a quiet voice, finally joining the conversation. "Your father. But he's gone, too."

"There has to be a mistake."

Her eyes find mine. "There's no mistake. I promise you, Owen, it's bad. It's worse than bad."

No. This is wrong. They have it wrong. "Maybe it was someone else. Maybe he was set up," I say.

"The authorities do believe there was someone else involved. No one believes he pulled this off without help, but they don't know who was helping him," Dr. Winston says, then throws a glance at Mom.

And Mom flinches like his comment actually hit her.

I can't hear this. I can't listen to this anymore. I have to get out of here. "Okay. Okay. Well, I'll go back to class now."

Mom puts her hand out, stopping me. A sliver of her usual confidence slipping into place. Something I haven't seen since I walked into the room. "I don't think you understand. You can't stay here."

Shaking my head, I say, "Of course I can. I haven't done anything wrong. Whatever is going on with him . . . is on him. Not me." If I can't stay here, I have to go home. No . . . not home. I'll have to go back to Lake Cane. But that isn't my home anymore. This school is. Sutton's has been my home since I was eleven years old.

I can't leave.

She stands and moves toward me but every step forward, I take one away from her. I can't look at her.

"You have to come home. There's no money for your tuition. There's no money for anything. Everything we had has been seized."

"No. This isn't right. There has to be some mistake." I take a step back and let out an unexpected laugh. "Did Jack do this? Oh, man. I've got to hand it to him. This is beyond any prank we've ever pulled. That has to be what this is."

Mom shakes her head slowly, back and forth. "This is no prank. And Jack has nothing to do with this. This is real. The things your father has done are real."

I want nothing more than to scream at her to stop lying. Dad wouldn't do this.

Turning to Dr. Winston, I say, "You have to let me stay. Surely, we've given you enough money over the years that you can let me stay."

Dr. Winston gives this bullshit expression like he feels bad for me. "It's not that simple, Owen."

"You can't stay here," Mom interrupts. "Your father used other people's money to send you to this school. And he used it to pay for all of the vacations and our home and our cars and jewelry. Everything we have was stolen from someone else. You can't stay here. I won't let you."

There's a knock on the door just before it opens. An older man pops his head inside and says, "Everything is loaded so I'm ready when you are."

Mom nods and thanks him just before he shuts the door.

"Who was that?" I ask. "And what does he mean, 'Everything is loaded'?"

"Dr. Winston? Can you give us a minute, please?" she asks. Dr. Winston nods, then leaves us alone in his office. She drops back down in the seat I just vacated. "That was Detective Hill. He's handling your dad's case. I don't think you understand how bad this is. Your father has disappeared but there are many people looking for him, including the local police, FBI, EPA, and IRS. And they are looking at me, wondering if I knew what he was doing since I worked there with him. They think I was in on it or I know where he is. . . ."

I lean against the wall, trying to absorb what she's saying.

"Detective Hill is along to make sure I come back. And to make sure your dad wasn't planning on meeting us here," she finishes quietly, then stands up and seems to be all business now. "They've already packed your room and apparently everything is loaded in the car. News of what he did is going public today. I thought it would be best for you to leave school before that happens so you wouldn't have to suffer any embarrassment in front of your friends."

"Just because I'm not here doesn't mean this won't be embarrassing."

Her hand rests on my shoulder. "This is going to be horrible for us both, but we have to remember, we didn't do anything wrong."

"I can't believe this is happening. Why did he do this?" I ask.

"I wish I knew. I'd like to think the first thing I'd do is ask him that but I'm afraid I would probably punch him instead."

She laughs quietly but it doesn't seem real. Nothing seems real.

"Do you know where he is? Have you talked to him?"

Shaking her head, she says, "No."

"When did he disappear?" I still don't believe he left willingly. There has to be an explanation for this. Something that makes this make sense.

"A couple of weeks ago," she whispers.

I push my chair, almost flipping it all the way over. "And you're just now telling me? You didn't think I should know about this sooner?"

"I didn't know what to do!" she yells. "I still don't. And I was hoping he would show up with some sort of explanation. I was hoping you would never have to find out what a coward and crook he is!"

Dr. Winston's head appears in the small window on his door. As much as I hate her screaming at me it's better than her blank expression earlier. She gives him a small wave, letting him know it's fine, but we're anything but fine.

"Owen, your dad was really stressed out but he wouldn't talk about it. He wouldn't talk to me no matter how many times I asked him what was wrong. The last time I saw him he was working late at the office. I haven't seen or heard from him since."

I nod but don't ask anything else.

Her eyes flash to the door again. "It's time to go."

"Give me a minute, please."

Mom nods and leaves the office but I don't move. While my mind races through everything she just told me, my hand slides into the front pocket of my backpack and pulls out a folded piece of paper I received in yesterday's mail on Dad's letterhead:

Hope things are going well at school. Just checking in on you. Thanksgiving break is coming up so you'll be home soon. Found a new place right outside of town called Frank's. Best burger around. They run a special on Wednesday nights. Maybe when you're in town during your break, we can check it out. It would be a great place to have dinner with your dad.

2

The news breaks when we're about thirty miles outside of Baton Rouge. We stop at a Denny's for a late lunch since neither of us had eaten breakfast and there are still a few hours on the road until we get home.

I'm not sure why I didn't tell Mom about the note. It's vague. He mentions my Thanksgiving break, which—if I was still enrolled in Sutton's—would start on the Wednesday before Thanksgiving. Is he trying to tell me he'll be at this place called Frank's on that Wednesday night? I have no idea why he'd want to meet up with me and not Mom, but for now I'm keeping it to myself.

Since I was eleven, I've only seen my dad on holidays, summer break, and the occasional parents' weekend at school. But even before that, he wasn't around as much as I wanted him to be. Work consumed him. It was his first love, the thing that got all of his attention and time, the thing he was the most scared to lose.

He told me all the time how he hadn't come from money so everything was sweeter now that he had it. And even though I didn't see him as much as I wanted to, he was generous with things: trips, cars, toys.

I'd like to think I know him. Know he wouldn't do this. Know he's not a thief. But the truth is, I know he would do anything to maintain our lifestyle. Anything.

I pull up the information for the restaurant on my phone and discover it's in the next town over from Lake Cane and the special on Wednesday night is two-for-one burgers starting at five. It's too close not to take the chance that he's sending me some sort of message.

"You're not touching your food," Mom says.

I nod toward her plate. "You're not touching yours, either."

We sit in silence. I push the mashed potatoes and gravy around until it's a soupy mess, mentally calculating what I would be doing at Sutton's if this hadn't happened. I'd be in English with Jack and Ray, thinking about lunch and practice after school and making plans for the weekend. My life is at Sutton's. My life is in New Orleans.

"Did you even think about what I'm missing at school? I had a cross-country meet this Saturday where I could have qualified for state. And lacrosse practice starts next week. And what about college? I'm in the middle of applications."

"I'm really sorry, Owen," she whispers.

"And what about my friends? It's not like they can just come over to visit."

Jack's family lives in Houston, where his dad runs a huge oil and gas company. I know Jack's dad did business with my dad on wells in this area, but I haven't heard if Dad screwed him, too. Ray is from New Orleans so even when he's not at school, he's still in the city. His dad is a sax player and his mom sings backup vocals for a jazz band and they're on tour more than they're at home, which is how he ended up in a boarding school in his hometown. Sai's family moved from Mumbai to Atlanta, where his dad is a neurosurgeon, and his family flies him home as often as they can.

Sutton's is our common ground. It's not like it would be easy for them to visit me or for me to see them.

"I'm sure we can figure out a way for y'all to get together," she says.

The TV in the corner of the room is on mute but it might as well be screaming through the room. An image pops up on the screen and my stomach drops. It's a picture of Dad and me with a little blurry spot over my face. We're both behind the wheel of the huge sailboat we rented for spring break last year in the Caribbean. The caption reads: *Louisiana CEO defrauds employees of millions, devastates small town* and underneath it says, *The Louisiana Enron?*

"Can we go?" I ask but don't wait for an answer. I'm out of my chair and halfway to the car before Mom catches up.

"Owen, wait. You can't run off like this."

I spin around, the gravel from the parking lot spraying in an arc behind me. "Do you believe he did it?"

Her shoulders slump and whatever fight she has left seems to bleed right out of her. "Everything points to him doing it. Everything."

I close the distance, my face close to hers. "But do you believe it?"

"I do. He's gone, Owen. Why would he run off if he didn't do it?"

I back away from her. Back away until my back hits the detective's Suburban. And then I notice him, several feet away. It's hard to make out his expression behind the mirrored sunglasses but it's close to pity. And I hate it.

"Owen, there hasn't been a mistake. There isn't anyone setting your dad up. He's not an innocent victim in this. He stole money from the people who worked for him. And then he ran."

The metal of the Suburban is warm, but it doesn't penetrate the cold that has settled inside me. I think about the note, torn into tiny pieces and buried in the diner's bathroom trash can. He owes us answers. He owes us the truth.

And if there's a chance he's going to be at that restaurant in fifteen days, then I will be there, too.

. . .

I'm not sure where I was expecting we would stay when we got to Lake Cane since Mom told me our house had been seized, but I'm shocked when we pull up to Aunt Lucinda's house.

"We're staying here?" I ask.

"Yes. And we're lucky she took us in," Mom grinds out.

I jump out of the car when it stops and move to the back, wanting to get my things before Detective Hill has a chance to help, but he's faster than I thought. He removes two of the boxes while I grab my big duffel.

He nods to the cross-country trophy that's sticking out of one of the boxes.

"You're a runner?" This is the first thing he's said to me since the diner even though he spent most of the drive eyeing me in the rearview mirror.

I nod. "I guess it's a family trait," I say back.

He raises one eyebrow. No laugh. Not even a smirk. But he does point down the street and say, "If you head that way and take a left two blocks up, you can be out of town pretty fast if you prefer running in open spaces. It's beautiful out that way and there's an orchard down the road worth checking out."

I mumble, "Thanks," and turn toward Aunt Lucinda's house but can't make myself walk up the path to the front porch steps. The last time I was in this house it still belonged to my grandmother and my entire extended family had gathered here after my grandfather's funeral. I was ten and I remember it like it was yesterday. I sat in the corner of the wraparound porch, eating chocolate pie and hiding from everyone else. Mom came looking for me, knowing how hard it was for me to be here with Granddad gone. She said, "Let's go for a walk and stretch our legs." We walked the neighborhood for hours, crisscrossing streets and lapping the house until everyone else had left. My grandmother died shortly after, apparently not able to handle being here without him, either. No one came back to this house after her funeral; they came to our house instead. Aunt Lucinda moved in not long after Grannie died.

The house looks the same but also different. The wraparound porch is still wide and full of rocking chairs and porch swings, but the old wood has been repainted a light blue with white trim, making everything seem screwed up somehow.

A screen door on the side of the house slams shut and I brace myself for this unwanted reunion.

"Well, well, look who's come home," she says. Aunt Lucinda is my mom's older sister and they've never been close. I'm sure the only reason she's taken us in is so she can be the first to know all of the gossip.

Mom nudges me as she passes and says under her breath, "Please say hello to your aunt."

"Hello, Aunt," I say. Mom shakes her head but doesn't look back at me.

I hear Detective Hill's big black car rumble away, but I don't turn around to watch him go. If I had a free hand, I would've flipped him off, though.

Mom stops inside the front door, waiting for me, her eyes begging me to come in, but it's not her look that gets me moving. It's the crowd that has formed on the sidewalk. A handful of women either jogging or pushing strollers has gathered in front of the house. Mom takes one look at them and flees inside. But Aunt Lucinda is beaming.

"Hey, y'all." She waves from the front porch. "Looky who's back.

My nephew, Owen, is home from that fancy boarding school in New Orleans." She's pointing at me and I turn to survey the group. One of the women holds up her phone and takes a picture of me.

This is fucking great.

Weighed down with bags, I make my way into the house. Aunt Lucinda waves good-bye to the women on the street and follows me inside.

"Since your mama is in the guest room, you're going to have to bunk down on the couch in the den. There's a closet in the hall where you can put your stuff. It's tiny but I guess it'll work since the police took all of your things."

She smiles at me and I have to think that anywhere in the world would be better than staying here.

I drop everything on the floor and head upstairs looking for Mom. It's not hard to discover which room Aunt Lucinda turned into the guest room since I could hear Mom's soft sobs the second I cleared the stairs.

I knock once then open the door. She jumps up from the bed and turns away from me, hiding the fact that she's wiping away tears.

"Did Lucinda show you where you'll be staying?" she asks when she finally turns around, a fake smile plastered across her face.

"We can't stay here. Aunt Lucinda is the devil." I turn and look into the hall. I'm going to ignore the fact that she was up here breaking down since she clearly is trying to hide it from me. "There's a reason why she never married. No one can stand to be around her for more than a minute."

Mom rubs a hand across her face and lets out a sad little laugh. She drops down on the edge of the bed, patting the spot next to her as an invitation for me to sit, but I choose the stool in the corner. Her disappointment hits me in the gut, but I'm holding myself together by a thin string and one touch from her will snap it apart.

"There is nowhere else for us to go. I promise you, I don't want to be here any more than you do, but until I earn some money and find us an apartment, this is it."

I'm shaking my head before she finishes. "What about the Blackwells? They would help us."

Her mouth tugs down at the corners and I'm afraid she's going to start crying again.

"He stole from every single person who worked for him. The company is shut down for now and will probably stay that way, which affects a lot of other businesses in this town, so our friends are hurt by this even if he didn't steal directly from them. And since there are so many environmental complaints, any well we fracked is shut down pending further testing. This affects almost everyone who owns land and receives royalties from gas sales, which is basically half the town. No one wants to help us."

I'm up and off the stool in a second. "I'm going for a run."

"Owen," she calls out but I don't stop.

"You can't just leave your stuff on the floor," Aunt Lucinda says from the hall the second I'm out of the door. The way she backed up when I came out of the room makes me think she was trying to eavesdrop on us. I throw her a look that tells her to go to hell as I rummage in my backpack for my earbuds. I'd already changed out of my school uniform into some athletic shorts and a T-shirt when we stopped at the diner.

I hit the front steps, glad the crowd is gone, and settle into a run in the direction Detective Hill suggested, cranking the music as loud as I can stand, hoping to drown out everything.

I run for miles. I run until my side is on fire and my knees are aching and I'm stumbling down the side of the road. But I don't stop and I don't turn back.

Some things are so familiar, like the Dairyette where we stopped for ice cream every Sunday after church, and other things are more of a blurred memory, like the old Kroger that seems to have been replaced with a newer and fancier version of itself.

Lake Cane isn't a big town and the old neighborhood where Aunt Lucinda lives is on the outskirts so it doesn't take long before I'm hobbling down a narrow country road with only the occasional passing car just as Detective Hill predicted I would. But the traffic isn't the only thing that has changed. The flat farmlands grooved with row crops give way to acres of land with trees planted in a perfect grid pattern. This must be the orchard he was talking about. Limping to the barbwire fence, I can't stop staring at the precision that must have gone into the planting.

The trees still have some of their leaves and the branches are heavy, some almost dragging the ground. I feel even more exhausted just looking at them.

"You lost?"

I fall back from the fence, trip over my own feet, and land on my ass in the ditch. The man sitting behind the wheel of a jacked-up golf cart laughs as I push myself to my feet.

Facing him, I answer, "No, sir, not lost."

He stares at me long enough for it to be awkward then rubs his hand back and forth across his mouth. His salt-and-pepper hair sticks up in places and the deep creases around his eyes show he's spent way too much time in the sun. He looks close to Dad's age or maybe a little older. Looking up and down the empty road, he finally asks, "Did you run all the way here from town?"

I manage to get myself out of the ditch and back on my feet before I answer. "Ran most of the way, walked the rest." I look back the way I came and don't see any sign of civilization. "I guess I didn't realize how far I'd gone."

The man looks me up and down. "You from around here?"

Here it goes. "I haven't lived here in a while but I'm back now." Please let him leave it at that.

He seems to consider this for a moment, then gestures for me to get in his golf cart. "C'mon. We'll ride up to the house and then I'll run you back to town in the truck. Doesn't look like you could make it another hundred yards in your condition."

I limp to the cart, thankful for the ride. Even though I've punished my body and will regret it for days, it's exactly what I needed.

He hesitates a second, then sticks out his hand and says, "I'm Gus."

I shake his hand and mumble, "Owen."

Gus turns off the road onto a wide gravel driveway that cuts right through the middle of the property. On each side are lines and lines of trees, the branches so full that they block out most of the late-afternoon light.

"What kind of trees are these?" I ask.

"Pecan. And it's almost harvest time," he says.

When his house comes into view, I'm speechless. It's like one of those old plantations you find around Baton Rouge and New Orleans, but this one is in such bad shape I'm surprised it's still standing. Every other window is missing a shutter and plants and vines are crawling up one side of the house like tentacles. The paint was probably once white but now it's just a dirty yellow, and the brick path leading to the front door is close to being completely overtaken by grass.

"Close your mouth, you're gonna catch flies."

I shut my mouth and turn to look at him. "Sorry. I was just surprised. . . ."

He nods toward the house. "That happens a lot faster than you think it would. And once it gets to a certain point, it's damn near impossible to set it back right."

He pulls the cart into an open bay in a detached garage on the side of the house. It's a two-story structure and is in much better shape than the big house right next to it. There's a small SUV and a couple of old trucks filling each bay. Gus gets out of the cart and gestures for me to get in the truck parked closest to the golf cart. I walk to the passenger side but he holds up his hand, stopping me.

"If you're interested, I'm looking for someone to help me around here. It's time to take that house back from this orchard and then I'll need help harvesting the crop. Maybe you could give me a couple of hours every day after school?"

This guy is clearly out of his mind. "You met me five minutes ago and you're offering me a job?"

I think he's not going to answer until he finally says, "Scraping bird shit and cobwebs out of that house is going to be more pleasant than spending your afternoons with Lucinda."

"So you know who I am." It's not a question.

"Of course. You look just like your mother." Gus hesitates a few seconds then asks, "How's she holding up?"

I shrug. "Hanging in there."

He stares at me for what feels like forever. "Your dad worked here, back when he was your age. Did you know that?"

I shake my head no. Is this why Detective Hill sent me out this way?

"He did. Lived a summer in the house in the Preacher Woods."

"What's the Preacher Woods?"

With arms stretched wide, he says, "The little grove where all this started."

"Why do they call it that?"

He leans against the side of the old truck, arms crossed in front of him. "Rumor has it, about a hundred years ago, there was an old man living in a run-down house on the edge of the property when Leonard

Trudeau bought the place and he didn't have the heart to kick him off the land. The old man never left and no one ever came looking for him. They say he wandered through that grove, Bible in hand, preaching to the trees as if they were his congregation, so everyone got to calling it the Preacher Woods."

"So he just stayed out there until he died?"

Gus cocks his head to the side and shrugs. "That's the damnedest thing. Leonard got to where he was checking on him every day, bringing him food and making sure there wasn't anything else he needed. By then, he was pretty old . . . paper-thin skin hanging off of him and hair so white it almost glowed, so the story goes. Then, one day, he was gone. Everything in that house was just like it had been the day before but the old preacher was never seen again."

I can't stop the rush of shivers that crawl through my body. "It's hard for me to imagine Dad here, living in a run-down house that belonged to an old preacher who disappeared into thin air."

"Your dad showed up here when he didn't have anywhere else to go. Funny how you've done the same thing."

I think about the job offer. It would be better to spend my afternoons here rather than at Aunt Lucinda's. And maybe I can learn more about Dad since Gus knew him. "I'd like to take the job, but I don't have a car. Not sure how I'd get back and forth every day."

Gus bangs a hand on the hood of the truck. "You can use this. It's not pretty but it's dependable."

I stare at the old truck. "You're not afraid I'm going to steal this truck and never come back?"

Gus pushes away from it and starts walking back toward the golf cart. "Is that what you plan to do?"

"Well . . . no . . . but . . ."

"Well, then stop saying stupid shit. I'll see you tomorrow."

Noah—Summer of 1999

"Here's your stop," the guy driving the truck shouts out of the window.

I throw my duffel bag on the ground then hop out of the back of the pickup. "Appreciate the lift," I call as he drives away.

He honks the horn then disappears around the curve while I start up the long winding driveway. When the house comes into sight, I'm tugging my hair back, stuffing it under my baseball cap, and taking a quick whiff of my shirt to make sure I don't stink too bad. I need this job and I'll screw up my chances if I look like a homeless person, even though that's exactly what I am.

I step off the driveway onto the wide brick path that leads to the front door. The house rises in front of me, blinding white in the sunlight, with huge columns going from the floor of the porch past the second-floor balcony, all the way up to the roof. The rosebushes are in bloom, giving the air a smell so sweet it almost makes me sick. There is a wide set of brick steps leading up to the porch with clay pots on each step overflowing with flowers.

This is the prettiest house I've ever seen.

I knock on the front door and rub my hands down the side of my pants so they'll be dry when I shake hands with the owner.

A black woman wearing a set of blue scrubs opens the door. "Can I help you?" she asks. She has a nice, friendly smile that makes my nerves quiet down just a little.

"Um, I'm here about the job? Saw the notice on the board in the diner next to the bus station."

Her eyes light up and I relax. "Sure, let me get Mr. Trudeau for you."

She turns away, leaving the front door open, but I don't step inside.

It's only a few minutes before she's back with a man I'm assuming is the owner trailing right behind her.

"Thanks, Betty, I'm stepping out for a few minutes but holler if you need me," he says to the woman. She squeezes his arm and gives him a soft smile.

"Take your time, I've got it covered here."

Betty moves away and disappears through an opening under the big sweeping staircase.

"You here about the job?" Mr. Trudeau asks. He's a white guy not that much older than me, maybe he's in his mid- to late twenties. Looking at this house and all the land, I was expecting an older man.

I nod. "Yes, sir."

He eyes me from head to toe, taking in my greasy brown hair that's falling out of my baseball cap, my faded Metallica T-shirt and ripped jeans.

"You ever work outside, with heavy equipment?"

"No, sir. But I'm a quick learner. And I'm not afraid of hard work."

Mr. Trudeau runs a hand through his dark hair and turns to look back at the house. "I normally take care of this place myself but I've got a lot going on right now. Need a little help keeping up with things."

He's still looking at the house and I'm wondering what's going on inside that's got him bothered.

"I can do whatever you need me to do," I answer. "You've got a beautiful place."

"Thanks," he says. "This orchard's been in my family for years." Mr. Trudeau points to some unknown thing in the distance. "My great-grandfather bought this land when it was just a small grove of native pecan trees near the river bottom. Then he started bringing in trees of other varieties of improved pecans—Moneymakers, Stuarts, Papershells, and Desirables. It's quiet around here now but come fall, we'll be shaking these trees and carrying pecans to town."

I don't plan to be here that long, but I don't tell him that.

He finally turns back to me and says, "I'll try you out for a week. See how it goes."

I nod but this is not what I wanted to hear. I need steady work. "Any chance you got a room to rent?"

He stares at me hard. "So you need a job and roof over your head. Hell, I don't even know your name. I was expecting someone from town to take me up on the job offer."

I dig my hands in my pockets. "I'm Noah and I'm from St. Louis, turned nineteen a few weeks ago. I'm the hardest worker you'll ever hire. I keep to myself and I don't cause trouble."

"How'd you end up in the middle of Louisiana?"

I kick a loose rock with my foot. "Thought about going to New Orleans. Bought a bus ticket for as close as I could get with the money I had. This was as far as I got."

Mr. Trudeau glances back to the house again before he says, "You still mean to get to New Orleans?"

"Maybe at some point. Just looking to make some money right now."

We stand there staring at each other a few seconds and I hope he doesn't see the sweat pouring down my neck, soaking my shirt.

"There's an old house in the back of the orchard. It isn't much but it's cheap. I'll take the rent out of your check."

"Thank you, Mr. Trudeau."

"Gus. Call me Gus. I'm taking a chance on you, but don't think I won't put a bullet in you if I think you're going to hurt what's mine."

3

Even on break from Sutton's, we rarely spent time in Louisiana. Some summers we stayed in Sun Valley while others it was a villa in Mexico right on the Caribbean. Christmas was always skiing in Aspen. So it's not surprising I get turned around and take a couple of wrong turns on my way to school. Landmarks that I thought I would recognize are gone, or changed in some way. Everything looks different. Feels different.

But the high school is exactly like I remember it. On those hot summer afternoons before we started middle school when there was nothing else to do, Pippa and I would ride our bikes here and roam around the grounds. The ugly gray building looks more like a factory than a school, but both us couldn't wait until the day when we would go here. Pippa even picked out what she thought would be the perfect parking spot . . . it was far from the front door but close to a side entrance that she hoped would be easy to sneak out of so we could cut for lunch.

She was always two steps ahead of where we were, always looking forward to getting out of here—to moving somewhere new and leaving this town behind.

But I was the one who left instead when my parents enrolled me in Sutton's for sixth grade.

God, I haven't thought about her in forever. Will she be here? Would I recognize her?

My phone vibrates as I pull into the parking lot at school. I click on the highly inappropriate picture of Jack that I assigned to his contact in my phone. It's his head, stuffed between an enormous pair of stripper's breasts. The picture was taken while we were out on a pass from Sutton's. We were wandering around the Quarter, looking to make the most of our first night away from school, when we passed a club. The guy working the door was unimpressed until Jack pulled out a wad of cash, so for double the cover price, we were in. It was our first time in a place like that. We were freshmen, young and stupid with braces and acne and it was obvious we were out of our league the second we walked through the door. Ray, Sai, and I put our money together and bought Jack a lap dance, mainly so we could do it to him before he did it to us. We laughed about it for weeks after.

Thinking about that night hits me in the gut.

I stare at the notification on my phone. Jack's been my best friend since we both started Sutton's and the only person that has ever come back home with me to Lake Cane.

I swipe open his latest message.

JACK: if you don't call me back I'm kicking your ass fucker

Have to admit that brings a smile to my face. I respond:

ME: not ready to talk

JACK: wtf get over it your dads a dick

ME: later

And I power my phone off. Jack means well but he has no idea what it's like coming home to this. If I thought we lived big, it was nothing compared to the Cooper family. We had a time share in Aspen and they had a house on top of the mountain with a private lift to get there. The only thing I regret is not saying good-bye to him before I left.

God, I would give anything if my only worry was if he papered the locker room with pictures of my bare ass.

Hunkered down on the couch in the den, I spent most of last night on the internet reading every news story, blog post, tweet, and Facebook post outlining Dad's greed and corruption. When Dad got out of college, he started working for my grandfather, my mom's dad, at his company, Louisiana Frac. Back then, it was a small fracking service that employed a couple dozen people. Natural gas drilling in Louisiana has always been steady but nothing compared to what happened when it was discovered that there was a lot of gas down deep a little more than ten years ago.

So business exploded. While a typical well needed about five frack tanks, a deep well needed around fifty. To help get the most out of a well, you have to frack it. That means you pump water, sand, and other fluids and chemicals down the drill hole to open, or fracture, the earth, then hold the fracture open for drilling. There is a lot of controversy around this process because water sources local people use can become polluted if there's a leak.

My grandfather had just passed away and Dad had taken over the company, and with the higher demand in business he expanded the operation and hired dozens more employees just as Dr. Winston mentioned yesterday. It wasn't long before Louisiana Frac was the biggest employer in our small town.

According to several articles, his theft is estimated at more than ten million. It's no coincidence that the boom in his business and the start of his theft was the same time we moved into the new house, the one that's been seized, and I was shipped off to boarding school.

The growth of Louisiana Frac launched other businesses as well, like transportation companies that hauled the frack tanks to different well sites and suppliers that sold us the materials we need to frack a well. Now that Louisiana Frac is shut down and the possibility of it running again very slim, those other businesses find themselves with problems.

Guys who worked under my grandfather, who were months away from retirement, are screwed because they're out of a job and have no money to retire on. And the guys who are far from retiring are just as screwed because they've worked all these years for nothing and have to figure out how to start all over in a town that doesn't have a lot of other opportunities.

There are also theories on the identity of the person or persons who is believed to have helped him, but the general consensus is that it was Mom. Most believe she knows what he was doing and she knows where he is, but she's playing dumb to stay out of trouble since he left town without her.

By midnight, I was ready to punch something. Or someone.

And then the comments started rolling in on my social media accounts. Every picture I had ever posted of us on vacation was targeted.

Wish I could spend Christmas in Aspen! Oh yeah, I could have if your dad hadn't stolen all our money. Dick.

Scuba diving looks so fun! You're welcome.

U and ur family totally suck

Your dad ruined our life

I was not expecting that. For hours, I watched the comments pour in. I was frozen . . . numb . . . with indecision. Should I reply to every comment, let them know I didn't know what he was doing? Would that make it worse? It was obvious those commenting were locals, so would I meet @gdogg4312 at school? Would he be sitting next to me in class and I wouldn't even know it? I had never faced anything like that. Had no idea how to handle it. So in those early-morning hours, I deleted every online account because I didn't know what else to do and I needed it to stop.

When I sat down across from Mom at breakfast, the one thing I was sure of was that she had no idea what was going on. Every charge against Dad was etched in a fine line across her face.

Fourteen days to go. Now more than ever I need to see him. Hear his side. Even with everything I read, I still feel like there's something more to this. Something I'm missing.

Since the school isn't too far from Aunt Lucinda's, Mom was going to walk with me so she could get me enrolled, but one peek out of the front window changed those plans. Instead of bored housewives, news vans were parked out front, cameras ready to go. One look at Mom and I knew how scared she was to leave the house. So Aunt Lucinda slipped out the front door to talk to them while I snuck out the side door and ran to the truck I'd parked down the street.

I haven't told Mom about meeting Gus and the loan of the truck because I know she'd make me give it back—not wanting us to take anything else from the people here.

And since Gus didn't specify it was only to be used to get to work, I decided it would suck to have the cameras catch me walking to school so I drove the short distance instead.

A group of girls trickles by, each peeking inside the truck as they pass. It's a small town and a small school so it's not surprising they are curious about this new addition to the parking lot. I slump down in my seat, but I can't stall any longer.

Ducking behind a group of guys who just stepped off the bus, I jump out of the borrowed truck and follow them up the meandering path toward the entrance. The main hall is as packed and chaotic as high school five minutes before first bell should be, but it's still nothing like I've ever witnessed.

I scan the space for a familiar face and am surprised when I actually recognize several people. I nod to a guy that I know pretty well. Seth Sullivan. We were friends before I left; we would spend nights hanging out on a regular basis. I remember we both loved to play Madden and hated Mrs. Tinswell, who taught us fourth grade.

But now he stares, then walks right past me. Damn—that sucks more than I thought it would.

I try a little harder with the next three people I recognize, making eye contact with them then throwing in a small smile to go with my head nod. Dirty looks, glares, and even a hard shoulder that nearly knocks me over when we pass are the only responses I get in return.

I guess this is how it's going to be.

With my new schedule in hand, I stop trying to find a friendly face and instead try to navigate the mazelike layout. I've never missed Sutton's more than I do in this moment. If I was back there now, my friends and I would be leaving the dining hall, laughing and joking as we made our way along the stone path to Hunter Hall.

I make it to second period before I get in my first fight. Coming out of class, some kid blindsides me with a weak-ass punch to the shoulder. After sitting through two classes being stared at, whispered at, pointed at, I lose my cool. I shove him, hard, and he skids across the floor. He stares at me for a few seconds before hopping up and taking another swing. I pivot around and his fist hits the locker behind me instead. He howls in pain then runs off in the opposite direction.

Since he threw the first punch, I could have whaled on him, but I didn't. I barely touched him. Yet every person in the hall is looking at me like I kicked a baby.

I hate that my dad is a royal son of a bitch, but I'm not taking a beating for something he did. By the time Mr. Roberts comes out into the hall, there isn't anything left to handle other than clearing the area.

When the other students start walking away, Mr. Roberts motions for me to follow him into his room.

"Have a seat, Owen," he says and shoves a chair in my direction.

I drop down and lean back, the chair teetering on the back two legs.

He circles around me, arms crossed, and I brace myself for the lecture I know is coming.

"Brian shouldn't have acted that way, but I don't think he'll be the only one to take out his anger on you. Your father hurt a lot of people."

I drop the front legs of the chair on the floor and it echoes through the room. "Just because my dad may have screwed people over doesn't mean I'm letting some kid take a swing at me."

Mr. Roberts holds out his hand and says, "I'm not saying that. You have to understand where he's coming from."

I hop up from my seat. "Got it. I have to take whatever they throw at me. Perfect. If there's nothing else, I don't want to be late for next period. I hear the principal is a real hard-ass."

By the time I walk into the cafeteria for lunch, I've had enough. No matter where I go or what class I'm in, the looks and insults don't stop.

"Asshole."

"Jerk."

"Thief."

I'm halfway to the lunch line when the last one registers. I turn around, taking a step toward the group hurling the names. "I'll take asshole. Even jerk. But I'm no thief."

A tall girl steps a little closer and lets out a really loud, horrible fake laugh. I know this girl. Went to school with her when we were little but she still seems like a stranger to me right now. "Oh, yeah, right. You may not be the one who stole from us but you sure as hell don't seem sorry. You should be kissing all our asses since our families"—she does a huge arm movement to encompass the group around her—"funded your entire life."

"Whatever. Maybe your parents," I say as I mock the huge arm movements, "should've been more careful with their money."

I swear I can hear gasps from every single person in the cafeteria. It's a low blow and a part of me burns with shame, but I still couldn't stop the words from flying out of my mouth. No one says anything else, but it looks like I'm one step from getting my ass beat.

"Whatever. Hate me. Make me the bad guy. Hope it makes you feel better." And then I'm gone.

I hear steps behind me just as I hit the parking lot.

"What happened to you?"

God, I'm so sick of this. I turn around, ready to decimate whoever has the nerve to keep this going, but I stop cold when I recognize her.

Pippa.

She's familiar but not, just like most everything here. Her hair is long and dark brown and straight as a board. Pippa was tall for her age back then but it seems she didn't grow much more since she barely reaches my shoulder. Or maybe it's because I'm more than a foot taller than when I left here.

Pippa and I were neighbors before my parents bought the big house that sits on the ninth hole of the Cypress Lake Country Club. The same one that was seized. I had my fair share of friends that were boys, including Seth, but there was something about Pippa. We were inseparable growing up. When I first left, we tried to get together when I was home for break but everything was strained and it wasn't just that I was in a different house, in a different neighborhood when she dropped by that first time to see me. I had gotten out of this town. It was the one thing she wanted to do and I did it.

I felt guilty telling her about all the things I had done with my new friends in New Orleans; the music festivals we always had passes to thanks to Ray's dad, watching the Saints play in a private box thanks to Jack's dad, and the gold card that paid for anything we wanted thanks to my dad.

By high school, we stopped trying. I told myself we would have drifted apart no matter where I went to school, but I'm not sure that's true.

"Good to see you, too," I say.

She shakes her head. "It's so wrong of you to come in here acting like an asshole." Pippa was tough back then and it seems like that hasn't changed.

"So I'm supposed to let everyone here say whatever they want? I didn't do anything to them."

Disgust washes across her face and I turn toward the truck, not wanting to admit how much I hate seeing that reaction from her.

"Your mom's had it pretty rough before you came home. Did you know?"

This stops me cold. "What do you mean rough?" The story with Dad only went viral yesterday.

"When your dad bailed a few weeks ago. At first, your mom made excuses when your dad didn't show up for work and no one could find him. It got worse when the Feds showed up and tried to figure out what was happening and the EPA started knocking on doors. And then she got kicked out of her house. They took her car. It was pretty bad. You may have just found out about this yesterday, but it's been bad around here for her for weeks."

I lean back against the truck. "Dad screwed up. Dad is a total asshole. I don't know what you want me to say."

Pippa shakes her head. Slowly. She's agitated with me. That is something else I remember clearly. "The Rutherfords, the Browns, the McKenzies, the Blackwells . . . all of their businesses are in trouble now and every one of your dad's employees lost everything. My parents' business is dependent on Louisiana Frac, Owen. We're as screwed as the people who worked for y'all."

I had forgotten about Pippa's family's business. They own a garden supply company that sells dirt, mulch, and anything else you would need for any landscaping project, but the biggest item they stock, the one thing that makes them profitable, is the sand Louisiana Frac needs for every well. I forgot that they would be affected, too.

"I'm sorry, I really am, but I didn't do this to your family. I barely saw Dad much less knew what he was doing. He screwed us, too. I get everyone needs someone to blame, but none of this is my fault."

She's disgusted, I can tell, but I'm not wrong. They need a punching bag but it's not me.

"Don't worry, your mom is taking most of the heat for you," she says and turns to walk away.

I grab her arm, stopping her. "What's that supposed to mean?"

Pippa jerks her arm free but doesn't walk away. "She let you stay at that school as long as she did because she didn't want to tell you the truth. She pulled you because she had to but she left you there as long as she could because of the threats."

"What threats?" I hate hearing this from her. Hate that Mom has left so much out.

"A lot of people here think she was as dumb as everyone else. But others think she knew what was going on. I mean, she worked there with your dad. Some people think she's got some of the money tucked away somewhere. Or knows where it is. It's been bad for her. And then you come back and act like an asshole."

For the second time, I try to stop her from walking away but this time she pulls out a move she learned when she signed up for self-defense class the summer before middle school. One I'm familiar with—and should have seen coming—since we practiced it together until she got it right.

She twists around, then sweeps her leg and I land on my ass while she walks away without a backward glance.

Noah—Summer of 1999

It only takes a few days to figure out what's got Gus distracted. She's wrapped in a big fuzzy pink blanket even though it's hot as hell.

Betty, the woman I met on the first day, pushes her out onto the front porch and locks the brake on her wheelchair.

"You want something to drink?" Betty asks her.

"I'd love a glass of lemonade," she answers in a weak voice. Gus's wife is bad off. Really sick. But she's got a smile on her face as she stares at the orchard.

Betty heads into the house and I concentrate on weeding the flower bed so I'm not tempted to stare at her.

"The bougainvillea is looking prettier than ever this year. Would you cut me a piece?"

It takes me a minute to realize she's speaking to me.

"Um . . . which one is that?" There are so many different plants in these beds and all of them look like they're doing well.

"The purplish-pink one there next to the steps," she says and points a skinny finger to a plant that is trailing out into the yard.

I find a full section and clip off a few inches, then bound up the stairs. The closer I am, the more I can see just how frail she is. I could circle her upper arm with my thumb and middle finger and still have room left over.

She holds her hand out and I place the flower in it.

"It's just lovely, thank you," she says.

"Of course."

I start to walk away but stop when she asks, "So you're the Noah I've been hearing about?"

Wiping my hands down the sides of my pants, I answer, "I guess so."

She laughs quietly. "My husband has been singing your praises. He may never let you know he's pleased with the work you're doing here, but he is."

"Thank you, Mrs. Trudeau."

"Just call me Abby."

"Thank you, Abby."

I jump down off the porch and dive back into the beds, yanking out everything that doesn't belong.

From what I can tell about this place, the only crop is the pecans on the trees and there's not a whole lot to do for them until the fall. Right now, it's all about keeping the orchard clean, fixing any equipment that needs to be fixed, and praying for the right amount of rain to fall.

Abby sits on the porch, sipping her lemonade, until she falls asleep in the wheelchair. Gus checks on her a few times on his way back and forth from the barn. Watching them, I realize they're both young enough that they can't have been married for very long.

And now she's dying. It doesn't seem fair.

Gus has me working close to the house over the next few days, but it's almost a week before I see Abby again. Just like the first time, Betty rolls her out onto the front porch and parks her there, then goes to get her something to drink.

Betty is basically the glue that's holding everything together here. She was the housekeeper when Gus's parents were alive, then became a certified caregiver when Gus's dad got sick, keeping him out of a nursing home while Gus was away at college. Since Gus's mom died when he was little, Betty has been like a second mother to him. She's here every day, all day, and I'm not sure how Gus and Abby would survive without her.

I've got a set of pruning shears and I'm trying not to destroy the shrubbery when Abby calls my name.

Moving closer to the porch, I pull a rag out of my back pocket and mop the sweat off of my face. "Yes?"

"I want to thank you for the flowers. I'm guessing you're the one who makes sure I have fresh ones every morning?"

I duck my head and run the towel across my face another time. "I thought you'd like them." After she asked me for a clipping, I realized she was probably the one who planted all these flowers. And now that she's sick, she probably misses them. I cut a few of the roses, mixed them with that purple plant she asked for the first time, and left them in a plastic cup near the front door the next morning. I'm not sure if it was Gus or Betty who brought them in but I've been doing it every morning since.

"Well, you've spoiled me now."

I nod again and move away, not sure what else I'm supposed to say. I don't know her, not at all, but it scares me how sick she is. There's no way she can last long looking the way she does.

I'm halfway back to the shrubs I was butchering before she calls my name and I stop, turning back to her. "Is it cancer? Is that what's wrong?" I ask.

She seems surprised by my bluntness but not offended. "Yes. Started as breast cancer but moved to everywhere else pretty fast."

"How long have you had it?"

Her head tilts to the side. "A couple of years. They found it right after Gus and I were married."

"That sucks," I say.

"Yes, it does," she answers back.

I bend down and grab the clippers from the ground where I left them and catch Gus on the side of the house. He's close enough that he heard what we said. Shit, he's probably going to fire me. And I probably deserve it. But instead, he gives me a brisk nod, then disappears around the back of the house.

4

By the time I get back on my feet Pippa is gone. Jumping into the borrowed truck I try not to think about how quickly she knocked me on my ass.

The number of news vans in front of my aunt's house seems to have doubled since I left for school. I park down the street, pull my baseball cap low, and keep my face hidden while I walk down the sidewalk. When I'm in front of the neighbor's house, I jump the short fence into the backyard, pushing my way through some overgrown azaleas until I'm in my aunt's backyard.

It's time for Mom and me to have another chat.

She's at the kitchen table, on the phone with the local phone book out in front of her. The back door is open but the screen door is closed. Her soft voice floats through the air so I sit down on the steps, listening to her end of the conversation.

"I would take any position you have available. And I can work any hours."

She's doodling on a notepad, listening to whatever is being said to her on the other end of the line.

"I understand. I really do. And I'm sorry. I really had no idea what he was doing."

She drops the phone and then chucks her pen across the table, where it bounces several times before hitting the floor. "Dang it," she mutters under her breath just as it rolls underneath the refrigerator.

I was ready to storm in here, demand answers, but seeing her like this sucks all of the energy right out of me.

Pippa was right. I have no idea what it's been like for her. What it's like for her now.

Even though Dad never went out of his way to see me once I went off to school, Mom did. She drove to New Orleans a few times a month, checking me out so we could spend an afternoon together or staying the weekend at a nearby hotel. Our favorite thing to do when she visited was check out every hole-in-the-wall restaurant we could find. The sketchier the better. And in New Orleans, we never ran out of places to go. It was our thing. I don't know anyone more adventurous than Mom when it comes to food. If she loved a place, she would write such glowing online reviews the restaurants would use them in local ads. There was nothing better than getting a call from her after she got a clipping I sent her. And I think her own cooking was inspired by all the places we visited because she's a genius in the kitchen.

She's always been there for me and I should have been here for her.

I stand up slowly and tap on the screen door just before opening it. I was hoping to alert her I was here but she's startled and jumps in her seat anyway.

"Owen! You scared me. Why aren't you at school?" she asks, closing the phone book and flipping over the notebook. Or maybe trying to hide all of the lines scratched through every local business that I'm sure won't hire her because of what her asshole husband did.

"I stayed as long as I could. It was . . . harder to be there than I thought."

She closes her eyes and keeps them shut. "Please tell me you didn't get in a fight," she says.

I wait for her to look at me before I shrug.

She gets up quickly from the table. "Well, did you get some lunch? Are you hungry?"

I slide into the chair she vacated and turn the notebook back over. "No one is going to hire you. They'll all think you'll steal from them. Plus, half this town is looking for a job and they won't give it to you over them."

She busies herself at the sink. "Yes. That is the general consensus."

"Tell me about the threats you're getting."

She finishes washing the mug she was just using for coffee, then turns to face me, shutting off the water. She scans my face but I don't know what she's looking for. Is she trying to decide if I can handle what she has to say?

"I haven't been getting any threats."

I'm out of my chair and next to her. "If we're going to get through this, you have to tell me everything. There can't be any secrets." And then I remember the note from Dad. The one I haven't told her about.

"I'm handling everything. I just need you to focus on school and try to get through the day without fighting."

"You're really not going to tell me?" I ask through clenched teeth.

Mom grabs a nearby dish towel and dries her hands. "There's nothing to tell."

I can see it in her eyes. Maybe it's regret or anger or something else but she's holding back. She's shutting me out and it pisses me off. I turn around and push through the screen door.

"Where are you going?" Mom asks.

"Out," I answer and sprint through the backyard and down the street before she has a chance to ask me anything else.

• • •

Gus is sitting in a lawn chair in the middle of the yard when I pull up in his truck. He's got one of those TV trays in front of him piled high with old parts and there are a few black marks streaked across his cheek and forehead where he's rubbed his greasy fingers across his face.

I thought the drive over would give me a chance to calm down, but I'm still so pissed off. Pissed at whatever threats Mom is hiding from me. She's probably convinced herself she's protecting me by keeping it a secret, but she's wrong. There's been enough secrets in this family already.

I pace back and forth in front of his little table while Gus silently tracks my progress.

Finally, he points to an empty chair beside him. "Sit. You're making me dizzy."

I drop down in the chair but still feel the need to move like an itch under my skin.

"What's got you all stirred up today?" Gus asks.

I shake my head. "Nothing. Family bullshit."

I'm expecting him to fire questions at me, poke and prod until he gets every little detail, but he doesn't even look at me. He either doesn't notice or doesn't care that I've shown up hours before he was expecting me. Instead, he hands me a small part and a wire brush.

"Run that brush through that opening until you get all that gunk out," he says.

The opening he refers to is so clogged with grease that I can barely get the brush inside. It's tedious work but after twenty minutes it's cleared out.

I hand the part back to Gus and he attaches it to the part on the table in front of him. Finally, he looks at me and asks, "Feel better?"

It takes me a moment to understand what he's talking about and then I realize I'm not as mad anymore. My anger fell away with every scrape of that wire brush.

"Yeah, I do actually." Leaning to get a closer look at the object in front of him, I ask, "What are you working on?"

"The weed whacker won't whack my weeds so I'm trying to figure out why."

He scoots the table to the side then launches himself out of his chair. He's in pretty good shape. He's tall, and if his arms are any indication he's muscular, which makes sense for someone who does a lot of physical labor. "Well, let me give you the five-cent tour and then you can get started."

I follow him up the front steps and through the wide front door. The smell hits me and I stagger back.

"Yeah, something died in here a while back but I can't seem to find it," he says.

It has to be a big something . . . a very big dead something to produce the stench that seems to coat every surface. I pull my shirt up over my mouth and thank God I didn't have any lunch because there's a really good chance it would end up all over the dirty floor.

We're standing in a massive foyer, a curved staircase wrapping around the room, and even through the chipped paint and years of neglect it's easy to see how beautiful this house once was. "All right, we got the dining room on this side and formal living room on the other," Gus says and he points right, then left.

There's trash and leaves and God knows what else littering the floor.

"Are you sure there's only one dead thing in here?"

Gus's head tilts to the side. "Well, no. Could be more."

I follow Gus down a hallway that opens up into a large room with windows all along the back of the house, where you can see rows and rows of pecan trees stretching out like fingers.

Gus points to the right and says, "Through that door is the kitchen and washroom." Then he spins around and points the opposite direction. "And down that hall is a study and the master bedroom. More bathrooms and bedrooms upstairs."

"You're not living in here, are you?" I ask.

"Hell no," he answers. "Staying in the room above the garage. It's been a long time since anyone lived in this house."

The amount of work it's going to take to bring it back overwhelms me. "We need about twenty more people helping if you want this place clean by this time next year, much less by the time you harvest pecans."

"Well, did you make a few friends at school that you could call to come help?"

My jaw clenches. "Not exactly," I grind out.

"Well, then, looks like it's just us."

"Why now?" I ask.

Gus acts like he doesn't know what I'm talking about. "What do you mean?"

I glance around the room. "What made you decide to clean up the house now? Are you about to sell it or something?"

Gus shakes his head and frowns. "I've been tied up with other things but it's time to make it right. It's been left like this for too long." He throws a pair of gloves at me that I nearly miss. "Start outside. Get those damn vines off the side of the house. I'm going to hunt up what's making that smell."

I'm down the hall and out the front door before Gus has a chance to change his mind and send me on the dead animal scavenger hunt.

My first mistake is not putting on the gloves immediately. It only takes minutes before my fingers are shredded from trying to pry away the plants clinging to the house.

"Shit," I mutter when I realize I've smeared blood down the side of the house. After I use the gloves to wipe it away, I pull them on, ignoring the sting pulsing in the tips of my fingers.

I work for hours. I work until my hands are numb and the ground is littered with broken pieces of vines and leaves.

"I think I found it," Gus says as he steps onto the porch. He's holding what's left of some animal with his gloved right hand while the fingers on his left hand pinch his nose.

The smell wafts through the air and I start to gag. I stumble away, desperately trying not to vomit. "What is that?"

"It was a raccoon. Not sure what got ahold of him. But he's got a few sisters and brothers up there in the same sorry state. One hell of a mess."

Gus walks across the yard, the dead raccoon bouncing with each step, and he dumps it in a large pile of debris in one of the only open spaces on his entire place. As he makes his way back to the house, he says, "Gather up all those vines and add them to the pile while I get the rest of those animals. Then we'll burn it. It's the only way to get rid of that smell."

By the time I drop the last armful of leaves and branches and vines on the burn pile, Gus steps out with what I hope is the last of the raccoon family. He throws it on the top and between the stench of the dead animals—there were seven raccoons in total rotting away inside—and the tentacled beast I fought all afternoon, I've never been so ready to light something on fire.

"I'll let you do the honors," Gus says as he hands me a small can of diesel and a pack of matches.

I step up to the pile and once more have to concentrate on not puking. As I walk around the mound of debris, emptying the can of diesel, I think about the last two days. The lies, the threats, the sadness, the guilt. And I'm so pissed. So pissed at everything. I step back, setting the can a good distance away, and then strike the match on the side of the box. I hold it one second then two, wishing I could get rid of all my problems as easily as we're about to destroy the dead animals and the creeping vines. Just before my fingers start to burn, I throw the match onto the pile and with a whoosh and a flash, the flames devour everything within reach. Smoke billows up through the opening in the trees, but some of it gets trapped under the nearby canopies then spreads down the row, looking for an alternate escape.

I turn back to the old wrecked house, staring at the section that is free and clear of intruders. I took back a piece of that house today. I ripped away what was hurting it. I destroyed what was trying to claim it.

Gus passes me on the way to the small garage but stops and moves toward the front porch steps. He bends down near a purple plant I uncovered when I cleaned off that area.

"Yeah, I was surprised to see something so pretty under all those vines," I say. "Not sure if it's a weed or not so I left it."

"It's bougainvillea," he says in a quiet voice.

"Well, whatever it is, I thought you may want to keep it."

Gus doesn't answer, just pulls his pocket knife out and cuts off a small portion from the end. He tucks the small bloom in his shirt pocket and says, "Good work today. See you tomorrow."

I nod and wave then turn back to watch the fire. I stand there until the smoke cleanses the foul air and everything is reduced to ash.

I stand there until I'm convinced I can reclaim a piece of my life just like I reclaimed part of that house.

Noah—Summer of 1999

I'm bushhogging the grassy areas in between each tree when I see a small black sports car pull up in front of the house. There hasn't been a single visitor since I got here and the only person who comes and goes from this house is Betty and the medical people who check on Abby every couple of days, so it's almost weird to see the little black car in the driveway.

Betty just pushed Abby back inside and Gus is on the back of the property so I hop off the tractor and jog to the front door so I can catch her before she rings the bell.

"Can I help you?" I say when I get to the yard near the front porch.

The girl spins around and almost drops what she's holding. "Oh, hi. My mom wanted me to bring this out. It's a casserole. We heard Abby isn't doing well so she sent food. Because that's what she does. She sends food."

The girl is blushing and shifting around from foot to foot. It's pretty cute.

"Here, let me take that." I move closer and reach for the pan. It's still warm and that surprises me, making me almost drop it. She makes a grab for it again and we're tangled up, the casserole jiggling between us.

I finally get a good grip on it and she pulls her hands away.

"Sorry," I say.

"Sorry," she says at the same time.

The dish is covered so I can't see what's inside but after getting a whiff of it, my stomach rumbles.

"What is this?" I ask. "It smells great."

She blushes and it's the cutest thing I've ever seen. "Oh, it's something I made up. It's jambalaya but instead of rice I use bow tie pasta."

"You made this? Well, if it tastes as good as it smells I know Gus and Abby will be glad to have it for dinner."

The pink on her cheeks deepens and then she cocks her head to the side. "Who are you? I don't think I've seen you before."

"I'm Noah."

She gives me a big smile. "Well, hi, Noah. I'm Margaret Ann. But everyone calls me Maggie. Nice to meet you." She points to my T-shirt. "Were you there?"

I look down to remind myself which shirt I'm wearing. It's from the last Rolling Stones tour. This one, like all the other concert shirts I have, came from Goodwill.

I shake my head no and say, "I wish, though. I've heard their shows are worth the insane ticket price."

"Hmmm . . . if I could go to any show, it would have to be . . ." She trails off like she's thinking about her answer.

"Oh God, please don't say Backstreet Boys."

She laughs and pushes my arm. "Give me a little credit. I was trying to decide between Springsteen reuniting with the E Street Band or Prince. But really, I wish I could go back in time to Madonna's Blond Ambition Tour. Can you imagine being in the audience for that show?"

I can't help but laugh. "Is that the one where she was on a bed onstage and . . . you know." I can't finish my sentence.

She laughs. "Yes. That's the one. She also dressed up like a nun and didn't act very nun-ly. I bet it was crazy." Maggie nods toward the house then back to the dish in my hands. "Maybe we should take that to the kitchen?"

I've never been in the house. Not once. Gus feeds me but it's by handing me a plate from the back door and I eat at the picnic table in the yard or I take it back to the old shack near the river on the edge of the property. But Gus isn't around and Betty is probably busy getting Abby settled.

"Sure."

She follows me up the front porch steps and I hope I can figure out where the kitchen is. I push open the front door and scan the area, looking for any clue to guide me in the right direction.

We pass through an arched opening on the back wall of the foyer, one I've seen Betty go through, and come out into a large den area. There are several couches scattered around the room along with some big comfy-looking chairs. And the walls are covered with pictures. Not just of Gus and Abby but of what must be their parents and grandparents.

I look left, then right, and wish I had a coin to flip. I pick left because why not and luckily when we pass through the door, we're in the one of the biggest kitchens I've ever seen. The fridge is wide and takes up the whole middle section of the wall, but when I open it, I find it's mostly empty.

"Looks like it's a good thing Mom sent me out. At least y'all have something for dinner tonight."

"Yeah, I know Gus and Abby will appreciate it." Actually, Gus is probably going to be pissed since it doesn't seem like he wants people nosing around in here, but it will make Abby smile to know someone was thinking about her.

"What's your number?" I ask. Then add, "In case Abby or Gus want to call and thank you and your mom." Yeah, that's why I want to know her number.

She gives me another smile and her cheeks get pink again. Maggie grabs a small notepad off the counter near the phone and writes down her number.

"You could call me," she says. "I mean, if you want to know where anything is around town. I've lived here my whole life so I know where everything is. I could show you one day. Or just tell you. You know, if you need something."

Maggie rambling nonsense is by far the best thing I've seen in a long time. I'm just about to take her up on her offer when Gus comes in from the back door. He looks surprised to see us in his kitchen.

He throws me a look like we'll have a talk about this later, and I'm worried if coming into his house makes the list of things for which he would put a bullet in me.

"Hey, Maggie. How are you?" Gus says.

"I'm good. Mama heard Abby wasn't doing well so she sent me out with a casserole." Maggie points to the fridge. "It's ready to eat, just need to warm it up."

"Well, that's really sweet. Tell her I said thank you."

Maggie nods and we all stand there in an awkward silence.

"Well, I guess I should go," she says, throwing me a look.

"I'll walk you out," I tell her.

We're almost out of the room when Gus says, "Come back in here when you're done, Noah."

"Okay," I answer and pray I didn't overstep my bounds here.

I walk Maggie to her little sports car, trying to think of something to say. We stop at her driver's side door and she holds her hand out.

"It was nice to meet you, Noah," she says.

"It was nicer to meet you, Maggie," I answer, slipping my hand in hers.

When she drives off, I head back toward the house and hesitate before letting myself back inside. Gus told me to come back so I push through the door and make my way to the kitchen.

He's got the casserole out of the fridge, sitting on the counter.

"Take this," he says. "It's yours. Betty will fix something for us for dinner." He pushes the dish across the counter and I grab it before it slips off the edge and crashes to the floor.

"You don't want any of it?" It smells good. Really good.

He shakes his head and moves toward the door that will take him back outside. "When people bring you a casserole, it's because someone's dying or dead, and we're not there yet."

And just like that, I don't think I can eat a bite of it either, even if Maggie was the one who made it.

5

I should go home. Mom's been texting me for a while. So has Jack for that matter. But instead I'm picking my way through her flower bed, trying to get to the window I hope is still hers. Because if I'm going to reclaim my life I need to know exactly what I'm up against, and this seems like the best place to get the truth.

Just before I knock on her window, I glance back at the house next door, the one I lived in until I went to Sutton's. Just like all the houses in this neighborhood, these two look just alike except our floor plans were mirror images of each other so my bedroom window looked out at hers. Most nights I crawled out of mine, crossed the small green space that separated us, and stood right here with my hand raised in front of the glass of her window.

Tapping lightly, I brace myself for some unknown face to yank the curtain back and the scream that will no doubt follow. But I'm startled when I hear steps behind me.

"It's been a long time since you've come knocking on my window, Owen Foster."

I spin around, trying not to get caught in the thorny branches of a nearby rosebush. "Hey," I say and feel lame.

"Hey," Pippa says. Her hands are jammed in her jean pockets and her head is tilted to the side.

"Can we talk a minute?" I ask.

She's still. No smile. Not even blinking.

"I'm not sure I want to talk to you. I'm afraid if you open your mouth again that I'll never get over how you've changed."

But even as she says that, she's looking me up and down with a confused look on her face. I came straight here from Gus's so I'm covered in dirt and soot and I smell like a bonfire and probably dead raccoon. I'm sure she wouldn't believe me if I told her how I spent my day.

Dragging in a deep breath, I say, "I need your help. I need to know everything. What you know about my dad. What you know about the threats my mom has gotten. How things have been. And not just the last few months. But since I've been gone."

Her eyes narrow like she's trying to find a trick in my request. And then she zeros in on my hands.

"What have you been doing?"

"Reclaiming things."

She waits for me to elaborate but I don't.

"Have you eaten?" she asks.

I shake my head. "Not since breakfast." And saying the words seems to unleash a growling hunger from the pit of my stomach.

She laughs quietly, and I've missed that sound more than I thought I would have.

"Come inside. My parents are at parent-teacher conferences for Pacey and Parker at the middle school. But she texted that dinner's on the stove."

Dodging the smaller plants, I step out of the flower bed and follow her to the front door. "Pacey is old enough to be in middle school?" I ask.

"Just started sixth grade."

I've been gone for so long. She was just a little kid when I saw her last.

Pippa's house is the same as I remember, just with more pictures scattered around every surface. I study a series of her little sisters and can't believe how much Pacey looks like Pippa did when she was that age.

"Come eat. I can hear your stomach begging for food from here," she says as she sets a bowl down on the kitchen table.

I take the seat opposite of her. Her mom made chicken and dumplings and it takes everything in me not to stick my face in it. Even using the spoon, I empty the bowl in record time.

"Want seconds?" she asks.

"Is there enough?" I ask.

"You know Mom always cooks way too much."

I'd forgotten that. I'd forgotten a lot of things about Pippa.

Grabbing my bowl, I help myself to more food, filling it until the excess spills over the edge.

I glance at the clock when I sit back down. "How much longer before your parents are home?" I've always felt comfortable here, but I'm dreading seeing them again. I know Pippa's mom won't throw her arms around my neck to hug me and her dad won't thump me on the back and tell me he's glad to have another boy in the house since he's always so outnumbered. Not after what my dad did.

Pippa's moving her food around but not actually eating. "Probably another hour."

"Will you tell me? Tell me what you know?"

She won't look at me. Just stares at her food. "I don't know that much."

"Please. Just tell me what you know," I beg.

"I heard your mom showed up alone at that fund-raiser they do every year for the football team. It's a cook-off and usually your mom's food is always the first to go. They said she stood there the entire time with all that food she made laid out on the table in front of her but everyone boycotted her because by then it was obvious your dad had run off with everyone's money. The news just wasn't public yet."

My fork bangs off the side of my bowl, landing on the table. I can picture her there, probably in a pretty dress with her hair pulled back. And I can only imagine the food she made, étouffée or maybe a seafood pasta and of course something sweet like pralines, all of it sitting there untouched. And what it must have taken for her to stay until the event was over.

"There were a few other things," Pippa says quietly. "She was asked to leave the committee she was on that plans that big party the country club does every year for New Year's Eve. You know, stuff like that."

Pippa looks at me, probably trying to gauge how I'm taking this. I want her to continue so I don't interrupt her. I need to hear this. All of it.

"And I ran into your mom right after her car was repossessed. She went into the grocery store and came out to find her car being towed away."

"They stranded her at the store?" I ask, forgetting my pledge to keep silent. "Why wouldn't they wait until she was home? Were they trying to embarrass her?"

Pippa shrugs and her eyes dart to mine once before she looks away again.

"She was sitting on the curb with a few grocery sacks scattered around her, trying to call a taxi on her cell. No one stopped to help her but everyone gawked at her when they went past."

I push my bowl away even though it's half-full. I should have been here.

"So I pulled my car up and helped her load her groceries. She held it together until we were alone. I could tell she was crying but she never said anything the entire way to your house. This was when she was still in the house at Cypress Lake."

Her words are like a gut punch. "Thank you for that." I reach across the table, my hand on hers for a few seconds before she pulls it away.

"I didn't do it for you. I did it for her. Growing up, she was like my second mother. It broke my heart seeing her like that. But when we got inside, you could tell someone had been there. Stuff was moved around and it was a mess. There was a note, too, that freaked her out but she wouldn't let me see it."

"Someone broke in the house?"

Pippa nods. "I stayed while she called the police. She was really shaken up."

I can feel the anger moving through me like a drug, racing through my veins. "Is that it? Or is there more?"

Her brown eyes are glassy like she's a second away from crying, which would normally make me panic. But instead it makes me want to reach for her again. But I don't.

"Some detective showed up. Talked to her. It sounds like there were other incidents. Something about a brick through a window and some threatening calls. She didn't really want to talk about it in front of me so I left. I checked on her a few times. Went by your house before she, um, had to move. I was there when she got another one of those calls."

I stare at the wall behind Pippa, trying to keep calm.

"Who do you think is calling her? Throwing bricks through her window? Breaking into her house?"

Pippa shrugs. "I really don't know. There are so many people angry with your dad."

"I get they're mad but they think it's okay to take it out on Mom? Dad stole some money from them, not her."

Pippa's eyes get big. "I agree that no one should be doing this to your mom but your dad did a little more than *steal some money*. For someone like Sarah Frazier, what your dad did changed her life forever."

Mr. Frazier is one of the stories I read about last night. Sarah is a year behind us so I'm sure I'll run into her at some point. Thankfully, her older brother, Reed, is older and off at college.

I'm not sure what I would say if I saw either of them.

"For a lot of people, their lives will never be the same because of what your dad did. But your mom was the only one here, the only connection to your dad, and they're all taking it out on her. You should have been here," Pippa finishes in a whisper.

I shift back in my chair hard enough that the legs scrape against the floor. "How was I supposed to know what was going on here? No one told me anything. She won't tell me anything. You should have called me."

"Me?" Pippa yells. She stands up from the table, taking her mostly full bowl of food to the sink. "Yeah, right. You and I haven't spoken in years. How was I supposed to know you didn't have a clue what was going on? For all I knew, you heard what was happening but refused to come home."

Her words cut, and the anger bleeds right out of me. "You really think I wouldn't come home if I knew what was going on here?"

"Owen, I don't know you anymore. We're not the same kids we were. You've changed. I've changed. We're not friends. We're more like strangers."

I stand up quickly, needing to be out of this house and away from her. "Tell your mom thanks for dinner. Or don't if you'd rather her not know I was here."

She doesn't stop me from leaving and that sucks as bad as the rest of it.

Mom's waiting for me in the backyard when I get to my aunt's house.

"You could have answered my calls. Or my texts. I was worried."

The only light comes from a lamp in the windowsill above the kitchen sink so it's hard to make out her face, but I can tell from her stuffed-up nose that's she's been crying. And by now I know she only does this when she thinks no one is around to witness it.

"I wish you would have told me what was going on after Dad left."

"You've seen Pippa," she answers. "I've always loved that girl. And she's the only one who doesn't look like she'd rather spit on me than speak to me. I should have known she'd tell you everything."

I drop down on the ground near her. "She's worried about you. Just like I am."

She sits up straighter and takes a deep breath. "And I'm worried about you."

"I should have been here the minute he left. You shouldn't have gone through all of that alone."

She's quiet, staring off into the darkness. For all of the things Pippa told me, the one thing that was clear was that my mother handled everything that was thrown at her with an amazing amount of grace. I would have fought and cussed and made things worse. But not her. She's the kind of woman that stands quietly in front of a table full of food for hours while others ignore her.

"Do you want to talk about it?" I ask.

"No."

I'm trying to keep my cool. Trying not to stand up and destroy things. "Has anything happened since you've been here?" I ask through gritted teeth.

She shrugs and picks at the hem of her shirt. "A few calls. That's all.

I think it's safer here for us. Lucinda is always around. Always has her nose in everyone's business. I think whoever is doing this knows that."

"Who do you think it is? You have to have some ideas. Someone who lost more than the others. Someone who'd lose it like this."

Mom leans back further in her chair, drawing her legs under her, and stares off into the night sky. "Everyone lost so much. I can't even wrap my head around how much money he stole. They're saying ten million but it'll probably be more when they understand the full extent of what he did. And I can't help but think of every trip we had. Was the money we used to go to Hawaii money that would have put the Barsons' kids through college? What about that boat we rented in the Caribbean? Maybe the Wellingtons could have retired and spent time traveling the country in a motor home like they've been talking about for years if we hadn't rented that boat."

I scoot closer to her chair, slinging the dirt and grass far away from me. "This is not our fault. We didn't do anything to those people."

"Owen, we may not have been the ones to steal from them, but our lives were made better by something that was theirs. I understand why someone would be so mad at us. I understand the desperation they must feel."

I stand up quickly, so quickly I almost fall over. "So you think you deserve those threats?"

She leaves her chair and stops right in front of me. Her hands reach up and she holds on to my shoulders, clenching them tightly. "No. I don't mean that. Whoever is doing this . . . it's not right. Not at all. But I'm not surprised that what he did drove someone to this. It's why I wanted to leave you at school as long as I could."

I step back from her and her hands drop to her sides. "We should leave this town. Go somewhere else. Somewhere where no one knows us."

"We can't leave. Not until the investigation is finished. Not until we've paid back as much as we can." She pauses a moment and I know there's one more thing she wants to tell me. One more bomb to drop on me tonight. "They set the date for the auction. Saturday, a week and a half from today."

"What auction?"

"Our house. And all our belongings. There will be a public auction where everything is sold and all the money will go toward restitution for the victims."

"Does anyone understand that we're victims, too? He left us with nothing."

Mom gives me a sad smile but doesn't answer. She's in the same pants she was wearing when she picked me up from school and a sweat-shirt that's seen better days.

"Did they let you keep any of your things?" It sucks I'm just now asking her this, just now noticing she's been wearing the same thing over and over.

She shrugs. "A few clothes. The ones not worth much. My makeup and toiletries. The things they can't sell."

"That's it?"

She nods. "That's it."

"That's not fair. Not all of your stuff was bought with stolen money."

She waves off my protests. "I don't miss most of it. And I certainly don't need designer clothes anymore. I do wish I could have kept a few things like the bracelet Granddad gave me when I graduated from high school."

I know the exact bracelet she's talking about. She wore it all the time.

She gets up from the chair and hugs me once more before disappearing inside the house. I stay out a while longer, thinking about everything she said. But mostly trying to figure out how to get that bracelet back for her.

Noah—Summer of 1999

No one ate the casserole. Not one bite. But I still have Maggie's mom's dish that she brought it in. Is that part of the gift? Here's some food because someone in your house is dying or dead and as a bonus you get a glass dish to remind you of this meal.

It's been three days and I still don't know what to do with it.

After Gus caught me in the kitchen, he started inviting me in to eat at the table with him for dinner. Betty usually feeds Abby once she moves her from the porch to the bed, and Abby doesn't want an audience for that. I guess Gus was tired of eating alone.

We just finished dinner and I'm eyeing that pad with Maggie's number on it. I should call her, lie to her, and tell her the food was delicious and ask if she wants the dish back. I mean, her mom could probably use it. Make another casserole, send it to someone else who's dying.

Yeah, that's why I need to call her. Not because I can't quit thinking about her. That smile, those pink cheeks, that rambling she does when she's nervous.

Before I can talk myself out of it, I pick up the phone and dial her number. I twist the cord around my finger, hoping she's the one who answers the phone.

"Hello."

"Maggie?" I ask.

"No, this is her sister, Lucinda. Who's calling?"

"This is Noah. Is Maggie around?"

"Noah who?" she asks, but before I answer, everything sounds muffled and then Maggie is on the phone.

"Hey!" she says.

"Hey, um, Gus and Abby wanted me to tell you the casserole was delicious. And we cleaned the dish. It's ready if you need it back."

"Oh," she says, sounding disappointed.

That's the only encouragement I need so I go for it. "And I wanted to see you again."

"Oh!" she says again but much perkier this time. "I'd like that."

Gus walks in the kitchen, a confused look on his face when he sees I'm on the phone. I point to the clean glass dish on the counter and then back to the receiver I've got cradled between my ear and shoulder.

His eyebrows shoot up and he shakes his head while he leaves the room.

"Are you there?" Maggie asks.

"Yeah, Gus just walked in. Sorry. Anyway, do you want to hang out sometime?" I've got nothing to offer this girl. Not a car to pick her up in, not money to take her out, nothing.

"Sure. When?"

I stare at the ceiling, willing something clever to come to me but I've got nothing. "Whenever is good for you. Can you come over here? I don't have a car," I mumble in the phone. There, I said it.

"Yeah, sure. How about tomorrow night? Am I coming to Gus's house? Is that where you live?"

I take a quick glance around the kitchen, making sure I'm still alone. "I live in a small house on the back of the property. I'll wait for you at the road and then ride with you to the back."

"Okay, I'll bring a pizza. How's seven?" she asks.

"Seven works for me," I answer and feel like such a tool. I can't pick her up and she's buying dinner.

"Great! See you tomorrow," she says, then hangs up the phone.

Shit. Now I'm nervous. I've got twenty-four hours to think about what a bad idea this is. I stick my head into the den, where Gus is sitting in a chair, reading.

"I'm leaving. See you in the morning."

"Maggie is a nice girl, but I can promise you her daddy doesn't know she's planning to hang out here alone with a boy."

"You mean a boy like me," I say.

Gus lets out a deep breath and drops his head for a second then looks back at me. "Yeah, that, too. It's a small town, Noah. Right or wrong, people are funny when it comes to their daughters and boys they don't know."

I nod and dig my hands in my pockets. "Trust me, I know how it is. I've been fighting my whole life for people to look at me and not see trash."

Gus gets up from his chair and moves toward me, putting both hands on my shoulders. "You've been better help around here than I could've hoped for. You're giving me time with her, and that's worth more to me than any amount of money. And anyone who takes the time to cut flowers every morning for a woman who is . . . very sick . . . isn't trash."

I hang my head but he nudges my arm until I'm looking him in the eye again.

"What are you running from?"

It takes everything in me to hold eye contact with him and not flinch. Somehow Gus has turned into the big brother I never had. "I'm not running from anything."

He can't know that it took me a few days to understand that weird feeling in my stomach was the fact that it was full. He can't know that for the first time in forever I've gone to sleep without the fear that I'd never wake up again.

"You haven't set foot off this place since you got here."

"You haven't set foot off this place since I got here, either. What are you hiding from?" I ask.

We stare at each other for a long moment before he says, "Everything I need is right here. No reason to go anywhere else. And I don't know what you're running from but you're safe here."

It's been a long time since I felt safe.

Gus drops back down in his chair and says, "That's enough talk for one night. Good luck getting your girl."

My girl. Is there any chance in hell that I could make Maggie Everett my girl? Probably not but damn, I'm going to try.

6

Mom thinks I'm running out of the door so I can make it to school on time, but I've got another destination in mind. The street is still packed with news vans but Aunt Lucinda is out there just like she is every morning. There's one reporter that's been overly flirty with her, probably just to get her talking, and she's fallen for it hook, line, and sinker.

No one glances my way when I come out of the side door and slip into the neighbor's yard.

The police station parking lot is full so I have to find an empty spot on the street and a few quarters for the meter. I spent most of last night digging back through the news stories I read a few days ago, but this time making a note of every person that has gone public saying Dad stole from them.

It's a long list.

There's an officer manning a security desk just inside the front door so I empty my pockets and walk through the metal detector, thankful nothing on me triggers the alarm. Once my change is back in my pocket and my belt is on, I walk to the information desk across the room and ask for Detective Hill.

"What's your name? I'll call him and tell him you're here," she says, the phone already in her hand.

"Owen Foster."

The officer does a double take when my name registers. "You can have a seat over there," she says and points to a small waiting area.

I drop down in the seat closest to the door and lean back. And wait.

Twenty minutes later, Detective Hill sticks his head out of another door and motions for me to come in. I follow him through a big room full of desks where other officers are either on their computers or talking on the phone. Every eye in the room lands on me and stays there until we cross through another door.

"You must be pretty high up to get your own office like this," I say. The office is small with barely enough room for his desk and chair and another small chair, which I drop down into before he has a chance to invite me to sit.

"What brings you by here this morning, Owen?" Detective Hill asks. He glances quickly at the clock. "Thought you'd be in school. Would hate if a truancy officer had to get involved with everything else y'all got going on."

"I need to know what you're doing to keep my mother safe," I say.

His face changes. The smart-ass expression falls away and he presses his lips tightly together. "Did she finally tell you what's going on?"

"The threats? Yes." I don't mention that I had to hear it from Pippa. Seeing Mom so upset last night I just couldn't push her for details, but that doesn't mean I don't want them. "I heard there have been some calls and a brick through her window. And that someone was in our house. Our old house."

Detective Hill nods like he's expecting me to say more. When I don't, he sits down in his chair, leaning back, and kicks one foot up on his desk. "To keep *you both* safe, I've got a tap on the house phone . . . at her request. We're also monitoring the incoming calls on her cell phone through her carrier. I've got patrols making regular rounds through your aunt's neighborhood."

I wait for him to say more but he just stares at me. "That's it?" I ask.

We stare at each other long enough for it to get uncomfortable. He finally drops his foot down to the floor and opens his desk drawer. He pulls out a plastic bag that has a piece of paper in it and another bag that holds the brick. I can't take my eyes off of it.

"We are taking these threats very seriously. I'm taking it very seriously. There are a lot of people who believe your mother knew what your father was doing. I'm not one of them."

I lean forward so I can see the note better. It's written on one of Mom's monogrammed notecards. Her initials are at the top in scrolly green letters. I remember these cards. They were in a flowery box on her desk and she always used them for thank-you notes. But I haven't seen that flowery box since I've been at Lucinda's house.

"The note on her stationery was the first threat she got. It was about a week after your dad took off. Your mom was trying to act like everything was normal. There was no forced entry."

I move in closer so I can read the note.

IF HE FUCKS OVER MY FAMILY, I'LL FUCK OVER YOURS

The words are written in black marker. The letters are thick and angry looking and my stomach rolls reading the words someone left for Mom.

"I'm guessing the black smudge all along the edge is where you dusted for prints?" I ask.

"Yes. We didn't find any," Detective Hill answers. "The brick came a few days later. Someone threw it through her bedroom window while she was sleeping."

Then I study the brick. The words are painted in red. It's crude and messy since the brick's rough surface wouldn't make it easy to write on.

WHERE IS THE MONEY

But it's the brick I'm studying more than the words. It's old with bits of blue paint on it.

"This is reclaimed brick," I say.

"Yeah, we figured that out," Detective Hill adds. He's trying to make me feel stupid for being here.

"Have you matched it? Have you even tried?"

Reclaimed brick is expensive. It's what people use when they are building a new house but want to make it look old. The bricks are salvaged when an old building is torn down and then reused on new houses. There's a chance a local builder would recognize this brick if it were used on a house around here, especially if the bluish-green paint color matches.

"We're working on it."

"So someone is threatening my mom. Who do you think it is?"

Detective Hill cocks his head to the side and studies me. "It's tough to say."

"Do you think the note and brick are from the same person?"

He shrugs. "We're looking into both options."

These are useless answers and I'm trying not to get pissed off. His phone rings and he spins around in his chair when he answers it, I guess to make sure I don't hear what he's saying. He digs around in a drawer while he talks and I take my phone out and snap a quick picture of the brick and the note before he ends the call and turns back around.

I stand up to leave. "On that first day, you told me where to go for a run. Did you know I'd end up at Gus Trudeau's house?"

He tilts his head to the side. "Depends on how far you could run."

"I guess you know my dad used to work out there. Live there."

Detective Hill nods slowly but doesn't say anything else.

"So you wanted me to meet Gus?"

He ignores my question and says, "I know you've heard from him."

"Dad? You think I've heard from him?"

Detective Hill nods slowly. "Yep."

Digging my hands in my jean pockets, I stand there and stare at him, shaking my head. "Nope."

The only sound in the room is the ticking from his wall clock. Almost thirty seconds go by before he speaks again.

"Did you know that fancy school of yours keeps a log in the mail room?"

It takes everything in me not to react.

"It's a new thing, and students and parents don't even know they're doing it. Last year, one of the students had his dealer mail him drugs. So now the mail is monitored."

Jason Holmes.

He's waiting for me to tell him about the letter I got. He can't know for sure it was from Dad but the timing is too coincidental, especially since very few people get snail mail anymore.

"Yeah, I knew that kid. He'd sell joints for twenty bucks each. Total rip-off."

Detective Hill smiles before he can stop himself.

"Owen, we're looking into everything. Every lead. Every threat. If you know something that could help, you need to share it with me. It's the only way to keep you and your mom safe."

Deep down, I know there's got to be more to what they say Dad did. And if he's as guilty as everyone thinks he is, I'll be the first one to turn him in.

But I need to talk to him first. I need to know why he wants to see me.

"We know you got a letter the day before your mom and I showed up at school. And we know it's the only physical mail you've received all year."

"That was a reminder from my dentist that it's time for a cleaning."

Detective Hill rolls his eyes. "You know I can check that out."

I shrug. "Check away."

And then I leave his office before I have to lie to him again.

I pull the truck into the school parking lot just as the bell rings in the distance. Checking the time, it's probably the end of first period or beginning of second.

I jog up the front steps and into the building, stopping to check in at the office.

"And why are you tardy this morning?" the woman behind the counter asks.

I could probably tell her I was at the police station and get an excused tardy but I don't want anyone knowing any more about us than they already do. "A reporter was following me when I left for school so I drove around until he got bored."

Her mouth hangs open slightly like she doesn't know how to respond to that. "Oh, of course. Um, we've just started second period." She checks the excused box and slides the slip across the counter.

"Thanks," I mumble and head to class.

Fumbling around in my backpack, I pull out my schedule to see where I'm supposed to be for second period. Trigonometry.

I pull the door open slowly, hoping to avoid making a scene, but there's no way every eye won't be on me the second I step into the room.

I only have this class on Tuesdays and Thursdays so I have no idea where I'm supposed to sit.

"Mr. Foster, please join us," the teacher says with his hand out, waiting for my tardy slip. "I'm Mr. Hanson. Take a seat." I hand the slip to him and survey the room. Pippa's in the back corner but after a brief glance at me, she ducks her head. The only empty chair is on the second row, nowhere near her.

I slide into my seat and fidget with my notebook. Hanson hands me a textbook and says, "We're on page forty-two. Not sure how far along you were at your old school so see me after class if you feel behind."

I turn to the page they're on and realize I'm a little ahead. We covered this a couple of weeks ago at Sutton's.

Hanson turns back to the whiteboard and finishes a problem that he started before I interrupted.

Most of the other students look back to the board or to their own textbook but a few are still staring at me. I want to flip them off. I want to tell them to turn the fuck around. I want to haul ass from the room.

But I stare ahead and focus on the calendar tacked up on the wall next to the whiteboard.

I have a little more than a week until every last thing we owned is auctioned to the public. Before strangers are walking through my house, looking at our things, judging their worth. Will people be there to buy something they really want or need? Or will they buy something just to have a piece of our downfall?

And then I think about the letter from Dad. If I'm reading the message he sent right, he'll be at Frank's in thirteen days.

It's not a far drive. Twenty minutes without traffic. I'm guessing since the Wednesday-night special starts at five I should be there by five.

Will he just walk inside and sit down next to me? Every person in this town—probably everyone in the state—is looking for him, everyone thinks he's run off with the money he stole, but could he really still be here, hiding out somewhere, waiting to see me?

I've already got a list of questions I want him to answer, and the first is did he start embezzling right away or was it something that just happened when he got into a financial bind? More than anything else, I want to know this. I feel like the only way I can someday come to terms with what he did is if he did it out of some sort of twisted desperation.

"Mr. Foster, are you with us?" Mr. Hanson asks. Half of the class is laughing that I've been called out.

"Yes, sir," I answer.

"Then come complete this problem so I know you're understanding this lesson."

I walk to the board and take the blue dry-erase marker from his outstretched hand. Quickly, I complete the problem, then drop the pen in the narrow metal holder at the bottom of the board.

Mr. Hanson moves closer to the board. "Wonders never cease."

"We covered this a month ago," I say, even though I know it makes me sound like an ass.

"Where did you transfer from?" Mr. Hanson asks.

"Sutton's," I answer just before I sit back down.

Mr. Hanson makes a clucking sound with his tongue. "Ah, very prestigious indeed."

There's a guy with a cool faux-hawk of short dreadlocks sitting next to me who says in a singsong voice, "Best our money could buy."

Seth, who's sitting next to him, laughs loudly and they bump fists.

Rage consumes me. I stand up quickly, almost knocking my desk over. The guy stands up too and we're chest to chest. We're evenly matched in height but I'm broader than he is.

"Whatcha going to do?" he says. "Gonna hit me for telling the truth?"

"David, Owen, both of you stop this," Hanson yells, then tries to wedge himself between us, but neither of us is moving.

I want to hit him. My fists clench and every muscle in my body is ready.

"O," Pippa says from behind me. There's something about the way that single letter sounds that makes me step back. I throw my hands up to show Hanson I'm not going to hit anyone but David flinches and punches me. I'm knocked backward, taking Pippa down with me. She hits her head on the side of the desk and there's a small cut above her left eye.

David drops down next to her. "Pippa, I'm sorry! Are you okay? I thought he was taking a swing at me."

She pushes his hands away. "I'm fine."

"You need some ice. And a towel," I say.

"Yes, Pippa, straight to the nurse," Hanson says as he helps her to her feet. He spins around to David and me. "And you two, straight to the office."

David storms out, mumbling how this was all my fault. Apparently, I'm to blame for everything that happens.

I try to help Pippa up but she pushes me away, too. We leave the classroom and I run ahead to the bathroom and grab a few paper towels.

"Here," I say when she catches up and hand them to her.

She presses it against her forehead. "Thanks."

We walk quietly down the hall until we're outside the office door. Pippa pushes through and heads left toward the nurse while I join David in the waiting area outside of the principal's office.

He doesn't say anything, just throws disgusted looks my direction every few seconds. He's wearing a lacrosse team T-shirt, and if we weren't sitting out here probably about to get suspended for fighting, I would have asked him if it's too late to join.

"Owen, David, please step inside my office," Dr. Gibson says.

Our principal is younger than I expected. He can't be more than thirty and he's tall enough that I have to look up at him, which is not something I normally have to do.

"Have a seat," he says. "David, tell me what happened?"

David's account is pretty accurate and he takes full responsibility for Pippa's injury and now I feel like a bigger jackass seeing how stand-up he's being about this.

Dr. Gibson watches us, watches me, then addresses David. "You're suspended for the rest of the day. And I want you here thirty minutes early tomorrow morning and every morning next week. You'll help the janitorial staff in whatever way they need you."

David slumps in his chair. "Seems a little harsh, Dr. G."

"I'm hoping word gets around that I'll not tolerate this any longer. Go home and cool off."

David nods and leaves his office without another glance at me. Just before David leaves the room, Dr. Gibson says, "Good luck on the upcoming season."

David throws him a smile then shuts the door behind him.

"Owen, this is your second day here and your second altercation with another student."

So he heard about the almost-fight yesterday.

"Yes, sir."

"I understand the situation you and your mom are in but it's difficult for your father's victims to have you here."

The words are like a knife.

"I'd like to promise you that no one will say anything to you, but we both know that's not something I can control. Something you can't control. But you can control your behavior."

"You call them victims. But Mom and I are victims, too."

"Yes, I know," he answers. "I never said it was fair that they're taking this out on you. It's not fair. But you are a constant reminder to them." Dr. Gibson throws his hands up. "Truthfully, Owen, I don't know what to tell you. This is a terrible situation for everyone involved."

I nod and stare at the ground. Maybe I should drop out. Get my GED. Work at Gus's full-time where it's no one but us out there.

"Have you spoken to your dad?" Dr. Gibson asks and my head pops up.

"Excuse me?"

"Has he contacted you? Do you know where he is?"

"No."

Dr. Gibson leans forward, resting his elbows on the desk. He's trying to determine if I'm lying but he doesn't know me well enough to read me.

"Did you know someone who worked there?" I ask him in a quiet voice. "Your parents? Maybe your wife? Are you wondering if Mom and I know where the money is?"

He leans back in his chair and crosses his arms. "I think you should take the rest of the day off as well. And why don't you join David and the janitorial staff. We'll see you tomorrow, Owen. And next time you're in any sort of fight, I'll recommend you be moved to the alternative school for those who need a bit more supervision."

I nod and leave the room before I get myself in any more trouble. Pippa heads out of the front door of school just ahead of me.

"Are you out for the day, too?" I ask as I sprint to catch up with her.

She throws me a glance over her shoulder but keeps walking. I slow down once I'm next to her but she won't look at me or speak to me.

"Is your head okay?" I ask.

Silence.

I nudge my shoulder gently against hers. "C'mon, Pippa. Talk to me."

She nudges me back but it's hard enough that I stumble away from her. "I don't want to talk to you. And anyway I'm not the one you should be making sure is okay."

I stop and say, "Pippa, please."

She takes another step then stops, too. She still has her back to me but at least she's not moving. "Maybe instead of taking the bait from David you should find out why he's so upset. Find out what your dad did to his family."

I close the distance between us until I'm right behind her but I don't know what to say.

"It probably doesn't matter anyway, Owen. I'm sure as soon as you can you'll be leaving again, so maybe there's no point."

Even though she says we're strangers now, she knows me well. The first chance I get, I'm out of here.

Noah—Summer of 1999

The headlights of the little black sports car sweep across me when she pulls into the driveway and she stops long enough for me to jump into the passenger seat.

"Hey," she says. "Where to?"

"Follow the driveway to the house, then veer to the right when it splits," I answer. She looks prettier than I remember. The smell of pizza makes my mouth water but I feel shitty I couldn't take her out tonight.

"I can give you money for the food," I say.

She shakes her head. "It's fine. You can buy dinner next time."

Next time. I like the sound of that. Gus's words seep through me and I ask, "Do your parents know where you are?"

She shrugs. "I just turned eighteen so I should be able to come and go as I want," she answers, but that's not really an answer.

"So no, they have no idea you're slumming it with me tonight."

She turns to look at me. "Don't say it like that. That's not what this is."

"What is it?" I ask.

She stops the car and we're in the middle of the orchard, halfway between Gus's and my little shack by the river.

"A cute boy asked me to hang out tonight and I said yes."

I can feel a smile tugging at my mouth but I hold it back. "It's that simple?"

"Yes, it's that simple."

She starts driving again and her features are bathed in the blue lights from the dash and I can see her watching the gravel path intently, like she's afraid she's going to somehow lose her way.

We curve around until we get to the little clearing where the house sits. Gus told me the history of this place and, not going to lie, sometimes I feel like that old preacher is still lurking around. Without a TV to watch, most nights I find myself wandering through these old trees and sometimes it's like I can hear his words whispering through the leaves. I don't know if there's a higher power up there somewhere, but the closest I've ever felt to one are those nights I'm here alone in the preacher's woods.

I've even got a favorite tree. One where the thick roots stick out of the dirt and curve around, creating small pockets of space. It's the perfect place to sit and think. To feel safe.

Maggie parks in front of the house and she tries to hide her reaction to where I'm living.

"Sorry, it's not much," I say. "But it's clean. And for now, it's mine."

She nods. "Then it's perfect."

We walk up the front steps and I push open the screen door. This place has electricity and basic plumbing but there's no air conditioner. Thankfully, there's usually a breeze at night that pushes cool air through the screened windows.

Maggie sits down on the old couch, putting the pizza box on the small coffee table while I move to the mini fridge Gus lent me when I first moved in, pulling out two bottles of water.

I hand her one then sit down on the other end of the couch. "Sorry, this is all I have to drink."

"Noah, stop apologizing. I'm happy to be here." Maggie opens the pizza box and hands me a slice on a napkin, then gets one for herself. We both take a bite then start panting, trying to cool down the hot cheese.

Maggie laughs and tries to talk. "It's super hot."

I laugh and nod, managing to get the scalding piece down. "Yeah, we may want to let that cool a minute."

It's really quiet in this little house and it makes it that much more awkward with Maggie here. I'm about to apologize for not having a TV but stop myself. Instead, I say, "You know how to play poker?"

She shrugs. "Not really. Can you teach me?" she asks.

I jump off the couch and grab the deck of cards that I found on the small bookcase near the bed when I first moved in. I've played a thousand hands of solitaire and I can't wait to put the cards to better use.

Maggie moves the pizza box off the small table while I shuffle the cards. "Okay, I'm about to teach you the best card game out there. Texas Hold'em."

"Okay, I'm ready. But I'll warn you, I have excellent luck, so don't be surprised if I beat the pants off of you."

I wipe the smile off my face. "So we're playing strip poker?"

Her eyes get big and dart toward the door and I fall back laughing. "I swear, I'm teasing you. But your face. I think you were trying to figure out the fastest way out of this room."

Her cheeks turn pink and she starts rambling. "Whatever, I knew you were kidding and even if I didn't I swear I'd be fully dressed by the end because I'm that lucky."

No, pretty sure I'm the lucky one. "Okay, this is how you play."

It doesn't take Maggie long to catch on and she wasn't joking when she said she's lucky. We're playing for matchsticks and her little pile could start a forest fire. She runs her fingers through her pile and gives her best evil laugh. "I warned you," she says.

I lean back against the couch, content with how good the last couple of hours have been. Just as I'm about to ask her for another date, she glances at her watch and hops up off the couch.

"Oh! I didn't realize how late it was. I need to get going."

She's moving to the door before I'm even off the couch. "Let me ride with you to the front gate. It'd be real easy for you to get turned around back here and end up in the river."

"Okay but how will you get back?" she asks.

"It's not a long walk."

I follow Maggie to her car and get in the passenger seat. She cranks the engine and pulls around in a tight circle then heads back toward Gus's.

"I had a lot of fun tonight," she says.

"Me, too. Can I see you again?" I ask.

She smiles and nods and I feel like I could fly. There's been so little that's gone right in my world and since coming here, I feel like that could all be changing.

We get to the front gate and I hesitate before getting out of her car. I want to kiss her but I don't want to push my luck on the first date. Before I can think about it any longer, Maggie is leaning toward me and brushes her lips across mine. It's gentle and innocent and one of the best kisses I've had.

"Can I come back tomorrow night?" she asks.

"I wish you would," I answer.

I hop out and watch her drive off, then make the long dark walk back to the house in the Preacher Woods.

7

I grab a couple of burgers on the way to Gus's. I don't want to tell him I'm out early because of fighting at school, but he's got to wonder why I keep showing up here long before the last bell rings.

Gus is back in the lawn chair with a table full of parts in front of him again when I come up the front walk. Again, he's not surprised to see me—maybe he gets what a struggle it is for me to be there—but he is happy to see the food.

"Looks like we've got some company," I say, nodding to the various work trucks littering the driveway.

"Yeah, got a few guys here fixing the stuff we can't handle. If we don't plug that hole in the roof, we're just asking for another family of raccoons to move right on in. I decided we needed to get the orchard in order and leave the house to those who know what they're doing."

I glance at all of the vehicles' business names splashed across their doors and it looks like we've got some carpenters, plumbers, and electricians, and even a janitorial company. But there's one thing they all have in common.

"You didn't want to use anyone local? All these guys are out of

Alexandria." Alexandria is the closest big city near here, about an hour away.

Gus looks back at the house and then at me. "No. People from town have always wanted to get a look inside that house. I'm not going to start letting them now."

"Do you ever leave this property?"

"Not if I can help it," he says.

"How do you get food and stuff?"

Gus doesn't look up. "Betty, a woman who worked here for years, comes out twice a week and brings me what I need. She used to work here full-time taking care of the house . . . and Abby . . . but now she has another job and just comes when I need her."

I wonder who Abby is, but by the way he said her name I don't ask. It's obviously someone he was really close to.

Something has kept Gus out of that house and away from town for years. Part of me wonders if he hired these people to fix it so he doesn't have to go back inside now, but what will he do when it's finished? Will he move back inside? And will he ever go into town or will he stay out here with just me and Betty as company?

The house really isn't as bad off as it looks. Once the broken windows are fixed, the shutters are replaced, and everything is cleaned, the house only needs some minor plumbing and electrical work to be livable.

We sit on the front porch steps, eating off of our laps, in relative silence. I've only been around Gus a few days but I've learned he doesn't make small talk.

And I'm realizing how much I like that.

"Where do you want me today?" I ask once I finish with my burger.

He crumples up the paper his food was wrapped in and drops it back in the bag.

"Before we get started, you're going to need a pair of boots. Can't do this kind of work in those dress shoes."

I look down at my feet and would hardly call what I'm wearing dress shoes although I do agree they aren't made for farmwork. Gus disappears into the barn for a few minutes then comes back carrying a pair of well-worn work boots.

"Here, see if these fit."

I kick off my shoes and slip on the boots. They're a little tight but not so much that they'd be uncomfortable.

"You need some old jeans and shirts you don't care about getting messed up, too. I've got some old clothes I can have ready for you tomorrow."

"Thanks," I say, pacing in front of him, trying out my new boots. "Looks like I'm ready to work. Where do you want me?" I ask again.

"How about you start raking the orchard today," he says.

Raking. Yeah, don't even have a clue what that means. "I'm going to need a little more to go on than that."

"Can't shake the trees until all the limbs and sticks are picked up from underneath them."

"Okay," I say slowly, "but how—"

"C'mon," Gus says, then walks to the nearest pecan tree. He points to the branches that have lost most of their leaves but are hanging heavy with pecans. "They're just about ready to pick but we don't want to wait for them to take their own sweet time coming off the trees. So we have a machine that shakes the tree. All the pecans will fall to the ground and then we'll come along with a harvester to pick them up. It's sort of like a big vacuum cleaner."

Gus points to the ground and kicks a limb that's right in front of us. "But if all these sticks and leaves are on the ground, then it's harder to pick up the nuts. So we need to clean up under each tree first. That's raking. You'll get on the tractor and drag that rake attached to the back of it around and around each tree until you got most of the debris caught in those fingers, then you'll drag it away from the tree."

"Okay, seems simple enough," I answer.

Gus watches to make sure I can get the tractor cranked then motions for me to back it out of the barn.

This should be a simple thing but it's not. I turn the steering wheel the direction I think I need to get out but the rake attachment doesn't go the direction I need it to. I pull forward and try again, getting the same results, almost jackknifing the rake.

I try again but slow my speed until I'm crawling and it's still not where I need it.

I try again but increase my speed until I almost take out the side of the barn.

Frustration simmers and anger threatens to boil over. It can't be this hard to back up a tractor and rake out of a barn. My hand goes to the key because I want nothing more than to shut this tractor down. I can't do this. I glance back at Gus, who is watching me with his arms crossed in front of him.

"Turn the wheel right to make the rake go left," he yells to me over the roar of the tractor.

"But that doesn't make sense," I yell back.

Gus shrugs. "Maybe not to you." He waits a moment, probably sensing I'm ready to give up, and says, "Try it once more."

I can quit or I can figure it out.

Even though it goes against every bit of logic I have, I turn the wheel the opposite direction I want the rake to go and damn if it doesn't work perfectly. Gus gives me a small smile and a nod of encouragement and I decide I'm not ready to quit just yet.

Going forward is definitely easier than going backward, and it's not long before I've finished making my first pass around the base of the closest pecan tree.

"Go around each tree, sweeping out from the base, about three to four times, until it looks pretty clean," he yells. "Then drag the debris away from the tree and leave it in the open lane before moving on to the next tree. We'll collect all the piles when you're done."

Gus walks off and somehow I feel like I've passed some little test. He's back in that chair in the front yard, working on whatever piece of equipment needs to be fixed, but I see his occasional glance as he makes sure I haven't wrecked his tractor.

After the first few circles, I fall into a steady rhythm. It's easy work but somehow gratifying watching those long metal fingers grab everything in their path. Since I got an early start on the day, I make pretty good progress. And since I only have to move forward, I haven't been tempted to drive the tractor into the river.

The sun hangs low, scattering light under the branches, catching the dust the rake throws up. It's hot enough that the back of my shirt is damp, but there's enough of a breeze so it's not uncomfortable. My mind wanders to Dad as it usually does and I wonder if this is something he did while he worked here. It would have been summer, so I'm not sure what's involved with the upkeep of this place when the harvest isn't right around the corner.

Did he take to this work or did he find it as foreign as I do? But even though things started out rough, just like yesterday I'm surprised at the sense of accomplishment I have when I can see what a difference I made today. Did he feel the same? Or was this what drove him to do something different with his life? Something that would guarantee he wouldn't make his living working outdoors? Even though most employees of Louisiana Frac worked on a well site, my dad was always in the office.

I'm halfway through this section when I see it. I kill the tractor and hop off while the engine sputters and belches and then follow the river by foot. The trees are older here; the trunks so wide it would take several people to circle around them.

The fading light bounces off the river and lights up the little clearing. It feels different here in this part of the orchard, or maybe it's my mind messing with me, thinking about that old man talking to these trees. I wonder what he said to them.

Did Dad talk to them, too?

I run my hand down the bark of the nearest tree thinking about the secrets hidden back here. What was going on with Dad that made him choose to live a summer here? I know so little about my dad's life growing up, even less about how my parents met. It's not something either talked about. Do these trees know the story?

The wind picks up, whispering through the leaves, and I pull my hand away while shivers race down my spine.

"Gus would be on the ground laughing if he saw me getting spooked like this," I say out loud. The air swirls around the trees then rushes over the water as if answering me.

I move toward the house. Wide cypress boards, gray with age, cover the outside and a narrow porch stretches across the front with thick wooden beams acting as columns, holding up the roof. A brick path, starting from nowhere, weaves its way to the front steps.

The doorknob is rusted, making it almost impossible to turn, and my straining muscles protest at any more use, but I've come this far. I've got to see what's inside.

With one final push, the door gives and I spill inside. It's just one big room and the only light comes from the few windows scattered down each side. Part of me believed I would discover Dad inside, hiding out here, waiting until he planned to meet me.

But it's empty.

A big couch sits in the middle of the space and an old black oven is against one wall, with a chimney shooting up behind it, disappearing in the ceiling. Next to the oven is a small counter made from the same graying cypress wood where an old washtub acts as a sink. Against the back wall is a small bed covered with what was once a brightly colored quilt but it's now faded. There's a small table with two chairs on the other side of the room. The back right corner is closed off and I'm guessing that's where the bathroom is.

Dust floats through the air, illuminated by the bright setting sun. I don't see any lights, not even sure if this place has electricity. Definitely no TV or phone. It's really hard to imagine my dad living here.

I walk across the room and stop in front of a small bookcase that's on the wall next to the bed. One shelf is full of old books, the spines so worn I can't make out the titles. But it's the top shelf that grabs my attention. There's a small framed picture there. I pick it up, wiping away the thick coating of dust, and drag in a deep breath. In the image, Mom is sitting on a blanket in the grass and she's got a huge smile on her face. She looks young and really happy. Happier than I've seen her in a long time.

I search the cabin for any other piece of Dad, anything, but there's nothing. There's nothing else.

I pick up the frame and flip it over, opening the back. It's one of those Polaroid pictures with the section of white across the bottom. Since part of it is stuck, it takes a few minutes to pry it loose without doing any damage. I want to remove the image, stick it in my wallet, but I'm surprised when I see the back of the white section.

Or really, by what's written there.

S6R9T4

I have no idea what it means. From the looks of the place, no one has been inside this house for years. But for some reason, this combination of letters and numbers meant something to Dad, and I wish I knew what it was.

• • •

I jump the small fence in the backyard and clear the steps leading to the back door. When I push open the screen door, Mom shrieks.

Her hand flies to her chest. She's so jumpy now.

"Sorry," I say. Seth's mother is sitting at the table next to her and she gives me a small wave.

She smiles and says, "It's been a long time, Owen. It's good to see you again."

"Hey, Mrs. Sullivan," I say. "Nice to see you again." I don't think it's the time to mention that Seth isn't dying to rekindle our friendship.

Mom hasn't had a visitor—that I know of—since I got here, so I'm curious what this is about. Mom has a legal pad in front of her, the page filled with her small neat writing.

Mrs. Sullivan pats the table in between her and Mom and says, "Call me if you think of anything I should add."

Mom nods and the first genuine smile I've seen on her breaks across her face. "I will, Elise. And again, I really appreciate this opportunity."

As soon as Mom is back from walking her to the door, I ask, "What was that about?"

"Elise heard I've been looking for a job. She can't hire me at the antiques store she owns downtown with Sheila Blackwell because Sheila isn't speaking to me anymore, but she does have a huge party coming up at her house and she's overwhelmed. Normally she uses Ardoin's, just like everyone else in town, but she said she wants to go a different route for this party and asked me to cater it for her."

"Oh, wow, Mom, that's great!"

"I know, right!" And there's that smile again. "From our conversation today, it sounds like money is tighter than it used to be since her divorce and I'm a fraction of the cost that Ardoin's would charge, but no matter what the reason, I'm thrilled she's giving me a chance."

She puts her arm around my shoulders and steers me to a chair at the kitchen table. "Are you hungry?" she asks.

"Starving."

She hasn't asked where I spend my afternoons and I haven't offered.

"I need to get Lucinda to go to the grocery store. We're out of almost everything. And I'll need supplies for Elise's party."

It's not lost on me that she won't even consider going to the store herself.

"Make me a list of what you need and I'll go for you," I say.

She gives me a smile and nods while I take a seat at the table. Mom pulls random things out of the fridge and throws together an omelet. She knows I love breakfast at any other time than breakfast time. Instead of working at Louisiana Frac, she should have opened a bakery or restaurant years ago. It's not surprising Mrs. Sullivan wants her to cook for her party.

"Now that you got a catering gig, maybe you should think of starting your own business."

She shakes her head quickly. "This is a one-time thing. And Elise has always been kind to me. She's just doing me a favor because she knows we need the money."

I shrug. "You may be surprised."

Instead of talking about it, she changes the subject. "So I heard there's a dance coming up at school next week."

"Yeah, that's the word around school."

She sets the plate of food down in front of me. The omelet is loaded with ham, two different kinds of cheese, mushrooms, and onions, and my mouth is watering just looking at it.

"You should go," she says. "This is home now, like it or not, and the sooner you settle in, the better it will be."

"I don't need to settle in. As soon as we're free to leave, that's exactly what we need to do." I pick up the plate and move toward the den that acts as my bedroom. "Thanks for the food, Mom," I say as I leave the kitchen. I'd rather eat alone than talk about making this place home.

Noah—Summer of 1999

She sits cross-legged on the end of the couch, facing me. "Tell me five things about you and I'll tell you five things about me."

Maggie has been here almost every night for the last week and a half. Sometimes it's just for a few minutes right when I get off work, and other times it's late at night and she manages to stay for a few hours. And every time she leaves, she brushes her lips against mine and asks me if she can come back tomorrow.

Tonight it's late and I know she's snuck out of her house to be here. But it's different this time. Something about Maggie is different. I turn and mimic the way she's sitting so I'm facing her. She only wants to know five things about me but I want to know a thousand about her.

I could go for the obvious. I'm nineteen, I'm from St. Louis, I'm hoping to save up enough money so I can go to college ... all the easy things. And most of these things she already knows.

But instead I say, "One: I left home and moved into an old run-down house with a group of guys I ran with when I was fifteen because my dad beat the shit out of me, and my mom didn't stop him. Two: When I decided I needed to get out of St. Louis for good, I stood in the bus station and looked at the map, trying to decide which direction to go. This was as far south as my money would take me."

Maggie's eyes are big, clearly expecting the easy answers. I push on, not thinking about how I'm probably going to run her off if I continue.

"Three: I've been in trouble with the law. One time it was because I was drunk and got in a fight with this guy. I beat him up pretty bad but he deserved it. I hardly drink anymore but I would still fight someone if they were hurting someone I cared about. I don't regret that part."

She bites her bottom lip then says, "I think you're trying to scare me off."

I give her a small smile. "Is it working?"

She shakes her head back and forth, slowly. "Two more to go."

"Four: Somehow, I screw everything up. No matter how hard I try not to, it always happens."

Her forehead scrunches together. "Now that seems like a warning."

I shrug but don't answer.

"One more to go," she says.

I take a deep breath. "Five: Even though I know I'll somehow screw this up, I'm glad you're here, with me, right now."

Maggie pulls her legs in close to her and props her chin on her knees. Her hair is pulled back and her face is scrubbed clean of any makeup. She probably acted like she was getting ready for bed before she snuck out of her window to come here.

"So we're going for brutally honest here, I see. One: My parents are really overprotective. So much that I'm hardly allowed to go anywhere without their approval of who I'm with and what we're doing."

This really isn't a surprise but it's the first time she's said it out loud. Her parents don't know she's here, with me, and they'd probably lose their shit if they did.

"Two: I dated the same boy all through high school. One my parents adored because he was the right kind of boyfriend. But they only saw what they wanted to see, not how he really was."

"Are you still dating him?" I ask, trying to keep my voice even.

"No. I broke up with him right after graduation."

I nod, and she continues: "Three: I can't wait to go off to college because I'm miserable at home. My sister and I fight all the time, my parents don't understand me at all. I feel like I'm suffocating there. But as much as I may want out of my house, I know it's nothing compared to what went on in yours."

Maggie pulls her ponytail in front of her, twisting her fingers in the long lengths. "Four: Someone like you scares me a little. You seem dangerous and you make me nervous."

Well, there's brutal honesty for you. I start to get up from the couch, not really wanting to hear the rest of where this is going, but she crawls closer, putting a hand on my arm, stopping me.

"Five: And even though you told me you would probably screw this up and even though I'm nervous as hell being here with you, I don't want to be anywhere else."

I pull her close and she's in my lap; her arms weave around my neck.

"I don't want to be anywhere else, either," I whisper back.

She leans forward, her lips brushing mine like they do every night just before she leaves, but instead of pulling away as she normally does, she lingers. I let her set the pace because I'm terrified of scaring her any more than she already is. As much as it may kill me, we could stay just like this, without going any further, and I'd be happy.

Maggie takes a deep breath and her eyes drift closed and she's kissing me the way I've been dreaming about. And I kiss her right back.

8

Taking my normal route through the neighbor's backyard to avoid the news vans out front, I jog to Gus's truck parked down the street. It's still dark since I'm leaving earlier than normal for detention this morning and the fog is thick but at least that helps hide me from all those cameras. I open the driver door and light from a nearby streetlamp catches on the window. Written in the condensation that formed are three words:

WHERE IS HE?

I drop my backpack and spin around. The small rivulets of water dripping from each letter haven't gotten far, so this wasn't written too long ago.

The fog that just moments ago felt safe now feels like it's closing in around me. Is whoever wrote this still here, hidden just a few feet away in the thick clouds? Are they waiting for a reaction?

The street is empty except for the caravan of news vans I can't see but know are a block away. I debate whether or not to show myself to them in the hopes one of them saw someone lurking here, but I'd give away my location . . . and they'll know what I'm driving.

Not to mention this would fuel the next news cycle.

But if I can't see them, then I know they didn't see whoever did this.

I snap a picture of the words and dig Detective Hill's card out of my wallet, texting him a copy of the picture and a quick explanation of what it is. As wet as the window is, I know there won't be any prints, but at least he can add this in with the rest of the evidence he's collecting.

Then I call Mom and she answers on the second ring.

"Hey, did you forget something?" she asks.

I don't want to tell her what I found. She'll find some reason to make me stay home, or worse, send me away somewhere "safe." And as much as I want to leave, I'm not leaving without her.

"No. Just forgot to ask you what you're doing today," I say as I jump into the driver's seat.

I hear the excitement in her voice. "Finalizing the menu for Elise's party. And doing a trial run on some dishes I haven't made in years."

I have another call coming through—Detective Hill—so I end the call with Mom saying, "Okay. Well, I'll see you later."

I switch calls and Detective Hill says, "Whose vehicle is that?"

"Gus Trudeau's. I got a job working for him. He's letting me use his truck so I can get back and forth from work."

"Did you see anyone near the truck?"

"No. But the message can't have been here long."

"I'll head that way. Wait for me," he says.

I look at the window. "The message is almost gone. Won't be anything left for you to see when you get here. And I need to get to school. Just get someone to keep a close eye on the house." I get in the truck and crank the engine.

I end the call, throwing the phone on the seat of the truck, and drive to school.

David and I arrive at school thirty minutes early, just as we were instructed. We walk nearly side by side, me following him to the part of the building where the janitors keep their supplies, but we don't speak. It's taking a lot for me to cool down after what happened this morning.

There's an older man waiting for us who looks as thrilled as we do about having the extra help this morning.

"Dr. G thinks he's doing me a favor by sending y'all to help, but all you're capable of is some busywork that I could do twice as fast on my own," he mumbles as he hands us each a garbage bag.

We both stand there, waiting for further instructions, and the man rolls his eyes. "They're trash bags. Go outside and pick up trash."

David moves away first but I'm right on his heels. Before I left the house this morning, before I saw the words written on the window of the truck, I thought about Pippa's words and how I should try to understand what Dad did to David's family. And I thought about what I would say to him, but I'm having a hard time getting back to that place of understanding. All I can think about is someone waited until they knew I was coming outside to make sure I would see the message, because the timing had to be perfect.

Even though I'm struggling, deep down I know Pippa is right, so I say, "Hey, man, sorry about yesterday." It's the best I can do right now. And since we're on trash duty for the rest of next week, I'll have plenty of time to try to talk to him when I don't feel like I want to beat the shit out of something.

David doesn't stop but does throw me a glance over his shoulder. "It's done," he mumbles back.

We step through a set of doors that leads to a small courtyard where most people eat their lunch. Neither of us is in any hurry so we both shuffle around, scooping up random pieces of trash that happen to cross our path.

I don't mind the silence. In fact, I'd be okay with not having to speak to another soul in this place.

Well, except Pippa. Ever since she told me we're not friends, all I can think about is trying to change her mind.

"I know I'm not supposed to say anything, but your dad completely fucked my family over. You didn't know what he was doing?"

I'm hunched over, grabbing a cookie wrapper when his words drift over to me. I take my time straightening up. Take my time trying to arrange the words to answer him so my anger over what happened this morning doesn't bleed into my conversation with him now. This is something I want to talk to him about but I don't know if I'm in the right frame of mind.

When I'm back upright, the bag hanging from one hand and the wrapper in the other, I answer. "No. Had no idea."

We stand there staring at each other, him weighing my words and me breathing in and out, hoping I can stop the explosion that's simmering right under the surface. "He fucked us, too." I know I shouldn't say this but I can't stop the words. "Me and Mom. We don't have shit. No money. No house. Nothing."

David's head cocks to the side. He watches me. Wants to see if I'll say anything else.

When he realizes that must be all I've got, he says, "My dad saved every penny. Always has. Working on a well site was hard work and he knew he couldn't do it forever. When your dad offered him the chance to buy stock in the company, he jumped at it. We didn't take many vacations. My parents didn't drive nice cars. Because we were saving. I always wondered if he had a magic number in his head or some goal he was trying to hit but I never asked. It's all he talked about . . . the things we would do when we had *enough*. And now it doesn't matter because it's gone. All of it. And every penny of my dad's money was spent on you doing all of the things I wished for . . . ski trips, beach trips, cars, boats . . . everything I wanted, you got, while I was waiting for it to be *enough*. So when you say we were both fucked, it's not the same. Not at all."

He turns and moves away from me, picking up random trash as he goes. He doesn't say anything else but his words hammer me harder than his fists ever could, and I drop down onto the nearest bench to catch my breath the second he turns the corner and is out of sight.

It's not my fault. I didn't steal all of that from him. Dad did. Not my fault.

But my words sound hollow and it's hard to hold on to the righteousness I felt before. I push away from the bench, grab my trash bag from where I dropped it on the ground, and move in the opposite direction from David.

Noah—Summer of 1999

"You're going to have to leave this place at some point," Maggie says. Her arms and legs are wrapped around me as I walk us deeper into the river. It took me an hour to talk her into the water but she's still scared of something "getting her."

It's high noon and hot enough that Gus told me to take a few hours off out of the heat and said we'll get the rest of the work done this evening when it's a bit cooler. I couldn't call Maggie quick enough.

"Why would I ever leave? I have everything I want right here." Gus said these same words to me and now I understand what he means by them. To emphasize my point, I pull her even closer. She didn't know we'd be swimming so she didn't bring a suit. She's got one of my Goodwill T-shirts on over her bra and underwear and I'm the happiest guy in the world right now.

Maggie has been here every day for the last three weeks. She'd bring a few groceries and Gus let her use his big kitchen. Maggie is a genius when it comes to cooking. It didn't take long before Abby was splitting her time between getting a little sun on the front porch and hanging out in the kitchen with us. And after Maggie made some simple soups that were easy on Abby's stomach but full of the good things she needs, Gus made sure Betty kept the pantry and fridge stocked with whatever Maggie needed.

But mostly Maggie sneaks over here at night after I'm done working and her parents are in bed. I hate the word *sneaking* but that's exactly what she's doing, so it feels good to be out in the sun with her, swimming and playing around in the water. It makes me wish we could do this every day.

"You can't stay in this orchard. There's a big world out there and you should come be a part of it."

"Gus stays here every day," I answer back.

"Well, it's not healthy for him, either. And now people are scared to come out here, especially after he lost it when those women from church showed up, wanting to pray over Abby."

Yeah, that wasn't a good day. Those women showed up by the carfuls, dressed in their Sunday best, holding their Bibles. Even before Abby was sick, Gus and Abby weren't big on going to church, but the shit hit the fan when one of the women mentioned they were here to get Abby to accept Jesus before she died so she could get into heaven.

I'm pretty sure all those women now think that not only will Abby go to hell, but Gus is the devil who will send her there.

I can't say I blame Gus, though. I've had my fair share of do-gooders try to "save" me over the years. Ones that would pull up in nice cars and tiptoe across the dirty sidewalk and crouch down in front of where I was sitting with my friends, careful not to touch anything around them. Acting like they understood how we ended up on the street. Making it sound like it was easy to change our circumstances.

They had no idea.

"It'll be fun, Noah!" She's pushing hard for me to come into town. Pushing me to hang out with her friends. But I know it won't end well. Her daddy will get wind of me, probably even look into my background if he's smart, and he won't like what he finds. My past isn't pretty.

I wish I could pull Maggie into the bubble Gus has created for him and Abby and me and none of us would ever have to leave.

I dunk us under the water and she comes up laughing. Her hands run through my hair, moving it out of my face.

"I need a haircut," I say. Can't remember the last time I cut it. Can't remember the last time I cared what it looked like.

"See, come to town. We'll get you a haircut, eat some pizza, maybe go to a movie. It'll be fun."

"You keep saying that," I say, pulling her even closer. As much as I want to stay here with her, it's not fair to her. If she wants to go to town, hang out with her friends, eat pizza . . . then that's what we'll do.

I shake my head, water droplets flying off of me and she lets out a surprised yell. She leans forward, pulling my face close to hers, and kisses me.

And I kiss her right back. Kissing Maggie is my new favorite thing to do. My hands slide up her back and she locks her ankles, pulling my hips right against hers.

We're moving into dangerous territory. Her wet clothes leave little to the imagination and it's impossible for either of us to ignore how turned on I am right now.

"You're killing me," I say between kisses.

"Good," she mumbles back. "You're killing me, too."

I move my hands to her face, pulling her back a few inches. "We need to stop before we do something we can't undo."

"I don't want to stop," she says, bending her head to kiss the side of my neck, then working her way up to my mouth. "Let's not stop."

Still holding her around me, I walk out of the river and up to the small house I call home.

9

JACK: Where are you

It's the third text from Jack asking where I am. I managed to get through school without an altercation. The snide remarks were whispers instead of shouts so I didn't feel the burning need to defend myself. But mainly because I couldn't quit thinking about David's words, which made me look at the face behind every jab and wonder what they gave up by saving rather than spending.

JACK: We're here. In town. Where are you

Shit. I should have seen this coming. I should have guessed Jack wouldn't let me hole up here and ignore him.

I push the last pile of debris onto the burn pile with the blade on the front of the tractor. I'm almost done raking the orchard and now I'm burning the sticks and leaves I've collected from underneath the trees.

They're here. In town. Driving through these streets trying to find me.

I send Jack my location before I can stop myself. It wouldn't be hard for them to stumble onto the news vans and I'd rather he come here than Aunt Lucinda's house.

I pull the truck around after I tell Gus I'm leaving and wait at the end of the driveway for my friends.

They must not have been too far away because it only takes another five minutes or so before I see Jack's Tahoe. He's one of the few that gets to keep a car on campus even though he rarely uses it. I wonder how they got a pass for Friday night since there's no way they'll make curfew.

He pulls the Tahoe next to Gus's old beat-up truck, and it's not hard to read his expression.

"Only gone a week and you already look the part of farm boy," Jack says.

Wait until he sees my stained Levi's and dirty work boots.

Ray's in the passenger seat and Sai is in the back but leaning forward enough that I can see his head poking out from between the first two seats.

"What are y'all doing here?" I ask.

"Came to see you, dumbass," Ray says.

"If you wouldn't have ignored us, we wouldn't have had to drive four damn hours to check on you," Sai adds.

I lean my head back against the headrest. I don't want anyone going out of their way for me. "You should go back. You shouldn't be here."

"Tough shit. We're here," Jack says. "Is this where you're staying?"

I shake my head. "No. This is where I work."

"Are you done? Anywhere we can find a beer around here? I'm ready to get out of this car," Sai yells from the backseat.

I don't know where anyone hangs out here. I don't know where the parties are. I wouldn't know which store looks the other way when a minor drops a twelve-pack on the counter or who has the best weed in town. And there's no one to call, no one to ask.

Jack must see all of this and more on my face because he throws me a sympathetic look and says, "I'm starving. Nearest pizza place?"

That I can do.

"Follow me."

I realize my mistake the second I pull into the parking lot of the local pizza place. I should have chosen one of the chains out near the highway but I haven't been to Joey's since I've been back, and the minute Jack said pizza, this was the only pizza I could think about.

The place is packed.

Jack and the others pile out of his car and head to the door before I can shut off my engine. I can't stop looking at the people inside, filling every table, all dressed in the school's blue and silver colors.

It's Friday night.

During football season.

Of course Joey's is packed. I've been away from here a long time, but some things don't change. Everyone will eat a few slices at Joey's then head to the stadium about a mile from here, where they'll cheer and scream for the home team.

Ray and Sai are waiting just inside the restaurant but Jack stands at the door, holding it open, waiting for me to join them.

With a deep breath, I get out of the truck and meet him at the door.

"How bad is it?" Jack asks.

He could be asking about Dad, he could be asking about the police or the IRS or the EPA, he could be asking about Mom. He could be asking about any of it. I don't know. But the answer would be the same.

"Worse than you could imagine."

We stand there a few seconds before a smile appears on his face. "Well, fuck 'em. I'm hungry."

The four of us wait at the hostess stand and most everyone in the room stares at us.

In a town where everyone knows everyone, of course Jack, Ray, and Sai stand out. They are the unknown. But the icy stares are directed at us because they're with me.

I recognize most of the people here my age and about half of the adults. David and his group are in the back corner while Pippa is in a booth with Janie McWilliams and Catherine Reynolds.

The room gets quiet when we slide into a booth that had just been vacated and cleaned off. It takes a few minutes but the volume in the room finally rises back to the level where it was before we got here.

"Clearly, they were stunned by my good looks when we walked in," Jack says.

"More like speechless when they saw those Mr. Potato Head ears," Ray says.

"Or it could have been his abnormally large head on his abnormally small body," Sai says.

Jack laughs and flips them off.

My friends are awesome. Seriously awesome.

To my surprise, Reed Frazier is our waiter. Why is he here? I thought he was off at school. Pippa mentioned his sister, Sarah, when we spoke in the parking lot but she didn't tell me Reed was in town. I should have figured I'd see one of them before long. I should have had something ready to say. But I don't.

"Hey, Reed," I say when he stops at our table.

He doesn't acknowledge my greeting. "What can I get y'all?" he asks, looking at my friends.

They study the menu but I'm watching Reed. "Reed, I just want—"

"Stop. Seriously. Don't say anything to me other than what you want to order."

The others look up from their menu and glance between me and Reed, trying to gauge where this is going.

I nod at Reed and place my order and my friends follow right behind me. Reed moves away from the table without another word.

"What's up with him?" Sai asks.

I shake him off. No way I can talk about it here with everyone in the restaurant watching.

Reed's dad worked for mine and they had been friends for years. According to the news articles I've found, after Dad took off, they started looking closely at Mr. Frazier to see if he was involved, too. There seems to be some evidence he knew what Dad was doing and even benefited from it. Mr. Frazier spiraled out of control, and before the cops could determine what he knew, he was dead. The last time anyone saw him alive, he was having drinks in a bar downtown and ranting about Dad to anyone who would stop to listen, saying that Dad screwed up his life like he did everyone else's. He was really drunk when he left and swerved into the lane of oncoming traffic, hitting an eighteen-wheeler head-on. He was killed instantly.

Reed's back at our table, passing out drinks, and I decide to try one more time to speak to him.

"Reed, I'm sorry about your dad," I say quickly before he can cut me off.

He sets Jack's drink down in front of him slowly and then turns to me. He's got me at a disadvantage since I'm sitting and he's hovering over me, but I don't let on that I'm uncomfortable with the situation.

Reed puts a hand on the back of my chair and his face comes close to mine. Almost all conversation in the restaurant drops to a low whisper and I can feel every eye on the two of us.

"Where is he?" he asks. His voice is so quiet that I doubt my friends at the table much less anyone else in the restaurant can hear him. "No one believes you and your mom don't know where he is. And no one believes she didn't know what he was doing. You want to talk to me? Tell me where he is or shut the fuck up."

He hesitates only a few seconds before he walks away from the table and it's hard for me to look at my friends.

"You okay, O?" Jack asks.

I nod and shake it off, not wanting to talk about how dirty I feel. Any thought that people will separate what Dad did and how they think about me or Mom is long gone. Part of me can't blame Reed. His dad is dead because he was at that bar drinking. And it was because of what my dad did. Another part of me wonders if Reed is so pissed that he's resorted to threatening Mom to get Dad's location. And I can't ignore that some of his first words to me were the same ones written on my truck window—*where is he.*

A waitress who looks like she drew the short straw and got our order as punishment delivers our food. Truthfully, I'd be shocked if Reed comes back to our table at all. Ray and Sai flirt with her when she brings the check and she's loosened up enough to invite us to a field party after the game. She got a jab in when she threw a look my way and muttered, "I guess you can bring him with you."

God, I have to get out of this town.

We go to the game but sit on the visitors' side because really, that's all I am here. A visitor. An unwanted one at that.

My school decimates the other team 48–0.

We leave Gus's truck in the stadium parking lot and ride in Jack's Tahoe to a field a few miles outside of town. It's not far from Gus's but I don't know the family who owns it.

"So have any of us actually been to a party in a field before?" Ray asks.

"I just hope there's beer. I mean, we can tip some cows or kick some shit, too, as long as there's beer," Jack adds.

I'm the only small-town guy I know at Sutton's but I'm no help here. I should be the one showing them a good time and it sucks I'm feeling as out of place as they are.

We pull onto a gravel road and follow it a few miles until we come to a clearing where there are no less than thirty other vehicles.

This is a bad idea. My friends got the message that I'm pretty much on my own and witnessed the utter hatred everyone feels for me, so I can't imagine things will be any better here.

I stay toward the back of the group as we make our way to where everyone is hanging out around a huge pile of wood bigger than the brush pile at Gus's. And just like I did a few nights ago, there's a guy named Daniel dribbling diesel along the edge of the pile. This fire is going to be huge when it catches.

Country music blares from some speakers set up in the back of a truck and there's a crowd in line to fill their red Solo cups with keg beer.

Ray spots the keg and turns toward it as if he's drawn to it like a magnet, stopping in front of the guy working the pump. I think his name is Jeff or James or something that starts with a *J*.

Ray motions to the keg and the guy says, "Five bucks." He hands him a twenty and says, "That should cover me and my friends."

The guy looks past him to me and says, "Not him."

Even though my friends know who he's referring to, they still look back at me to make sure.

Jack steps up between Ray and this guy and says, "C'mon, man. We don't want to cause any trouble. Just looking to hang out. Meet some people. See what y'all got going on around here."

Jack Cooper is the politician. No matter the situation, he gets a read on what's happening and starts working on how to make it swing his way.

"I'm not trying to get in the way of your good time. Only his."

Jack keeps trying to smooth things over but I step away when I spot David on the other side of the huge pile of wood. He's sitting on the tailgate of a truck and laughing at something a girl next to him says. You wouldn't know by looking at him that his family lost everything. He's here hanging out with his friends, having a good time.

I pull on Jack's arm and say, "Let it go, man. I'm good. And we need someone to drive anyway." There's no way I'm going to ruin anyone's good time and be the cause of any trouble here tonight.

Someone throws a match on the pile and the fire blazes. Even though it's November, it's not cold enough for a fire this size, so it's not long before everyone starts backing up, trying to get a little distance from the heat.

Sai spots the girl from Joey's and we make our way over to where she's sitting with a group of girls. They're all smiles for my friends but ignore me completely. Even though it sucks for me here right now, I'm relieved to see they aren't holding it against my friends.

I lean up against the back of an old Toyota 4Runner nearby, happy to keep my distance and let the guys enjoy their night.

"I'm surprised to see you here," Pippa says. She must have come around from the front of the car because I didn't see her when I scanned the group hanging on every word my friends were saying.

"I'm surprised to be here," I answer.

She's wearing an old pair of cutoffs, the denim frayed like it's been washed a hundred times, and a plain white V-neck T-shirt. I haven't given myself permission to check her out because it's Pippa. But standing here, the front of her lit up by firelight, it's hard not to. She looks good. More than good. Her hair is pulled back into a sloppy bun but half of it has fallen down around her shoulders. Her eyes look a little glazed over. Maybe that's not her first cup of beer. And that's probably the only reason she wandered over here to talk to me.

"Your friends are a big hit," she says, nodding toward them.

"They're good guys. It's hard not to like them."

She moves closer, steps around me, and stops at the back window of the 4Runner, tracing her name in the dust coating the glass. "You were a good guy once."

I laugh but it sounds hollow. It guts me that Pippa thinks of me like that. I was a good guy *once*.

Then she starts tracing my name next to hers in the dust, circling the *O* so many times it looks more like a doughnut than a letter.

"I'm not a bad guy," I whisper to her. I don't care what anyone else thinks about me except her.

"I wouldn't know. We're strangers, remember."

I slide down the side of the car until I'm only a few feet from her.

"Let's play a game," I say.

"What game?"

"The *How well do I know Pippa* game. I say a fact about you and if I'm right, I get a point. If I'm wrong, the point goes to you."

She rolls her eyes. "This is stupid." Pippa has moved on from my name and is now drawing some sort of flower. "What does the winner get?"

"Whatever the winner wants," I answer.

She side-eyes me. "That sounds dangerous."

"Scared?"

She stands a little straighter. "How many points to win?"

I have to think for a minute . . . strategize . . . because there's no way I'm not winning this.

"Three."

She bites her bottom lip. "Five."

"Done."

She holds a finger up. "Rules, though. Every fact has to be about something that's happened since high school started. No pulling out something from our childhood."

"Not a problem."

"Oh, shit. I'm going to regret this."

I laugh again but this time it feels good. Jack must hear me because he turns to face us, raises his eyebrows, and nods his head toward Pippa.

"Are you too scared to start?" she asks.

I look away from Jack and focus all my attention on Pippa. "Every college you applied to is at least a four-hour drive from here."

Her hands drop down by her sides and she leans against the 4Runner, facing me. I can tell by the smirk that I'm right.

"One point to Owen," she says.

I study her, think about her, recall everything I once knew about her.

"You've got more than ten journals under your bed where you've written on every available page." By the time I left before middle school the count was four, but I can't imagine she's stopped writing.

She closes her eyes and scrunches up her forehead. "That's two."

I rub my hands together like I'm an evil mastermind rejoicing over my plan for world domination.

"You secretly watch that reality dating show, the one with the roses, but would deny it to anyone who asked."

Her eyes widen and her mouth pops open, and I can't help but stare at her lips. I may be the one who regrets this.

"Three," she says.

I lean even closer, only inches away from her. "You've got a playlist with nothing but old country, and I mean Hank and Waylon and Merle, but you only listen to it when you're sad."

Now she's back to biting her bottom lip.

"I'm guessing that's point number four, right?" I ask since she's working that lip and staying quiet. I can tell she's worried about what I'll want when I win this.

She nods and I smile.

"Okay, so last one." We stare at each other while I debate what I want to say next. "You may act like you're pissed I'm back but you stand up for me to every person at school who talks shit about me. Or my mom."

I hold my breath. This one is a gamble, one I hope is true but could just as easily not be. Her head drops and I can't read her.

She waits a second, five, then ten, before looking at me again. "You win."

I know the smile that breaks out across my face looks ridiculous. It feels ridiculous but I'm not pushing it away.

She crosses her arms in front of her and asks, "So what do you want?"

A kiss is the first thing that pops in my head, pushes against my lips, trying to escape. But that would be wrong. No matter how attracted to her I am right now, that's not where we are. It's not something I have the right to ask for from her. And if I ever do get the chance to kiss her, I want it to be because she wants to kiss me, too, not because she lost a bet.

"Eat lunch with me every day next week. I'm tired of sitting alone. It doesn't have to be in the cafeteria where everyone can see us together."

She stares at me and I wonder what she would have done if I'd have gone with my first choice.

"Fine. Lunch. We can sit in the cafeteria. Doesn't matter to me," she says then turns, moves away from me.

Just before she gets too far, I say, "We're not strangers."

"We're not friends, either," she answers.

"Not yet," I whisper and watch her disappear into the darkness.

Noah—Summer of 1999

"Maggie, you gotta get up." I nudge her but all she does is snuggle in closer. She's been staying later and later every night, and I'm getting scared we're pressing our luck.

"It's close to morning, Mags." Brushing her hair back from her face, I kiss her cheek, then her neck, until she's laughing.

"You know that tickles," she says in a sleepy voice.

"I know. That's the only thing that will get you moving."

She jumps up and almost falls out of the narrow twin bed. "What time is it?" she asks.

"Five a.m."

"Shit!" Maggie jumps out of the bed and grabs her shorts off of the floor, trying to put them on and walk at the same time. "Shit! Noah. My dad's going to be up in thirty minutes."

I swing my legs over the side of the bed. "I've been trying to get you up for forty-five."

She drops to the floor, digging a flip-flop out from under the bed, and says something I can't understand.

"What?" I ask.

"I said I'm picking you up at seven. No excuses. Be ready." She's shoving her feet in her shoes and grabbing her bag off of the small table.

"This is not a good idea," I say for the hundredth time.

"Well, too bad. I'm not taking no for an answer." She runs back to the bed and kisses me quickly on the lips. "I'll make it worth your while after."

I groan and she laughs, skipping out of the house and down the front steps.

I'm sitting on the front steps of Gus's, waiting on Maggie. It doesn't make any sense for her to drive all the way back to my place to turn right back around and head to town. Plus, I haven't seen Abby in a while. She took a turn and hasn't gotten out of the bed in the last week, but today Betty has her back on the porch.

"Your haircut looks nice, Noah," Abby says.

I run my hand across the back of my hair where it feels like stubble. "Betty cut it for me this afternoon. All she had was Gus's electric razor so that's why it's really short."

"Well, I like it. Are you going out?"

"Yeah, Maggie is picking me up. Not sure where we're going."

Abby smiles and it transforms her face. "I know you'll have fun. I'm glad you're getting out of here for a while. And tell Maggie thank you for the smoothie she left for me yesterday. It was delicious."

When Maggie found out Abby wasn't able to get out of bed, she was even more determined to find things she could eat.

"I'll tell her," I say and stare back toward the end of the driveway, smoothing out the wrinkles in my shirt.

The only clothes I own are ripped jeans and tour shirts from concerts I'll never be able to afford to see. But when Gus saw Betty cutting my hair, he asked what I was getting cleaned up for, and when he found out Maggie was taking me somewhere in town, he brought me a pair of his jeans and a button-down shirt, saying, "You're going to need a little armor if you're facing those people."

So here I sit in clothes that aren't mine, with a haircut that makes me look completely different, willing to hang out with people I'll never feel comfortable with just to make my girl happy.

"He's not going to handle it well, Noah."

I turn back around. "Who?"

She nods her head toward the house. "Gus. When I'm gone. He won't handle it well. He lost his mom when he was young and his dad a couple of years ago. Now this entire place sits on his shoulders."

It feels like my stomach bottomed out.

"He hasn't left this place in months," she says. "If it wasn't for Betty, we would have starved months ago."

"Why won't he go to town?" I ask.

"He's so private, Noah. When his mom died, he said he felt like the house was invaded. Then when his dad died, it was the same, but Gus put his foot down. I was already sick and not up to fighting with him about it. We had a private funeral in the little cemetery on the back of the property. Just us and Betty. That's what he wanted. That's what he'll want for me."

"Is that what you want?" I ask.

She gives me a small smile. "I want whatever is easiest for Gus to handle. Although I don't think anyone will try to come here after he ran off those women from church a few weeks ago. Just don't let him go too far over the edge where he can't find his way back."

I can't make this promise. A promise that ties me to this place. But I answer, "Okay."

Abby falls asleep a few minutes later and Betty moves her back inside the house. Gus comes out on the porch a few times, looks around, then heads back in, not saying anything about the fact that I've been waiting half an hour for Maggie to show. I think about Abby's words and I can't look Gus in the eye.

Just when I'm about to give up, Maggie's little black car pulls up in front of the house. I meet her halfway down the front walk and I can tell she's been crying.

I pull her in close and she buries her head in my shoulder.

"What's wrong?" I whisper.

She shakes her head. "I don't want to talk about it. Is that okay?"

I pull her back so I can look at her. "Did someone hurt you?"

She shakes her head no and then she seems to take in my appearance. She runs a hand through my short hair. "Look at you. I like it. I can see your face now."

I pull her hand away from my head and hold it close to my chest. "Mags, talk to me. What's wrong?"

"Family stuff. I don't want to talk about it. It'll make me cry again."

I should push her, make her tell me what's wrong, but her tears are killing me and I don't want to do anything else that brings on more of them.

"Okay. But you would tell me if someone did something to you? Hurt you?"

She nods but doesn't say anything else.

"So I'm guessing we're not heading into town?"

Maggie runs both hands down the front of my shirt. "Can we just go to your place?"

"Of course. Whatever you want."

She smiles and the panic I had when I saw the sadness in her face when she first got out of the car subsides a little. I don't know what happened but whatever it was, it was enough to make her change her mind about bringing me to town.

And that makes me feel worse than I thought it would.

10

Jack and I have to carry Ray to the car. I knew after that last keg stand he wouldn't make it on his own. Sai isn't much better but at least he's still upright.

Once they're settled in the back and I'm in the driver's seat, I turn to look at Jack in the passenger seat. "I can't take y'all to my aunt's. But there's somewhere else we can go. It's kind of rough but it's all I have."

Jack nods and says, "Lead the way."

Once I get to the orchard, I cut the lights off until we pass the big house and the garage apartment where Gus is living.

"It's spooky as hell driving in between these trees in the dark," Jack says. He's almost as sober as I am since he switched to water a while back. Knowing him, he wasn't sure we wouldn't end up in some sort of brawl before the night is over and he can't fight for shit when he's drunk.

"Just be glad the moon's out or I probably would have plowed into one of these trees by now."

I flip the lights on once we get close to the river and they sweep across the front of the preacher's house when I turn into the clearing.

"What's this?" Jack asks.

"The only place I could think to bring us."

The small cabin is no bigger or cleaner than it was a few days ago but it's easy to ignore the dirt in the dark. We get Ray and Sai out of the car and onto the couch, one head on each end.

"Come back out here," Jack says and I follow him to the porch, sitting next to him on the top step.

The one thing about being out in the country is how dark it is at night. Even with the almost full moon shining down on us, you can't see past the tree line or out into the river.

"You can come back to Sutton's if you want," Jack says. "Dad said he'd cover you."

And just like that, there's my old life, handed to me on a silver platter. A breeze blows off the river, snaking around the trees as if it, too, heard Jack's offer and wanted to offer its opinion.

I run a hand across my face and blow out a deep breath. "Shit, Jack," I whisper.

Jack and I would be roommates again. I could leave and not look back. And if I'm being honest with myself, I've been expecting this since I got Jack's text telling me he was in town.

"Is that a yes?" he asks.

"It's not that easy," I answer.

"It is that easy," Jack says. He turns toward me, drawing one knee up and leaning against the porch railing. "Dad talked to Dr. Winston. All you need to do is catch up with your classes from last week. You could head back with us in the morning." It makes sense now, how they got out for an overnight. They were sent here by Mr. Cooper to bring me back to Sutton's.

But what about Mom? She's stuck here with Aunt Lucinda and getting threats from someone who thinks she knows something. Could I leave her here to handle that on her own?

"I don't think I can leave the parish. You know, the investigation . . ."

"Dad's handling that, too. He talked to that detective. It's not like you're skipping the country; you'll actually be watched closer there than you are here. Dad was going to call your mom tonight. He knows she left you at school as long as she could, so we figure she'd rather you be back there if possible."

He's right—Mom will probably jump at the chance to send me away, thinking she's protecting me. And Detective Hill probably thinks there's a better chance Dad will contact me again if I'm back at school. Maybe he's thinking he can intercept another letter or something.

I drop my head in my hands, my mind spinning.

Jack nudges me with his foot. "Dude, it's not like you have anything going on here."

I can see how it seems that way to him given how everyone treated me, but there's Gus and this orchard. I told him I'd help bring the crop in and I know there's no way he can do it alone.

And Pippa. Pippa who agreed to have lunch with me every day next week. We're not strangers but we're not friends, either. If I leave again, I'll be forever in that in-between space.

But none of that may matter after I talk to Dad. Maybe he's got a plan to clear all of this up.

"I thought you'd jump at the chance to go back."

Me, too, I think.

As painful as it is, I can't stop David's words from drifting through my mind . . . *everything I wanted, you got.* Is there anyone out there offering to give him the things he wanted, the things his dad was saving up for, like Jack is offering me my old life back?

If Jack had asked me this the first day I got back here, I would have jumped at it.

"As much as I want to, I can't go back," I whisper.

He doesn't argue. We sit and listen to the things we can't see . . .

the crickets and the rushing water of the river and the soft snoring from inside the cabin.

Jack will build his case, think through the things he thinks are holding me here, work out a solution so I can't refuse him a second time. He stares off in the darkness. "Anything you need, O. You know that."

There's a lump in my throat that's hard to swallow past. After this week, I'll never take my friends for granted again. I clear my throat and say, "Tell your dad thanks . . . for everything."

He leans forward and punches me in the shoulder. "Things aren't always going to be this bad."

"Things will never be as good as they were, either."

Jack gets up and jogs down the stairs toward his car.

"Where are you going?" I ask.

"Sleeping in the car. The couch is full and no way I'm sharing that twin bed with you." He opens his door and looks back at me. "And I still owe you for the *Playboy* picture," he says, then jumps inside.

• • •

Mom rushes me the second I push through the back screen door the next morning. She's pissed but also hugging me, then pounds her fist against my arm a few times.

"You scared me to death, Owen! You can't stay out all night!" She's squeezing me so hard and I can feel her shaking against me. "Not with what's going on."

"I texted you that Jack, Ray, and Sai were in town and we were staying with a friend."

She pushes away from me. "A friend? You've barely finished a full day of school! Have you even made it past lunch since you started?"

"I will for sure next week since I'll be eating with Pippa," I say.

That surprises Mom, and she stumbles over her next words. "Well . . . still, who was this *friend* you stayed with?"

I take a deep breath and answer, "Gus Trudeau. We stayed in that old house that Dad lived in that summer."

"Oh," she says. She drops down in the chair and rubs her hand across her mouth.

"You seem surprised." Shocked is more like it.

She shakes her head. "I am surprised. How did you end up out there? Have you met him? How is he?"

"He's fine I guess. I have no idea what to compare him to. I mean, he doesn't leave the orchard. He doesn't like visitors. He says very little."

She lets out a quiet laugh. "Yeah, that sounds like Gus."

"I'm surprised he gave me a job. Thought I would run into the same trouble you did but he hired me . . . sort of. He's letting me borrow his truck in exchange for helping him in the orchard. He remembers you, you know, from when you hung out there with Dad."

Mom is staring at me and she looks like she's about to cry, which is surprising because she's usually the queen of hiding those tears. I can't take seeing her upset so I move to the fridge to grab something to drink. When I turn back around, Mom seems to have regained some of her composure. "So tell me how you like working there."

I start at the beginning and fill her in on how I've spent my week. She's staring out of the kitchen window, lost in her own thoughts.

"Who's Abby?" I ask.

This question snaps her out of wherever her mind drifted off to. She gives me a sad smile and says, "Abby was Gus's wife."

Mom starts clearing off the table and I grab a blueberry muffin off a plate on the counter.

"That's all he told you?" she says. "That your dad used to work there?"

"What else is there?" I ask.

She closes her eyes and shakes her head. "Nothing."

Mom moves from the table to the sink. There's something she's not telling me. So, hoping to get her talking about it, I say, "It's hard to imagine Dad living there in that small house. There's no TV. And I can't see him on a tractor."

Her head drops and her shoulders cave forward. She shuts off the water and dries her hands on a dishrag. "I can't talk about him, Owen. I can't talk about this."

She turns to leave the room but stops. "I think you should go back to Sutton's. William Cooper offered to cover your expenses. As much as I don't want to take another dime from anyone, I'm willing to accept his help."

"Do you really think I would just pick up and go back to school, leaving you here to deal with all of this?"

"I can deal with this. Your life isn't here anymore. You've been saying that since you've been back and you're right. At Sutton's you have a real chance to move past this. To be happy. To be safe."

"If I'm not safe here, then neither are you. So I'll leave when you do."

She's turns around. "I could make you go," she says.

"You could try," I answer.

She runs a hand through her hair. "I'm trying to do what's right. That's all I've ever tried to do for you. From the very first moment, every decision was supposed to be the right one. But none of it is right. I'm not sure it ever was. And I don't know what to do anymore. God, I should have done so many things differently. . . ."

"Like what?" I ask.

Her head pops up. "What?" Her eyes are frantic.

"If you could do one thing differently, what would it be?"

She lets out a deep breath, hesitates another moment. "I would have been braver," she says, then disappears from the room.

Excerpt from the diary of Leonard Trudeau:

Step two—Shaking the trees

In years past, I patiently waited for the pecans to fall to the ground of their own accord. I discovered that the ones that fell early were near rotten by the time the rest were free from the trees. So now, we shake the trees, knocking loose every nut, no matter how ferociously they cling to the branch. It's delicate work but important and the payoff is worth the effort you expend.

Noah—Summer of 1999

Abby died quietly in her sleep on an early Tuesday morning in mid-July. I knew something was wrong when the flowers I cut for her sat untouched on the front porch. Betty called all the necessary people and now they've come and gone, taking Abby away with them.

Gus hasn't set foot out of the house and I can't bring myself to go in.

I'm sitting on the front porch steps, cutting off every person that shows up so Gus and Betty don't have to talk to them. They come in a steady stream, bearing casseroles, cakes, salads, and every other type of food no one that lives here wants to eat. The second they leave, I dump it all into a garbage can around the side of the house, dish and all.

Maggie is one of the last to arrive, but she's with her mom and we act like strangers. She's crying hard and I can tell her mother doesn't understand why.

Just before they leave, Maggie turns around and says, "I can come back for the dish later."

I nod and once her mom's car turns onto the main road, I dump the food.

The dish, too.

11

I'm nervous walking to the cafeteria on Monday even though the school day so far has been one of the better ones I've had since I've been here. No one here is trying to be my friend but most have stopped spewing hate right to my face. Maybe they're as exhausted by all of this as I am.

I pull open the door to the cafeteria and see Pippa across the room, near the corner. She gives me a small wave when we make eye contact then points to the lunch line with a questioning look, but I hold up a brown bag, letting her know I brought my lunch. I cross the room and stop a few feet away, just enough that someone wouldn't automatically assume we're together. Even though Pippa said she didn't care about being seen sitting with me, I'm going to give her the option to go somewhere else.

"We don't have to eat in here," I say.

She pulls out a nearby chair and throws her bag on the table. "Here's good."

I sit across from her rather than next to her, with my back to the rest of the room. I know everyone will be looking at us but I don't want to look at them.

She pulls one of those insulated bags out of her backpack and starts unpacking it. Sandwich, water bottle, string cheese, and a pack of Reese's Peanut Butter Cups, her favorite.

"I thought *eat lunch with me* meant you were actually going to eat," she says after she swallows a bite of sandwich.

I laugh and dump the contents of my brown bag on the table. Mom wasn't feeling well this morning and I was running late so Aunt Lucinda offered to pack my lunch. I didn't consider at the time that since she doesn't have kids, she's never had to pack a lunch in her life, so I'm not surprised that Pippa's eyes get big when she takes in the odd combination on the table in front of me. Mom and Aunt Lucinda are different in a lot of ways, but none so much as their culinary capabilities.

"I'm not sure if it's the can of tuna fish or the Vienna sausage that's got me the most concerned," Pippa says, then takes another bite of her sandwich.

"Definitely the sausage," I answer. "I'm pretty sure these were left over from when my grandparents were still alive. And it's not a pop top so I have no idea how I'm even supposed to open it."

She lets out a shy laugh then pushes the Reese's across the table. "I'll split these with you."

I give her a big smile and tear open the package. I eat half the peanut butter cup in one bite and she rolls her eyes. "You're eating it all wrong."

I knew this would get her. She's funny about the way she eats anything that has chocolate in it. For Reese's she likes to punch the center part out, leaving behind the solid chocolate edge so she can save that for last.

"It's mine and I can eat it any way I want," I answer before shoving the rest of it in my mouth.

She gives me a smile but her eyes keep bouncing from me to whatever is going on behind me. If I had money to bet, most everyone in the room is watching us, trying to figure out why she's sitting with me. And probably her friends are motioning to her and trying to mouth questions at her. I'm glad I can't see any of it.

"Tell me what's going on with you," I say and her eyes fly back to mine.

"When? Today? The last six years?"

I slide the Reese's package back across the table to her. "Any of it. All of it."

She shrugs and plays with the cap to her water bottle. "You guessed right about the journals. I'm still writing. I'm also in the drama club. I submitted a play I wrote at the end of last year and it was chosen for this year's school play."

This seems like a really big deal but she says it like it's not. She watches the top spin and refuses to look at me, so I wad up the brown paper bag and throw it at her.

"Hey!" she says when it hits her in the forehead. "What was that for?"

"The play you wrote is going to be performed by this school and you said it like you're letting me know what's on the menu for the hot lunch tomorrow."

"It's not a big deal. There were only two entries. I'm pretty sure they're regretting making it a contest. It's not going so well."

"Why?" I ask.

She shakes off my question. "I don't want to talk about it."

"Okay, what else do you want to talk about?"

She shrugs again. "I don't know. You're the one who wanted me to sit with you."

Pippa seemed comfortable when I first sat down, but I can tell the crowd behind me is getting to her. I want to talk to her, hang out with her, but not like this.

"It's cool. I'm not really hungry." I stand up and throw the unopened cans in my backpack. "I'm going to head to the library and finish my English homework."

It's like she wants to say something but the words won't come out. I step away from the table and I hear a soft "O."

I look at her over my shoulder. "Really, it's cool." I should let her out of the bet since she seems so uncomfortable, but I don't. I can't. "We'll try again tomorrow."

She nods and her friends rush the table before I'm halfway to the door, peppering her with questions. She doesn't seem to answer them, or maybe she's just waiting for me to leave first.

I spin around and exit the cafeteria. The need to ditch and head to Gus's is strong, but the fear of being sent to an alternative school is stronger. I'm heading to the library when I recognize a girl off to the side, sitting at one of the picnic tables in the common area. She's reading a book and seems oblivious to everyone and everything around her.

I shouldn't talk to her. I shouldn't go anywhere near her, especially after how bad things were between her brother and me, but the feeling that I should try to make things right with at least one person who was hurt by my dad pushes me toward her table.

"Hey," I say when I'm a few feet from Sarah Frazier.

She snaps the book shut and stares at me. The pain on her face almost brings me to my knees, and I realize no matter what, I can't invade her space like this. "I just want to say I'm sorry. About your dad," I say then turn away.

I should have learned my lesson after my run-in with her brother. I get a few feet from her before she says, "I'm sorry about yours, too."

This stops me in my tracks. Spinning around, I search her face, waiting for her to blast me or curse me or something, but she just watches me closely.

I move back toward her table and sit down on the bench across from her. I haven't seen Sarah in a long time. Not since our families vacationed together after my freshman year in Mexico. Reed was a couple of years older than me and treated me like some stupid kid, but Sarah was just a year behind me so I spent most of my time with her. She looks the same, though. Same brown hair, same freckles, same brown eyes.

We watch each other and I can tell she's trying to gauge what I want, but even I don't know what that really is.

"I'm so mad at him, you know. For getting in the car in that condition," she says. "I keep thinking that if he had called a cab he would be alive, and then he could prove to everyone he didn't know what your dad was doing. Now that's all anyone will remember about him."

I swallow hard. "Yeah, I feel the same way about my dad. I mean, not that it's the same. Not that my dad running off is the same at all. I mean I'm mad, too . . . at what he did."

She nods and gives me a small smile. "No, I get what you mean. They both left in ways we don't understand."

"Yeah, that's it. Are y'all going to be okay? I mean, not okay with what happened but . . . I should just stop talking right now." God, when did I become so awkward talking to a girl?

She laughs this time and it feels good to hear it. "We're waiting until Christmas break and then we're moving to Jackson, Mississippi, where my grandparents live. There isn't anything left for us here and it's been really hard on Mom and my brother. Me, too. But I didn't want to transfer halfway through the semester, so they're waiting for me to be done."

"I saw your brother. I thought he was off at college."

Sarah bites her bottom lip. "Mom needs him here. She's not handling things well. He's hoping to go back next year," she adds. "He's working down at Joey's right now and hating it."

Yeah, I got that vibe.

With nothing left to say, I get up from the table.

"They stare at me, too. For different reasons, obviously, but it's all the time. It sucks." She holds up her book. "It helps to have something to block it out."

"Thanks," I say. She was nicer to me than I deserve. "Even though it's usually a painful experience, I'm here if you ever want to talk."

"Thanks, Owen. I tell myself every day . . . I'm not my dad. And you aren't yours, either."

. . .

In my daily ritual of googling Dad's name to see if any other information has been uncovered, I run across the ad for the auction of our house and all of the contents. Every piece of furniture, every pot and pan and mirror and rug . . . everything is listed for sale. I click on the tab "Boy's Room" and see all of my things laid out for the public's inspection. The bed, the matching side tables and lamps, my desk, and even the bedding are up for grabs.

I feel sick.

"Did you get finished in section four?" Gus asks. He stops the golf cart a few feet away from the tractor and I shove my phone in my pocket, pushing away the fact that even the books on my shelf are for sale.

"Yeah, just finished," I answer.

I spent all of Saturday and Sunday raking under the trees and finished up the last section this afternoon.

"Good. We can start shaking by the end of the week then. Pecans look ready. The only section that needs to be cleaned is the Preacher Woods." Before I can crank the tractor, he says, "Next time you and your friends stay in that house, you need to let me know."

My mind scrambles for an excuse but he holds his hand up before I can get the words out. "I get it. Sometimes you just need a place to crash. But give me a heads-up next time, okay?"

"Okay, thanks." And before I can talk myself out of it, I say, "Tell me what Dad was like when he lived here."

Gus leans back in the seat and props one foot up on the short dash. He stares off, his gaze getting lost in the distance. Finally, he turns back to me and says, "He was a damn fool for your mother. Fell for her hard."

"I always thought they met in college."

Gus shakes his head. "Your grandmother sent your mom out here to deliver a casserole when Abby was sick, and your dad was working on one of the tractors in the yard."

"I'm sorry about Abby," I say. I saw the small cemetery near the back of the property earlier today. One of the names on a tombstone was *Abby Trudeau*, and based on the engraving, she's been gone a long time.

Gus rubs a hand across his mouth and nods. "She was a wonderful woman gone way too soon." He seems lost in thought for a moment.

"So Mom hung out here, while Dad lived here?"

Gus nods. "Yeah, she did." He's about to pull away but he stops when I keep talking.

"Mom's been getting some threats. I'm thinking it's someone who lost a bunch of money and thinks she knows where it is. Or they think she knows where Dad is."

Gus leans forward on the steering wheel. "What kind of threats?"

"Phone calls mainly. Someone threw a brick through her window at our house. Our old house."

"She's told the police, though, right? They know what's going on?" Gus asks.

I nod. "Yeah, but they don't have any idea who it could be. There's this one guy, Detective Hill, who seems like he halfway gives a shit, but that's it." I'm not sure why I don't mention the note that was left on my window. Maybe I'm worried that if he thinks someone might mess with his truck, he'll take it back.

"So this detective thinks it's someone lashing out and there's no real danger?"

I shrug. "I guess. That's what he told me when I asked him. I keep trying to think of who it could be but the list of people is so long that it could be almost anyone in town. Any guess who it is?"

Gus drums his fingers against the steering wheel. "Well, since I don't go to town, I'm not sure who's still there, but I know the list of people who lost money is long."

"Did he steal from you, too?"

It looks like my words physically hurt him. "Yeah, he stole something from me." Gus pulls the cart around, back toward the house. "You got about an hour until dark. See if you can get the trees in the Preacher Woods raked."

I crank the tractor and slowly make my way to the back of the orchard. It's been killing me knowing that Dad screwed Mom over so badly, but it's almost worse that he did the same to Gus. Just one more reason why I need to find him.

Noah—Summer of 1999

The soft knock on the door doesn't come as a surprise, but I can't force myself to get up to open it.

Maggie pushes the door open and searches for me in the dark.

"Noah, are you here?" she asks in a quiet voice.

"Over here," I answer.

She moves through the small room and sits on the edge of the bed, her hand resting on my arm.

I bite the inside of my cheek, hoping the pain is enough to stop me from breaking down. Pushing to a sitting position, I maneuver around her until I'm off the bed and across the room. I know I've hurt her by moving away from her, but I can't handle her consoling me right now.

I shouldn't need consoling. I mean, one look at Abby and you knew she didn't have much longer here. Hell, I barely knew her. I shouldn't care that she's gone. I shouldn't care what Gus is doing in that big house all alone. I shouldn't care that Maggie wouldn't hardly look at me when she was here with her mother.

"Noah," Maggie says in a near whisper. "It's okay to be upset. I'm upset, too."

"Abby's family is insisting there be a visitation at the local funeral home before the burial here. As much as Gus hates the idea of that, he doesn't have it in him to fight them over it. So when we're at the funeral home, and I'm standing there making sure Gus doesn't freak out on everyone, or run off or fall on the damn floor, are you going to be able to talk to me? If I feel like I'm about to fucking fall apart because a woman I barely knew had the ability to take a chunk of me with her when she died, will you be able to hold my hand?" I spit out. I'm being mean on purpose. I can't get any more attached to this place. I'm leaving as soon as I have enough money saved, no matter what I promised Abby.

She jumps up and races across the room to me, throwing her arms around my waist. "I'm sorry. I just didn't know what to say. My parents . . . you don't understand how they are."

"I understand you're ashamed of me. Don't get me wrong, I get it. I'm not the kind of guy you bring home. Just one you fool around with while you're killing time before going off to college. I just wish you never would've acted like you wanted me to meet your friends. To go with you to town and let everyone see us together. You changed the game on me."

She hugs me tighter while my arms just hang loosely by my side. "No, it's not like that. I'm not ashamed of you."

"The last time I talked to Abby was the night I waited for you to pick me up. She liked my haircut. She told me to look out for Gus . . . after."

"I know she was glad you're here." Her hands roam up my chest and around my neck. "I'm glad you're here."

"Let's be honest about what this is. You're not going to bring me home to Mom and Dad. They're never going to know you spend most of your time here. When it's time for you to go off to college, you're going to leave and not look back."

She buries her head in my neck. "I don't think I can do that. And I don't want you to be a secret. If Abby dying taught me anything, it's life is short. Too short. I want to bring you home. I want my family to know where I spend most of my time. When I go off to college, I want you to go with me. I want us to be together."

I believe she believes every word she's saying, but I don't know if she's got it in her to follow through with it. Something is going on in her family, something that has her showing up here crying, but she won't let me in.

Her hands run up my back and around my neck, pulling me closer to her. She kisses me and I kiss her back. I can't stay mad at her.

Maggie leads me back to the small bed and I follow right behind her.

12

Pippa's waiting for me at the same lunch table the next day. There's a package of peanut butter M&M's, my personal favorite, and a can opener on the center of the table, and I can't help but laugh when I see them.

"What's in the brown bag today?" Pippa asks when I take the seat across from her.

Mom was up before I was this morning and had my lunch waiting on the counter when I came down. As I dump it out on the table in front of her, she seems disappointed the can opener won't be needed. I untie the brown piece of twine then unwrap the white butcher paper to find half of a muffaletta. She used the bread she baked last night and the melted cheese and olive mix make my mouth water. There's also a huge chocolate chip cookie and a bag of chips. The contents of my brown bag rival anyone's in the school.

Her hand closes over the small appliance and she pulls it toward her bag.

"I never thought I'd wish I had a can of Vienna sausages in my bag. But thanks for bringing the opener."

She shrugs like it's no big deal, but to me it's a big deal. It means she thought about me at some point while she was home—in a good way—and that's progress.

"So what's on the agenda today?" I ask. I know there are people behind me watching us but Pippa doesn't seem as bothered by them today as she did yesterday.

"You," she answers. "I want to know what the last six years have been like for you."

This is not the subject I was hoping she'd pick. "Not much to tell."

She throws a chip at me. "Start talking or I'll start walking."

I think about where to start.

"Going off to school sucked at first. I missed my parents, my house . . . the one next to you . . . and my friends. I missed you." I pull a chunk from the thick fresh bread and find it's easier to talk without looking at her. "I had trouble sleeping when I got there. Weird bed, strange guy sleeping five feet from me . . . it sucked."

"But you obviously got past that," she says in a quiet voice.

I finally look up and I can tell the rest of the room has faded away for her and I've got her full attention. "I did. I think I would have gone crazy or run out of there crying if it hadn't been for my roommate, Jack. We raided the kitchens after hours and snuck out of the dorms. I joined the lacrosse team and the debate team and ran cross-country. Slowly, that first year, I started to feel like Sutton's was my home, my family. When I started that August of sixth grade, I wanted nothing more than to come back to Lake Cane, be here with all of you. But by the time the school year was over and I was headed home for that first summer, I wanted nothing more than to stay at Sutton's."

"I could tell," she says.

I debate continuing in the direction this conversation is going, but if Pippa and I are going to get back to a good place, we need to air out what happened back then.

"I know," I say. "You were mad at me and I didn't know why. I mean, I didn't ask to be sent off."

"I don't think you get how hard that year was for me. You had just moved to that ridiculous house in Cypress Lake when you told me you were going to Sutton's. Did you know there is an all-girls boarding school not far from yours?"

I nod. St. Ann's. We have dances together and they are the cheerleaders for our football team.

"I found out everything I could about that school. I begged my parents to send me there. And I didn't understand why they said they couldn't. They said we didn't have the money for that. Everything had been the same for us since we were little. Same street, same school, same trips to Gulf Shores for summer vacation, so I didn't understand why your parents had enough for you to go but mine didn't have enough for me. And then everything changed. We didn't live on the same street anymore, or go to the same school anymore, and while we still rented the same three-bedroom condo, you were going to Europe and South America. You were different after you came back. You had friends I didn't know and you talked about places I've never heard of and I realized things would never be the same for us."

"I'm so sorry, Pippa. . . ."

She holds her hand up, stopping me. "No. I'm sorry. It wasn't your fault that your family's situation changed any more than it was my fault that my family's didn't. And you did what you had to do. You were in a new place and you made it home. And I'm glad you did."

We sit in silence long enough for it to get uncomfortable.

"I didn't mean for it to get so deep," she says with a laugh. "I thought you were going to tell me about all the pranks I'm assuming go on in boarding school and sneaking out to see girls or stealing liquor from the headmaster."

"Well, there's that, too. When you have that many guys with that much time on their hands, there's no shortage of trouble to get into."

"So what's the wildest thing you did while you were off at school, Owen Foster?"

Just like it gets me when she calls me O, there's something about the way she uses my full name. And I don't really want to answer since it involves a girl and little to no clothing so I deflect. "I can't give away all my secrets. We still have three more lunches to go."

"I can only imagine what you did. If you had a chance, would you go back to Sutton's?"

I could tell her I do have the chance. I could tell her I turned it down but all I say is, "No."

"So you're going to be here awhile?"

"It looks like it," I answer. The case against Dad doesn't look like it will be resolved anytime soon. "How's the lacrosse team?" I ask. If I am stuck here I might as well try to find something to do. Not sure how much Gus will need me after all the pecans are harvested.

"Really good. They make it to the playoffs every year." She looks confused. "Are you thinking about joining?"

I lift one shoulder. "Yeah, thinking about it."

She nods and her gaze catches on something behind me. Before I have a chance to turn around or ask what's got her attention, Seth drops down in the seat next to me.

He angles his chair away from the table so he can look straight at me. Shit. I don't need another fight on my record.

"Hey, man. What's up?" he asks.

Oh, so now he's going to speak to me. I slide my chair to the side so I'm angled toward him, too, and lean back. "Not much, man. What's up with you?"

"Just checking on my girl Pippa. Making sure she's good," he says.

His girl. I look to Pippa and she seems surprised by his comment. "Owen, do you remember Seth Sullivan?"

"Yeah, I remember," I say. I'm determined to keep my cool so I don't ruin Mom's catering deal. Neither of us speaks and neither of us looks away. We're having some sort of pissing contest.

"This is so stupid," Pippa says. "Y'all can sit here and stare at each other all day but I'm done."

I look away in time to see her push her chair back and grab her bag. Seth makes no move to follow her. Once she's gone, I turn back to Seth.

"You got a problem?" I ask. I can't get into another fight. No matter what he says. No matter what he does. I'm not fighting with him.

"Yeah, I do. Pippa is my friend and I don't want to see her hurt."

I nod slowly. "Pippa's my friend, too, so it looks like we're on the same side of this."

He lets out a sharp laugh. "I can promise you, we're not on the same side of anything." He pushes out of his chair and walks away, and I relax every muscle in my body.

• • •

I make a detour on the way to Gus's after school. The guard at the Cypress Lake Country Club gatehouse stops me, one hand pulling up his utility belt while the other rests on my open window.

"Can I help you?" he says.

The security here looks intimidating, but you really just need to know what to say.

"Yes, sir. I'm here to fill out an application for the grounds maintenance position." There is always an opening for this job and the applications are turned in at the clubhouse, which is in the same direction as our old house.

He taps the roof of the truck twice. "Right at the stop sign, follow the road until you see the clubhouse."

I nod and tell him thanks. Even though it's called Cypress Lake Country Club, you won't see any cypress trees until you get to the lake. Most of the houses are big but similar, all drawing from the Louisiana Creole style that this area is known for. I turn down a side street that leads to where our seized house sits.

Not sure why I'm here. It's not like this house holds a lot of memories for me. I've never lived in it full-time—only spent time here during a few holidays and parts of summer. But I can't quit thinking about all of our things just sitting inside, waiting for this weekend when strangers will pour in and snatch them up for the lowest possible price. Most of my personal belongings are safe, tucked away at Lucinda's. My laptop, my lacrosse gear, a watch my grandfather gave me . . . all safe. I'm not sure if the people in charge forgot about my stuff that was with me at Sutton's or if Detective Hill turned a blind eye to them. But Mom has nothing and I can't quit thinking about the only item she wants from her old life, the bracelet her dad gave her for her birthday. And I have a burning desire to rescue that one item for her. To save the one thing that was hers before our entire life is wiped away.

The house comes into view and the driveway is full of cars. Great. I park down the street and watch the house. The law enforcement guys are easy to pick out since most have a gun or badge in plain sight and it doesn't take long to figure out who the rest of the people are since they're all wearing matching shirts with the same company logo. They're the ones getting ready for the upcoming auction. Not only are they selling every item inside the house but the house itself is for sale, too. In fact, it's the first item to go. I guess they're hoping whatever fool buys the house will also want to keep some of the furniture and art inside.

I watch for a few more minutes before pulling away. There may be only one way to get in that house—the same day everyone else in town will be here.

. . .

The first tree I pull up to in the shaker is a monster. The shaker is a little dune buggy–looking vehicle with a massive arm that stretches out in front of it. Basically, the purpose of this machine is for the grip on the end of the arm to grab the tree and then the engine sends vibrations down the arm that "shake" the tree, which causes all of the pecans to fall off the branches and hit the ground.

It's insane.

There is a steel cage around the top of the vehicle but I'm not sure if it's strong enough to protect me from one of those massive branches if it decides to fall while I'm shaking this tree. I go over the instructions Gus gave me in my head: line up straight to the tree, extend the shaker's arms to the trunk, close the grip.

I watched Gus shake three trees and he watched while I did three more but this is the first one I'm doing on my own. The first tree I tried to shake ended with the same results as when I tried to back the tractor and rake out of the barn. Complete fail. I didn't have the grip right and once I hit the lever to shake the tree, the arms slipped off the tree and the shaker damn near rammed the tree trunk with me in it. Thankfully, Gus hit the kill button in time. I'll never understand why something that looks so easy is actually so complicated to operate.

"Here goes nothing," I whisper to myself. I push the lever forward and the arm attached to the vehicle starts to vibrate, shaking the trunk of the tree and the vehicle I'm sitting in. Pecans and leaves and sticks rain down on me and I can feel my teeth rattling. Gus told me to shake the tree until I don't hear the nuts hitting the roof anymore, just like you time a bag of popcorn in the microwave. A few limbs hit the ground next to me and I pull back slightly until the arm stops vibrating. I feel like I'm in the center of a snow globe with the last of the leaves floating down around me.

I pull the arms back into the vehicle, then back away from the tree. There are little sweepers in front and back of each tire that brush the pecans out of the way so I don't roll over them, crushing them. This is probably the coolest piece of equipment I've ever seen.

I shake trees for the rest of the afternoon and thankfully no huge branch comes crashing inside, but my whole body is aching from the constant vibrations. I figure at this rate, we'll be ready to start picking pecans by next week.

By the time I park the shaker back in the barn, it's almost dark. I sit in the small vehicle listening to the pings and sputters as the engine cools, and for this first time, I actually think, *What if I don't try to meet Dad?*

Not getting answers would suck, but would it be so bad to let it go? Embrace what we have here? Because if there's one thing I'm honest about—I want to find Dad to get the truth but I don't want a relationship with him. If he offered for us to flee with him, I wouldn't go. He distanced himself from me years ago and I feel less connected to him now than ever.

The barn is completely dark when I swing open the door to the shaker and my whole body protests as I push myself out. I'm definitely going to feel today's work when I wake up tomorrow.

Stepping out of the barn, I scan the grounds for Gus but he's nowhere to be found. I've never left for the day without speaking to him, and from my knowledge he doesn't leave the property, so I go off in search of him.

I jog up the front steps of the main house, knocking once on the front door before opening it. I flip the light switch by the door and only make it two steps in before I'm stopped short, staggered by how different everything looks. The biggest change is how clean it is. I remember thinking that this place just needed a good cleaning but really, it's amazing how different it looks with the trash and debris gone and the floors and walls scrubbed to a shine. That janitorial staff worked a miracle in here. I wander around, partly looking for Gus and partly checking the place out. This is the first time I've been inside since I got the tour when I first started working here. Workers have been here for the last week and they've made unbelievable progress.

I walk through every room and look in every closet but never come across Gus. There's still a lot of work to be done upstairs but it's going to be incredible when it's finished.

Turning out every light on my way out, I walk across the yard to the shed. I'm guessing Gus is in the upstairs apartment. I've never been invited up there but I hate to leave without telling him everything I got done today.

Each step creaks and I'm expecting him to open the door any second, stopping me from seeing inside. Is it going to be as dirty as the main house was?

I knock on the door and wait.

Nothing.

"Gus?" I call out. I get a funny feeling and look over my shoulder, expecting him to be right behind me, but there's just the empty stairs.

I knock again and try the handle but it's locked. Why would it be locked?

"Are you looking for me?"

I spin around and almost fall off the top step. Bracing myself against the wall until I find my balance, I say, "Yes, just wanted you to know I've finished for the day."

Gus stays on the bottom step while I move down to meet him. Yeah, he definitely doesn't want me to go inside the apartment.

When we're both on the same level, Gus hesitates a second, then pats me on the back. "You've done good work here." He moves past me, up the stairs, unlocks the door, then disappears.

Noah—Summer of 1999

I've got to get Gus out of here. He's like a wounded animal that's been cornered and the only thing standing in between him and the roomful of visitors is me.

Abby's parents are across the room and her mother is sobbing loudly. They aren't from here but that doesn't stop all of the local older ladies from comforting her, the same churchgoing old ladies that Gus threw out a few weeks ago.

I felt really bad for Abby's parents when they first showed up. Her mom fell apart and her dad looked like he wanted to punch someone. In fact, he did try to punch someone. He tried to punch Gus. I didn't understand it at first, I mean, here are Abby's parents, crying on the front porch, and Gus is all but taking a beating from her dad without even trying to defend himself.

Then Gus told me later that night that Abby had a falling-out with them when Gus and Abby had eloped after only knowing each other a short time. They hadn't spoken in years. Abby reached out to them after she got sick and they came to visit her once early in her diagnosis. But it was horrible. Sounded like Abby's parents couldn't set aside the old issues and Abby was relieved when they finally left. When Abby got worse, she wasn't up for another visit and Gus backed her decision not to tell them how bad things were.

It's all kind of screwed up, but shitty relationships with parents are something I totally get. If I was at death's door, there's no way I'd call my parents. But then again, they wouldn't show up for my funeral, either.

The second fight between Gus and Abby's parents was about the visitation. Her family wanted an open casket and Gus was against it.

Truthfully, Abby was against it, too. She told Gus she didn't want anyone to see just how badly the cancer had changed her. But Abby's parents insisted it should be open. So the tradeoff was the casket would be open for just her parents, her older brother, Douglas, and a cousin named Robert who showed up with them, but it would be closed once the visitation officially started.

Gus has been standing guard by the casket just in case her family decides to go against Abby's wishes.

The line to pay respect to Abby is out of the door and around the corner. I didn't understand why Gus was so against this but now I get it. There are so many people here. They're staring at Gus, staring at her family, whispering about the friction between the two of them and most of them never even met Abby when she was alive.

"How much longer?" Gus asks. He was very clear with the funeral director that the visitation was over precisely two hours after the doors were opened, no matter who was still in line.

"Twenty minutes," I answer.

An older couple steps up to the casket. The wife says, "Gus, we're so sorry for your loss. How are you holding up?"

I can see the tic in Gus's jaw. This is the dumbest question people can ask. And the most common question he's gotten tonight. How's he supposed to answer that?

I'm fucking miserable, but thanks for asking?

Instead, he says, "Fine. I'm fine."

The woman moves closer and puts a hand on Gus's arm. "If there's anything we can do, please let us know. It's a shame Abby was taken so young."

And that's the second most common thing I've heard tonight. *It's a shame Abby was taken so young.* Again, what are you supposed to say to that?

Gus nods at them and they move on only to be replaced with another couple mumbling the same words. And on and on and on it goes.

I glance toward the back of the room and I see Maggie in line with her mom, who I recognize from the casserole delivery a few days ago, and a man I'm guessing is her dad. He's a big guy. Looks like he was a linebacker back in high school with his broad shoulders and height but then let himself go once he was done playing and now sports a big gut that hangs over his belt.

We watch each other from across the room and I know it's crazy for me to expect her to walk toward me, claim me in front of her parents and all of these people, but that's all I really want her to do.

"Are we almost done?" a voice behind me asks.

I glance over my shoulder and see Robert, Abby's cousin. He's a couple of years older than me and seems like a decent guy.

"Yes, thank God," I answer. He's the only rational person in Abby's family.

"Let me know when we're shutting the doors. I'll take Aunt Susan and Uncle John out of the side door. You take Gus out the back. I think it's best if we keep some distance between them," he says.

I nod. "Thanks for your help. I'm not sure I could have handled all of this without you."

"Yeah, same here." He slaps me on the back and says before walking off, "It's almost over."

Robert moves back to stand next to Abby's parents and brother while I count how many more people Gus has to talk to until it's Maggie's turn. It's excruciating waiting for her to make it to the casket. Gus notices her when they're still a few people back, then calls the funeral director over.

"Yes, Mr. Trudeau. What can I do for you?" he asks. This has to be the most difficult funeral this guy has ever had to plan.

Gus points to Maggie and her family. "After them, we're done. Time's up. I want everyone out of here and I want Abby brought to the orchard."

The guy swallows hard, glances at the long line still stretching out of the door, and then to Abby's parents across the room. He straightens his shoulders and steps in front of the people behind Maggie's family.

"Okay, folks, I'm sorry but we'll be moving Mrs. Trudeau to the private burial. I know you've been waiting to pay your respects but please respect the wishes of Mrs. Trudeau's family."

Confused looks are passed between people and groans fill the room. Abby's dad looks like he's about to protest, but thankfully Robert pulls him aside and talks him down. He can't stop Abby's mom's loud cries, though.

The director starts herding people toward the door just as Maggie and her family step up to Gus.

Maggie's mom says, "Oh, Gus, we're so sorry. How are you holding up?"

"How do you think, Mom?" Maggie says. "This is completely devastating for him." She moves past her mother, who's frozen with a shocked look on her face, and hugs Gus. "This sucks so bad," she whispers to him. "Really sucks."

He hugs her back and for once this afternoon, he doesn't look like he's about to kill someone. He looks sad but grateful not to have to exchange pleasantries. "You have no idea how bad this sucks."

Maggie moves away from Gus and steps up to me, then throws her arms around my neck. I hesitate only a second, because honestly I'm stunned, then I wrap my arms around her.

"Maggie, honey, I don't think we've met your friend," her dad says.

Gus answers for her. "This is Owen. He works for me and he and Abby were close before she . . . died."

Maggie's mom says, "Oh," but you can tell she still doesn't understand how Maggie knows me.

Sooner than I'd like, Maggie pulls away and walks to the exit, her parents following close behind her.

Abby's family is long gone, ushered out by Robert a few minutes ago, so now it's just Gus, Abby, and me.

Gus puts his arm around me, leading me toward the director's office. "Let's get Abby home."

13

I'm hoping our third lunch together actually lasts all the way through lunch. This time, I get to the table first and most of the students in the cafeteria are over it and don't seem to care that I'm waiting for Pippa. I'm taking this as a small personal victory.

I glance at the sign-up form for the lacrosse team I picked up from the office on my way to lunch. Luckily I already have gear, but there's a two-hundred-dollar fee to join since it's a club sport. Folding the paper and shoving it in my pocket, I decide to worry about how I'm going to come up with that money later since Pippa is heading toward me.

Her bag hits the table and then she drops down in the seat across from me. I slide a package of Reese's across the table and she stops it before it flies off the edge. "Think we'll make it all the way through lunch today?" she asks.

I smile. "Just wondering the same thing. I guess it depends on if any of your boyfriends decide to check on you again."

"You're baiting me and I'm not falling for it." Then she ruins her brush-off by looking behind me to see if anyone is approaching the table.

I pull out my sandwich and she does the same. "Since the school is doing your play this year, I'm guessing you're involved with the group putting it on?"

Pippa tilts her head to the side. "What do you mean 'involved'?"

"I mean, you're part of the production, right?"

She shrugs. "Yeah, I guess although they've just announced auditions so there's not that much going on right now. Why?"

"I have a favor to ask."

"You want a part?" she asks, laughing. "There's a ghost in the story but he only hangs around during the first act before he disappears for good. You'd be perfect!"

I grab my chest and fall back in my seat. "Your aim was perfect," I whisper as if taking my last dying breath.

She covers her laugh behind her hand.

I straighten back up and say, "Uh, no. I want you to help disguise me."

Pippa takes a bite of her sandwich and looks at me while she chews. I take a bite of mine and watch her just as closely. When she finally swallows down her bite, she asks, "Why do you need to be disguised?"

"So I can go to the auction on Saturday. The one where they're selling every possession we have. Or I guess, had."

She puts her sandwich down and props her chin in her hands. "O, I don't think it's a good idea for you to go to that. Are you even allowed to be there?"

I shrug. "Why wouldn't I be allowed to be there? It's open to the public. And I am part of the public. And I have to go."

"No. You don't. There's nothing good that will come from that." She puts the rest of her uneaten sandwich in her bag.

"Nothing is going to stop me from going, but it'll make it a lot better if I'm not recognized. I hate when I walk in a room and everyone stares at me then starts whispering." At some point yesterday after I tried to visit the house I got it in my head that I had to be there when they sold our things, and it's probably the only way to get something for Mom. Whether I have to buy it or steal it.

She throws her napkin at me, making me look up at her. "So you think you'll put on a wig and a fake mustache and no one will recognize you?"

"I don't know," I say and throw the napkin back. She's smiling and I can't stop smiling back at her.

"If you want to go, go. But go as you. Hold your head high and walk through your house. Look every person there in the eye. Don't be an ass to anyone, because seriously, everyone will be expecting that. Just be you. Or at least the Owen I used to know."

I nudge her foot under the table. "*I'm* the Owen you used to know."

She shrugs. "You know what I mean. No one wants to blame you for what your dad did, but you made it so easy for everyone to do just that when you walked in here with that huge chip on your shoulder. Like you're so much better than the rest of us. Don't be that guy."

"So you don't think it's crazy for me to want to go?"

"No. I get it. But I still think it's a bad idea. But if I were you, that's the way I'd handle it."

"That's what you'd do, huh? Just march right into that front door and stand there while people paw through all of your things and smile at them."

She nods. "Yep. It's the only way to do it."

"Will you go with me?"

This catches her off guard but it'll be hard for her to say no after that little speech.

She drops her head on the table, covering it with her arms, and lets out a low moan.

"Do I take that as a yes?"

She lifts her head and looks at me. "Well, I can't very well say no now, can I?"

I pop the last bit of sandwich in my mouth. It will be hard for me to walk in there but maybe with Pippa by my side, I won't completely freak out. "Perfect. Auction starts at ten on Saturday. I'll pick you up at nine thirty."

"So we're really doing this?"

"Yes, we're really doing this. And how bad do you think it'll be if I actually bid on stuff?"

Pippa rubs her hands across her face, clearly frustrated with me. And I may be egging that on just to see her reaction, but I'm serious about bidding on something. In the end, it's better than stealing it, but there's no way I'm leaving there without getting that bracelet for Mom. "What are you going to pay for it with? Do you have any money?"

"Not much." Gus has been paying me even though I tried to refuse it, saying the use of the truck was enough, but he insisted I was earning more than the use of the truck was worth. Truth is, Gus told me if I didn't take the money not to come back.

"But people are going to think you're buying stuff with their stolen money."

I lean forward, getting as close to her as the table between us will allow. "Pippa, they're going to think that about me for the rest of their lives no matter what I do."

She chews on her bottom lip. "But you're not, right? I mean, of course you're not."

I scoot my chair back and grab my stuff off the table. I've got to get out of here because it completely crushes me that she has any doubts about whether or not I'd use any money Dad stole.

"I'm sorry, O. I shouldn't have said that. I don't think that."

"Maybe tomorrow will be the day we make it all the way through lunch," I say before leaving the cafeteria.

. . .

Gus ordered a part for the cleaner, whatever that is, and he'd gotten word yesterday that it was in so I stopped by the small local hardware store on my way to work to grab it for him. I'm stopped at a red light and realize I'm a block away from Mr. Blackwell's office. Mr. Blackwell owns a transportation company that mostly just moves frack tanks from well to well. And in the fenced yard behind the building is row after row of almost brand-new trucks. Trucks that should be out for the day, earning money for his company, but have nowhere to go since Louisiana Frac is shut down.

If any business has been hit hard with Louisiana Frac closing, it's got to be Mr. Blackwell's.

And if there's anyone, other than Mom, who knew Dad best, it's Mr. Blackwell. He was one of Dad's closest friends before all of this happened. And just like whatever is inside me that's pushing me to go to the auction, that same force has me turning the wheel and pulling into the closest parking spot.

"Hi, I'm Owen Foster. I'm here to see Mr. Blackwell," I tell the woman at the front desk. Even though Dad screwed up his business, I'm hoping he'll still talk to me.

She gives me a look, then motions for me to have a seat. She makes a quick call and then says, "He'll see you in a moment."

I can feel her staring at me while I stare at the floor. A few minutes later, a side door opens and Mr. Blackwell stares at me. He's a small guy, probably not even five eight, and really lean.

"Come on back," he finally says. He doesn't seem happy to see me.

Maybe this was a bad idea.

I follow Mr. Blackwell back to his office and sit in the chair in front of his desk. He takes a little longer to settle in and then we're both staring at each other.

"I haven't seen you in a while," he starts.

"Yes, sir," I answer. By his expression, I can't figure out if he's pissed I showed up or pissed I waited this long to come by. "I'm sure you're wondering why I'm here."

He shrugs. "Not really." He leans back in his chair and waits for me to continue.

"Well, I wanted to come see you, to ask you if you believe what the police say. That Dad stole all that money. And if you do, why do you think he did it?"

"I do believe he did it. As for why . . . I have no idea. I wish I did," he says. Then he cocks his head to the side. "I really wish I knew where he was."

There's no mistaking the meaning behind those words.

"Yes, sir. I do, too." I hesitate a second before asking my next question. The one that's on the top of the list when I see Dad. "Do you think he started embezzling from the company right after he took over or do you think he did it later, once he started having money problems?"

This question makes Mr. Blackwell lean forward. He props his elbows on the desk and takes a deep breath.

"Son, honestly I don't know. I thought I knew your dad. I considered him one of my closest friends. I think when he offered the initial stock options to the employees, it was a legitimate offer. He couldn't have captured the business he did without using that influx of cash for inventory, supplies, and new hires."

"I can't believe he did that to all his employees."

Mr. Blackwell nods. "Me, either. I'm thinking he didn't handle things like he should have and I imagine at some point found himself in a bind. I bet the first time he skimmed some money from the company, he thought he'd pay it right back. But then that hole just got deeper and deeper. Money has a way of corrupting like nothing else."

I know he's trying to make me feel better, but I feel like I want to punch something.

"Everyone believes he had help. Do you think Mr. Frazier helped him? Or someone else?"

Mr. Blackwell shrugs. "You know, it's hard to steal that much money without leaving behind a trace of where it went or how it was done. He didn't just drain those accounts right before he ran away, he's been taking from them for years. Could he have done it by himself? Maybe so, but he would have had to have hidden it from a few key people. Frazier being one of them. Your mother being another."

"Mom didn't know what he was doing," I say. "Things have been tough for her."

Mr. Blackwell's forehead creases and he pinches his lips together but doesn't say anything. I can tell he has his doubts about her innocence.

"She didn't. If you saw her . . . talked to her, you'd know that. She's devastated over this. Won't leave my aunt's house. Doesn't sleep. Jumps at every sound. You have no idea."

Mr. Blackwell nods, but he's placating me.

"Have you heard Mom's been getting threats? Someone is calling, harassing her, breaking into our house."

He seems genuinely surprised to hear this. "I didn't know. I'm sorry, Owen."

"Do you have any idea who it could be?"

"Maybe someone who worked for your dad? Or someone who

believes she was involved. I just don't know." Mr. Blackwell leans back in his chair, lost in thought. "You know, I remember a couple of months ago we were playing golf and your dad was on the phone with someone. I don't know who it was, but he was yelling so loud I thought we were going to get kicked off the course. I asked him what that was about when he got off and he said someone from his past was in town. Made it sound like he had a real problem with the guy and wasn't very happy to hear he was back."

"What do you think that means?" I ask.

Mr. Blackwell shrugs. "I asked him that very question. He said the guy left here a long time ago and he thought he wouldn't have to ever deal with him again but now he's back. Sounds like he was bracing for trouble."

I soak in everything he's saying, trying to match it to what I know about Dad's past. "Do you think that's who it could be?"

"Who knows? But I don't think I've ever seen your dad that mad in all the time I've known him."

"Thank you for being up front with me. And for what it's worth, I'm really sorry that this has been hard on your business."

Mr. Blackwell stands up and reaches across the desk to shake my hand. "You're in a tough spot, son. That's your dad and I know it's gotta be hard hearing all of this about him."

I shake his hand and nod. "Yes, sir. It's been tough. Well, thanks for talking to me," I say, then show myself out of his office.

I'm pushing through the front door when I bump into the last person I expect to see in Lake Cane. William Cooper, Jack's dad.

"Mr. Cooper! What are you doing here?"

Mr. Cooper shakes my hand while pulling me in close, slapping me on the back. "Owen, it's good to see you."

He lets go and I step back. "Why are you here?"

"Checking out some things. I'm sorry to hear you didn't take me up on my offer to go back to Sutton's. I know Jack misses you."

I nod but don't want him to get away with changing the subject. "Thanks for your offer, but my mom needs me here. But I really am surprised to see you."

"Well, there are a few things here that need my attention."

I have no idea what that could be, but it has to involve Dad. He's the only link Mr. Cooper has to Lake Cane.

Mr. Cooper steps closer and puts a hand on my shoulder. "You've been like a brother to Jack all these years. You know that, right?"

"Yes, and I think of him like a brother, too," I answer.

"I've known your family a long time. Knew your grandfather when he was running the company and truthfully, I'm glad he's not alive to see what's happened to his business."

Mr. Cooper is more my grandfather's age than my dad's. Jack is a product of his third marriage and has siblings that are almost twenty years older than he is. The oil and gas company Mr. Cooper runs did business with my grandfather and then with my dad after he took over. Any wells Mr. Cooper's company drilled in Central Louisiana, our company fracked them. That's how my parents heard of Sutton's, because Mr. Cooper was telling him that's where Jack was going.

He pulls me just a bit closer. "You haven't heard from your dad, have you?"

There's something about the way he's asking me this that makes me nervous.

"No, sir. I haven't."

If I tell anyone about the note, it would be Mom. Until I know who's threatening her or what the note means, I'm not trusting anyone.

"You'd tell me if you did, wouldn't you?"

I nod, then ask, "Did you know what he was doing?"

His hand drops away from me and he cocks his head to the side. "If I knew what he was doing, that'd make me as bad as he is."

Then he pivots around and walks into Mr. Blackwell's office.

• • •

It's late when I get to Aunt Lucinda's. Mom's in the kitchen surrounded by cookbooks and there are pots and pans and every kind of utensil you can imagine scattered across the countertops.

She gives me a frazzled smile when I drop down in one of the chairs at the table.

"Long day?" she asks, then skims my face and clothes.

Shaking trees is dirty work. Even though I'm inside the shaker, the dust and dirt seem to find me and cling to me.

"Yeah. But it feels good, you know. I like looking down a row of trees and seeing exactly what I did today."

Mom smiles. "That's how I feel when I cook. Feels wonderful knowing people enjoyed something I created."

I nod to the mess around her. "Is all of this for Mrs. Sullivan's party?"

"Yes," she says. "She's coming by in the morning to approve the final menu and I thought it would be better if she had a little taste of a few things I'm suggesting she serve."

"I don't think you need to win her over; you already have the gig."

Her head bobbles from side to side. "I know, but I've been thinking about what you said. Maybe I can do this—cater parties. But I need to hit it out of the park. So everything has to be just right."

Even though she'll probably be up all night, I'm glad it's because she's working toward this than because she's staying up with worry over what Dad did.

She slides me a plate containing a trio of appetizers. "I'm sure you're starving. You can be my taste tester."

Holding up a little mini-sandwich-looking thing, I say, "This looks good. What is it?"

"Pork tenderloin with a Creole mustard sauce on a homemade biscuit. We had something like it at that little restaurant off Magazine Street when I visited you last spring, remember?"

I don't, but that's not surprising. I ate a lot of good food when I lived in New Orleans.

"In the mini glass mason jar is my take on a shrimp boil. You get a couple of peeled boiled shrimp, slice of sausage, and a quartered potato topped with a spicy corn relish. And the last sample is a BLT-stuffed cherry tomato. There are a couple of other items that will go with these plus a couple of sweets like mini pecan pies and petit fours. I wanted dishes that could be made ahead since she'll be picking everything up a few hours before the party."

Cleaning my plate, I say, "I could eat a dozen more of each. People are going to go nuts over this."

Her smile is big and has the power to warm me just by being near it.

"So, have you made plans to go to the dance on Friday? I really think you should try to go."

"Doubt it," I answer. When she's busy at the stove, I steal one more of the pork biscuits.

"Owen, you should go. It could be fun."

We need a change in conversation. Quickly.

"I went to talk to Mr. Blackwell, and I can't stop thinking about something he said."

And this does it. Mom's eyes are big when she turns around to stare at me. "Why did you go see him?"

"Wanted to talk to him about Dad."

"Oh, honey," she says, moving closer to me. "I'm sorry about what I said earlier. You know you can talk to me about him. I've just been so wrapped up in my own feelings. . . ."

"It's fine. I just had some questions I thought he could answer. Like if Dad set out to screw everyone over from the beginning."

Mom frowns. "What did he say?"

I lean my head back. "He thought he got into a bind and *borrowed money* at first. Then it got out of control. He may have been saying that just to be nice."

"For what it's worth, I don't think he set out to steal from everyone, either. What else did he say?"

"I asked him if he knew you were getting threats."

Mom stiffens next to me. "O, I wish you wouldn't talk about that to anyone. You know how they like to gossip in this town."

"Sorry," I say. "I was really trying to see his reaction. See if he was the one doing it."

"I can't imagine Peter Blackwell running through our yard in the middle of the night chucking a brick through my window."

I can't help but laugh at that mental image. "He's such a little guy, he'd probably have a hard time throwing it that high, much less hitting the window."

Mom giggles and I'm happy to hear it. But my next words steal the smile right off her face. "He said they were playing golf not long ago and Dad was on the phone and was super pissed. Screaming at someone."

"Who?" Mom asks.

"Dad told Mr. Blackwell it was some guy who left here a long time ago that he thought he wouldn't have to ever deal with again. That's all he said."

"Oh, God," she says.

Some of the color has drained from her face.

"Do you know who he was talking about?" I ask.

She chews on her thumbnail and seems to be lost in thought. "Your dad has lived here a long time. I don't know. . . ."

"Could it be someone from that summer he worked at Gus's?"

"I don't know. Owen, I just don't know." But her expression tells me that she has someone in particular in mind. "But whatever doubt you have of his guilt, you need to let it go. He's guilty. He did exactly what he's accused of . . . and then some."

Noah—Summer of 1999

Abby's parents won't leave. It's been three days since we buried her in the small cemetery in the back of the orchard and they're still here. Her brother left as soon as he could, saying he couldn't take off any more work. Robert, Abby's cousin who's been staying with her parents, is still here but it seems like he's at their mercy.

Gus spends his days working on the second floor of the new barn he had built last year. I joked that he was probably trying to enclose it so he could live out there and not have to go back in the house with his in-laws. He didn't laugh so I'm guessing that's exactly what he's doing.

Last night is the first night Maggie's been by since the night Abby died but she didn't stay long. Seems like her parents are keeping a closer eye on her ever since she hugged "that stranger" at the funeral home.

"Can I help?"

I like Robert, but damn he's always got a funny way of sneaking up on you.

"Uh, sure. Grab that branch and throw it on the trailer." We're out in the orchard, clearing limbs that have fallen. It's busywork but I'd rather be doing this than playing referee at the house between Abby's parents and Gus.

"How much longer are y'all going to be here?" I ask Robert.

He pulls a limb to the trailer and tries to pick it up but it's more than he can handle. I grab one end and together we throw it on top of the pile with the others.

"I have no idea. I'm on break from school for the summer and was working for Uncle John at his office. Then when we got word that Abby died, we all loaded up and headed down this way. I think Aunt Susan is ready to leave. She's so depressed and being here isn't helping because she's regretting the falling-out they had years ago. But I think Uncle John is staying because he knows it's driving Gus crazy."

I jump on the four-wheeler and slowly drive the trailer to the next tree while Robert follows behind me, picking up smaller branches as he goes.

"What are you studying in school?" I ask him.

"Business. Want to get my MBA after I finish my undergraduate degree."

He's got a plan and I can't help but be a little jealous of him. I bet Maggie's dad wouldn't curl his upper lip when she hugged me if I had my shit together like Robert does.

"That's cool. I'm hoping to go to college one day. I'm working here, saving up so you know . . . this won't be it for me." I'm trying to justify working here to him and I hate myself for it. Hate that I feel like I'm not good enough for Maggie because I'm not like him, but Robert is a cool guy and it's hard to hold it against him.

He helps me with the limbs for the rest of the day and I can tell it's been a long time since he's done any work like this, if ever.

"I'm probably not going to be able to get out of bed tomorrow," he jokes, but he's right. He's gonna be hurting.

"Yeah, this work isn't for everyone."

Robert hops up on the trailer while I drive the four-wheeler back to the barn. Once we get everything put up, Robert brushes the dirt off his pants although it's going to take more than that to get clean.

"What are you doing later tonight?" Robert asks. "Want to get away from here for a few hours?" I know Robert hates being stuck in the house with Abby's folks and it's not like Gus is any company.

As bad as I feel for him, I can't do this. I can't let him in, tell him what I do in my private time. And I don't want him to know about Maggie's late-night visits.

"Not much. I'll just probably crash," I answer.

He's hanging around, probably hoping I'll invite him to my place for a beer or something, but I guess he gets tired of waiting when he says, "I think I'll head to town. See what's going on. I'm going stir-crazy out here in the country."

And I feel bad. If things were different, I'd want to hang out with him. He could probably help me figure out the quickest way to get into school. But between Gus and this orchard and Maggie and everything else, I'm barely holding it together. So I watch him walk away and try not to think about how much I wish I was him.

It's late when Maggie shows up. I'm almost asleep when I hear the door creak open.

"Are you still awake?" she whispers into the dark room.

"Yeah," I whisper back.

She moves across the room and slips in the bed beside me, throwing an arm and a leg over me.

"I wasn't sure you were coming." I sound pathetic.

"I wanted to get here earlier but I had to go to this thing at the country club with my parents. I left as soon as I could. Sorry."

I pull her close. "I didn't mean it like that. Don't apologize."

She buries her head in my neck. "Maybe you should come by my parents' house. Meet them. Let them get to know you. Then we don't have to sneak around like this."

My jaw clenches. As much as I hate having to go kiss up to her parents, I will if it makes things easier on her. "Okay."

She pulls back and looks at me. "You will?"

I smile. "Maggie, there's very little I wouldn't do for you."

If she needs me to be more like Robert to impress her parents, show them I can take care of her, then that's exactly what I'll do.

Robert's on the front porch with a cup of coffee when I show up at the big house the next morning.

"Good night?" he asks, with a smirk.

"Pretty good," I answer back.

"Late-night visitor?"

I drop down in the chair next to him. "Are you spying on me?"

He laughs and takes a sip of his coffee, then says, "No. I was coming in late myself. Saw a little black car driving through the orchard in the direction of that house you're staying in. It's that girl from the funeral, isn't it? The one who hugged you by Abby's casket."

I nod but don't say anything.

"I saw her last night. I met a girl in town and she brought me to some party at the country club to kick off the Deb season. That girl was there."

"What's Deb season?"

"Debutante season. You know, when all the rich families parade their daughters around, introducing them to society. There'll be party after party until the big one sometime later this year."

I take a few steps back and turn to look out at the orchard. There's a whole part of Maggie I don't know. In fact, all of her life outside of her visits here, I know nothing about.

"What was she doing?" I hate I'm asking this. And I hate he knows the answer and I don't.

"The normal stuff at parties like that. Hanging out. Dancing with her friends. Looks like she's one of the ones being presented this year."

I'm going to lose her. It's the one thing I know for certain. No way I can fit into that life with her.

Unless I swallow some pride.

I turn back to Robert and say, "I'm not good at that stuff. You know, fancy parties and talking to parents."

He nods and I know he gets what I'm trying to say. "I can help. It's not hard. All you have to do is tell them what you think they want to hear."

Relief flows through me. Maybe there is a chance I can be someone Maggie would be proud to introduce to her parents.

Robert stands up. "Want some help today? I can't stay in this house with Aunt Susan and Uncle John. And we can go over how to look good in front of your girlfriend's parents."

"Sounds good."

I hop off the porch and head to the barn. A few minutes later, I hear Robert following behind me.

14

"*I'm not sure* why we're attempting lunch," Pippa says as she unpacks her bag. "One of us is bound to get pissed off and leave and if the pattern holds, it's me."

"But this is the best twelve to thirteen minutes of my day," I say.

She laughs even though she doesn't want to. "So we've talked about me and we've talked about you. What's left?" she asks.

"How are things going with the play?"

Pippa drops her head to the table and lets out a moan. "Auditions started and let's just say it all sounded better in my head than it does onstage."

"That bad?" I ask. "Maybe it's like hearing a recording of your own voice? You know, you think you sound horrible but really it's not that bad."

She tilts her face up. "It's that bad."

"Whatever. I've read things you've written and you're very talented."

She closes her eyes and groans. "You haven't read anything I've written since before you went to Sutton's."

"So you've only gotten better," I say back to her. She gives me a small smile and I take that as a victory. "Actually, I have another favor to ask," I say.

"I'm already going to the auction with you," she says. "I don't know if I like you enough for two favors."

"You like me plenty. You just aren't ready to admit it."

She doesn't respond to that but does ask, "So what's the favor?"

"It's an easy one. I've heard rumors there's a dance this Friday."

Pippa glances around the cafeteria at all of the homemade signs advertising the upcoming dance and game. "Rumors, huh?"

Tonight's football game is the last game of the regular season and on a Thursday night instead of Friday, so Friday night the school is throwing a dance to celebrate making it to the playoffs.

"Yeah, I'm not sure why this school isn't making a bigger deal out of it," I say. Literally every announcement, every poster, every conversation is around the upcoming weekend festivities.

"What do you need me to do?"

"Are you going?" I ask.

"Yes, I'm going with Seth."

Ah, now it's all coming together. "Is he your boyfriend?"

"No. We're friends. I like Seth. He's cool."

"Cool." Now I hate him more than ever.

Pippa spins her water bottle around. "So what's the favor?"

"Mom is on me to interact with people from school so she's driving me nuts about going to this dance. Keeps telling me to get involved. So can I tell her I'm going with you to get her off my back?"

She frowns. "Can't you just tell her and have that be the end of it? Why do you need a favor from me?"

"I can. And I will. I just thought on the off chance she calls you, you'd be ready. It wouldn't surprise me if she checks up on me."

Pippa bites on her bottom lip, thinking about what I'm asking of her. "I don't like the idea of lying to your mom."

"I highly doubt she'll call. I'm just covering my bases."

"So what are you going to do while she thinks you're at the dance?" She pulls out a Snickers bar and I stare at it, because Pippa eating candy is the best thing ever. She's not even paying attention as she smooths out the square plastic bag her sandwich was in. Pippa pinches the candy bar gently, separating the chocolate shell from the inside filling. I know after she eats the chocolate, she'll separate the nougat layer from the caramel and peanut layer, eating them separately.

Pippa catches me watching her and drops the bar, now completely bare of chocolate, on the plastic bag. "It's weird, I know. I can't help it."

"I like it. It's your thing and that makes it really cool."

She blushes, then ducks her head so I don't see it. Too late. I like that I'm breaking through her resistance. I want nothing more than for us to be friends again.

She realizes I haven't answered her question so she asks it again. "What will you be doing while she thinks you're at the dance with me?"

I shrug. "I'll be around." I don't tell her that I don't have any plans, but doing nothing would be better than going to that dance. I'll probably end up back at Gus's. Maybe bring him some food and hang out there.

"Where do you go every day after school?" she asks. "Because I know it's not your aunt's house."

"Are you checking up on me?"

"You wish," she says with a smile. "I babysit two little girls after school every day until their mom gets home from work and they live down the street from your aunt's house. That truck you drive is never there. Just wondering where you go because . . ."

She doesn't finish although I could probably finish for her. *Because you have no friends or because you have nowhere else to go.* Either of those could work.

"I work for Gus Trudeau in his pecan orchard every day."

She nods. "I've heard of him but I've never been out there. He's quite the recluse. Everyone talks about how he's only left that house once since he buried his wife. The cops showed up at his house for some reason, brought him to town, and he lost it on everyone in the station. He hasn't been back to town since."

Now I want to know everything she knows about him. I forget how small this town is and how everyone knows everyone else's business.

"So you've never met him?" I ask.

She shakes her head. "No. My parents knew him way back. They all went to school together. I think my mom met his wife before they were married and then saw her a few times after but no one saw her once she got sick."

"She died pretty young, didn't she?"

"Yeah. I heard they met at some concert or music festival or something like that. It was one of those love-at-first-sight kind of things. Got married soon after they met and then she got diagnosed with cancer. It was really fast. Everyone says he was never the same after that. Wouldn't let anyone come over, never came to town. It's really sad."

It is sad.

"How'd you end up with a job out there? That seems so random."

I hate for her to hear how pathetic I was the day I got back to town but there's really no other way to explain it. "The day I got back I couldn't stand to be at Aunt Lucinda's, especially with all the people standing on the sidewalk, gawking at Mom and me. So I took off running. Ran all the way to his place. Talked to him awhile and he offered me a job in exchange for using the truck."

She looks surprised. "I've always heard that you'd get shot if you showed up there. Or that his wife haunts that pecan orchard."

I think about how spooky it feels sometimes in the Preacher Woods but I don't think it's because of the ghost of Gus's wife. It's more like the ghost of my father, taunting me with a past and a present I don't understand.

"It's really pretty cool out there. You should ride out. I'll give you a tour."

Her shoulders shake like just thinking about it gives her the shivers. I had no idea Gus had that reputation.

Pippa puts all her lunch trash back in her insulated lunch bag. "So back to lying to your mom—"

I cut her off by saying, "Most likely she won't call you."

She waits a few seconds, then repeats herself. "So back to lying to your mom, you'll just be *around*?"

"Yes. And I owe you one. Say the word and whatever you need, you've got it."

She nods and then we're both startled when the bell rings.

We made it through lunch.

• • •

I scan the aisles, checking the prices and hoping there is at least one pair I can afford. This store sells everything from sporting goods to electronics to home décor and is the only place in town I can find what I need.

"Want to try something on?"

I glance over my shoulder and try not to look surprised when I see David. He's wearing a shirt with the store's logo with a name tag pinned above it.

"These are a little out of my range." It's hard to say this. I'm not sure that I've ever looked at something and worried I couldn't afford it. And then I realize what a jackass that makes me.

David stares at me a moment then says, "What type of shoes are you looking for?"

I hesitate telling him because he's on the lacrosse team and I don't know how he'll feel about me joining. I don't really want to get too involved at school but I'm also thinking I need to keep busy. And then there's college. I'm not sure how I can pay for college now that we don't have any money. My grades are good but not good enough to get a full ride. And I can't join the cross-country team even though that's my best sport because the season is almost over and I missed qualifying for the state finals. But lacrosse starts soon and since it's a club sport, there are no eligibility restrictions. Not sure I can get a scholarship since it's not like lacrosse is a huge sport in college in the South, but I'm desperate enough to try anything.

"I need some cleats," I answer. "For lacrosse." My old pair are shot from last season.

He raises his eyebrows and looks at me. "You're joining the team?"

I nod.

"What position do you play?"

"Attack."

David looks me up and down as if he's seeing me for the first time. "Are you fast?"

I nod again. Thanks to cross-country, not only am I fast but I have the endurance to maintain my speed throughout the entire game.

"Follow me," he says.

We move away from the shoe display and turn the corner until we're in the back corner of the store where there's an entire wall of discounted items.

David gestures to a pair of cleats. "We have a bunch of these left over from a couple of seasons ago."

The price is slashed and more in the range I can afford. "Thanks, man. I appreciate it."

"What size?"

I tell him and he digs in the pile until he finds the ones I need. I flip open the box, pull the shoes out so I can try them on, but then we're both distracted by the TVs in the electronics section right next to us.

Every set is tuned to the same station so all of them show the local news anchor cutting into the episode of *Jeopardy!* with a breaking story on my dad.

With both of us glued to the TVs, the anchor says, "Police are on the scene at Louisiana Frac. There was a break-in last night and investigators are trying to determine what, if anything, was taken."

The screen switches to a reporter on the scene who is interviewing Detective Hill.

A microphone is shoved in his face and he says, "We are looking into what happened here. Almost everything of value had already been seized and removed from this location so there's not much left to steal. This may be more of a case of vandalism than burglary. There will be a police presence out at Louisiana Frac from now on to deter anyone else from trying to destroy this property."

The camera pans the interior of Dad's office and it looks like a hurricane blew through there, papers everywhere, chairs turned over, light fixtures torn out of the ceiling.

"It looks like someone went in just to tear the place up," David says.

"Or maybe they were hoping to find something the Feds missed."

David looks at the screens a little differently now. "What would they be looking for?"

"I'm sure they were looking for something that could point them to the missing money. Maybe a file or bank account info. That's all anyone wants to know. And it's probably the same person who has been calling and threatening my mom."

"Your mom has been getting threats?" David asks, looking at me.

I nod. "Yeah. Some calls and shit like that."

"Man, that's not cool." And by the way he says it, I know he means it.

"Thanks," I say, turning back to the shoes. "I'll get these."

David nods and I follow him to the register. He rings me up and I hand over my very hard-earned cash. I hate parting with it but I feel good that I was able to buy them myself.

I'm just about to leave when David says, "Welcome to the team."

• • •

"Did you see the news today?" I ask Gus.

Not only was there the story of the break-in at Louisiana Frac, but it also turns out a few more companies have come forward saying Dad owes them a ton of money for work they did or products they sold him that he never paid for on a set of wells in North Louisiana. But records show he was paid in full for fracking those wells, so it's clear the money went straight into his pocket.

His theft keeps growing.

"Yep," he answers. One of the arms on the shaker was acting funny so Gus is working on it while I watch. We're in the back of the orchard, close to the preacher house, and it's about thirty minutes from dark. I was hoping to get this section done, but the left side wasn't gripping the trunk tight enough to shake the tree.

"This is going to make it so much worse," I say, back to thinking about Dad. "Before, I bet most people believed he'd spent all of the money, but now it looks like there's probably a stash somewhere. He's definitely stolen more than he's spent."

"That's what it sounds like."

I kick the shaker's tire. "What am I supposed to do now?"

Gus looks up from where he's working. "What do you mean? I don't think there's anything you can do about any of it, is there?"

I can find Dad. I can confront him and try to talk him into giving whatever he stole back. Or I can turn him in if he doesn't. But I can't say any of this so I answer, "No. Not really."

"Well, try to quit looking at the news and let the people in charge worry about finding him and the money." He waits a moment, then asks, "Y'all haven't gotten any more threats, have you?"

I shake my head. "No." I lean closer to get a better look at what he's working on. "What are you doing?"

"I'm taking the arm off and cleaning it out then putting it back together. Hopefully, that's all that's wrong with it."

Dad never really taught me how to do anything like this—not change a flat or the oil in my engine.

"Big plans this weekend?" Gus asks.

I shrug and try to look casual. I'm afraid my plans for the weekend are all over my face. "No. Not really. Just hanging out."

"Good. We could be done shaking by tomorrow. I was thinking we could start harvesting this Saturday. We could get two full days in before you go back to school on Monday."

Shit. This is not good. Gus has done so much for me . . . the truck, the paycheck . . . and I'm going to have to bail on him because there's no way I'm changing my plans.

"Well, I'm going to the auction on Saturday."

Gus stops what he's doing and looks at me. "You're going to the auction?"

I shrug. "Yeah."

"Why?"

"Just want to look around before it's all gone."

Gus gets back to work on the shaker and the silence is killing me.

"Will it throw you off too bad if I'm not here to help?" The guilt is filling me up quickly. He's bent over, working on the shaker's arm so he doesn't see my panicked look.

"Nah, it's fine."

I'm waiting for him to tell me not to go or what a bad idea it is to be there but he doesn't say anything else.

Gus finally takes a step back from the shaker and says, "We're going to need a little oil to grease the gear. Ride back up to the barn and grab it from the shelf on the back wall. It'll be in a small blue can."

I nod and sprint to the golf cart parked off to the side. It's a short trip back to the barn and I pull the cart into an empty spot next to the shelf, looking for the oil he needs. I scan the shelves three times and don't see anything that resembles what he's asking for. I search the rest of the barn and come up empty. The only place I haven't looked is in the apartment upstairs and even though I really don't think it would be up there, it's the last place I haven't checked. I move to the bottom of the stairs and look up at the closed door.

I jog up the stairs before I think too long on whether or not Gus would be pissed if I walk into his private space. If I'm being honest, I've been dying to see what it's like in there.

I turn the knob and the door opens. It's not locked this time. Pushing it open farther, I step inside. It's one big room, very similar to the house in the Preacher Woods with the kitchen, sitting area, and bed all in view. But this room is cleaner and more modern than the old shack since there's a huge TV mounted to the wall and the kitchen is full of the usual appliances.

I take a quick look around but I'm not surprised when I don't see the blue can. I'm just about to turn to leave when something odd catches my eye. The side of the refrigerator is covered in pictures. Curious, I move across the room hoping to learn more about Gus but I'm shocked to see he's not in any of them.

Instead there are pictures of a bunch of different people. Some I guess at, like the woman sitting in a wheelchair, wrapped up in a blanket, must be his wife that died. And the woman in scrubs standing beside her must be Betty.

And then there are the pictures of me. A couple of me as a newborn, a few more when I was in grade school, and then on to Sutton's. The last image is one of Mom and me when she dropped me off at school back in August.

Why are these here?

I move around to the front of the fridge and there's a Christmas card taped to the front. In Mom's neat handwriting and dated a few months after I started Sutton's in sixth grade, it says:

Gus,

Thinking of you this holiday season! Owen is settled at Sutton's and we're looking forward to seeing him during the break. As much as I wanted him to go, it was hard sending him off to school but it's where he needs to be. I'm hoping he can get some distance from here. I'll send more pictures when I see him in a few weeks.

There's not a day that goes by that I don't think about that summer and everything that happened. I'd love for you to meet him. I think you'd really like the young man he's become.

Maggie

I stagger back to the small table in the kitchen area and drop down in the chair. I stare at the card, rereading it until it's memorized. I always thought Dad was the one who wanted to send me off to boarding school, but it seems it was Mom who wanted me to go. Why did she want me to have some distance from this town?

What summer is she talking about? The one when she met Dad here?

For some reason, she never brought me to meet Gus and she's never mentioned "that summer" or anything that happened.

Then I remember what Mr. Blackwell told me. There's a guy from Dad's past that had Dad bracing for trouble. Could that be the same thing Mom was talking about in her note? Something that happened that first summer they met?

Just when I thought it wasn't possible for me to have more questions, I do.

I hear the rumble of the shaker outside the small window and I jump up from the chair and hurry across the small room, shutting the door on my way out. I barely clear the stairs when Gus walks into the barn.

"What's taking you so long?" he asks. He looks from me, up toward the apartment and then back at me.

"I've looked all over but can't find a blue can," I say. Keeping my voice calm and steady, I bite back the questions that are lodged in my throat.

Gus passes me as he walks to the shelf behind me, the first shelf I searched, and pulls out a small blue can partially hidden behind a box of random parts. He searches my face, trying to read what's going on in my head, before he turns around and starts walking out of the barn. Just before he gets to the door, I say, "What happened that summer?"

By the jerk in his shoulders, he knows I've seen the card. He doesn't turn around, just shakes his head slowly back and forth.

He starts to walk away but I stop him when I say, "I have a right to know."

Gus finally turns around. "You're right. You do. But not today. And not from me."

Noah—Summer of 1999

"I look like a dumbass," I say, staring at the mirror.

"You'll look exactly like the rest of those boys in town," Gus says.

I'm dressed in khakis and a button-down shirt, both pressed so stiff I'm wondering if I can actually move in them. My hair has grown out a bit since Betty cut it and Gus let me borrow a razor so I could shave. After working here the last couple of months and getting regular meals, I've bulked up some, and Gus and I are the same size. We're in the small apartment he's been working on in the barn. It's almost finished and it's nicer than I thought it would be.

"So where is she taking you?" Gus asks.

Maggie and I are actually going out on a date in town. And because I'm trying to do things the right way, I'm going to meet her parents when I pick her up.

"I think we're going to eat somewhere then stop by some party her friend is having."

Gus makes a grunting noise as he hands me a pair of shoes that look like they belong to someone going boating.

"I have to wear these?" I ask.

"What else are you going to wear? Those muddy boots? Sylvia will love you when you track dirt across her polished wood floors."

Not going to lie, I'm terrified to meet Maggie's parents. I feel like our entire future hangs on this meeting.

"Got any pointers for meeting the folks?"

Gus laughs. "Well, you can see I did a terrific job in that department," he says sarcastically. Abby's parents are still here and showing no signs to leaving. "Just be polite. Shake Martin's hand. Don't be afraid to look him in the eye. You're a good guy. They'll see that."

I nod along to what he's saying until he gets to the *good guy* part. I'm not a good guy. Have never been a good guy. And if they decide to check into my past, they'll see that.

"Why don't you take Abby's car? It's cleaner and nicer than the truck."

Abby's car is a black SUV with all the bells and whistles that's the envy of every person who sees it. "Gus, I can't . . ."

"You can. She'd be happy to help you win over Maggie's parents." Gus moves to a small chest on the cabinet and pulls out a set of keys. "Don't let anyone make you feel like you're not worthy of them."

I nod and he drops the keys in my hand.

I make good time since it's a short drive to Maggie's house, following the directions she gave me. I pull up outside and stare at the two-story house complete with wraparound porch and white picket fence while I'm in someone else's clothes, driving someone else's car.

I feel like such a fraud.

"Here we go," I mumble when I get out of the car. The front walk stretches out in front of me and I can see the curtains move in an upstairs window. Someone's been watching for me.

I ring the bell and it's opened almost immediately. Maggie's mom pulls the door wide and says, "Come on in. I'm sure Maggie is just about ready."

"Thank you," I say and step into the house.

The house is spotless. I can almost see my reflection in the wood floor and I'm glad I didn't wear the boots. The rooms I can see from the foyer are full of fragile-looking antique furniture that I'd be scared to sit in for fear of breaking something. Maggie's mom looks as prim and proper as I remember her being the couple of times I've seen her. Her dark hair is short and styled in neat curls like she just left from getting it fixed. I don't think gale-force winds could knock a hair out of place. Her khaki pants are as pressed as mine and her white blouse has ruffles and bows and a lot of other useless fabric all over it.

"Hey!" Maggie is bouncing down the stairs and I've never been happier to see someone in my life.

"Hey," I answer back. Her mom is eyeing me so I refrain from touching her in any way once she's close.

"Mom, I don't think you've officially met Noah. Noah, this is my mom."

Her mom extends her hand and I gently shake it.

"Who's this?"

Her dad comes in from a side door, looking me up and down like he can see through the borrowed clothes.

I close the distance between us, look him in the eye like Gus suggested, and shake his hand. "Hello, Mr. Everett. I'm Noah. Nice to meet you."

He shakes my hand, gripping it tight, and we hold eye contact for longer than I would think is normal. He's a big guy. His chest barrels out and I have to look up at him. He's dressed like he's been working in the yard, worn jeans and T-shirt with holes in it, and I watch for Mrs. Everett's reaction when his muddy tennis shoes leave marks on the clean floors. A simple glance is all I get, but I can tell the second I'm gone she'll be out here with a mop cleaning it all up.

He lets go of my hand but points to the small gathering of chairs in the next room. "Come have a seat. Tell me about yourself."

Mrs. Everett says, "Wouldn't y'all be more comfortable on the front porch?" She may start sweating at the thought of him sitting down in one of those fancy chairs as dirty as he is.

Maggie rolls her eyes and says, *"Dad,"* in a pleading voice.

I give her a look that I hope lets her know I'm cool with this and follow Mr. Everett into the room. I lower myself gently in the chair but then don't quite know what to do with my arms so I end up letting them rest in my lap. It's awkward looking, I know.

"So, Noah, Gus called and vouched for you. I've known Gus his whole life, knew his dad, too. Said you're one of the best employees he's ever had and that he trusts you completely."

Trying to hide my shock that Gus went out of his way for me like that, I say, "Yes, sir. I really enjoy working out there but I have plans to go to college soon. If not this fall, hopefully by January."

Mr. Everett nods. I glance around for Maggie and see her and her mom having a quiet conversation by the front door.

"What do you plan on studying when you go to college?" he asks.

Remembering what Robert said, I answer, "Business. Then try for my MBA."

He looks impressed and I start to relax. "And what are your plans for tonight?"

I look back at Maggie and thankfully she comes to my rescue. "We're going to eat at Geno's then going by Annie's house. She's having a few people over."

Mr. Everett nods, looking between the two of us. "I want you home by eleven."

"Eleven?" Maggie says. "That's ridiculous. I'm a month away from going off to college."

"I'll have her home at eleven," I say.

Maggie rolls her eyes again and says, "Fine," then storms off to the front door.

I gently get out of the chair, thankful it didn't collapse while I was in it, and follow her. Mr. Everett stops me before I get too far.

"I don't know you or where you came from but the only reason I'm trusting you with my daughter is because Gus Trudeau vouched for you."

"Yes, sir. I understand."

Maggie and I walk to Abby's car with a respectable distance between us.

"That was brutal," I say when we're finally inside.

"Sorry my parents are so weird. And I can't believe I have to be home by eleven. You should have let me talk him into letting me stay out later."

We pull away from the curb and she scoots closer to the center console and threads her fingers through mine.

"It's a miracle your dad let you leave with me. I wasn't going to push for you to stay out any later."

"I can always sneak back over to your place after you drop me off."

She gives me directions to the restaurant and I pull into a spot in the side parking lot. Before she opens the car, I say, "Maybe we shouldn't risk it. If your parents bust you and know you're coming to see me, then any progress I've made with them will be lost. We need to do this the right way."

Maggie turns around in her seat and faces me. "I get you want to impress my parents but they're wrong. They treat me like I'm a little girl. They only want me to date boys from families they've known their whole life."

"They might not know my family but I can become the kind of guy they'd be happy to see you with."

Her eyes squint. "So you'd change who you are for them? For their approval?"

"I'd do anything to be with you. If being accepted by your family and this town makes that possible, I'd change in a second."

"But I don't want you to change. I want you just the way you are. And they can only control my life for a few weeks more . . ."

"And then you're gone," I finish for her.

"Baton Rouge isn't that far away. You can come visit and I'll be back."

"Yeah, to stay at your parents' house."

"You could come with me," she says.

I don't say anything else. I want that more than anything but it will take a miracle for that to happen.

She leans over and kisses me on the cheek. "We're not worrying about all of that right now. Let's enjoy tonight and the fact we're going on our first real date. I'm going to introduce you to all my friends and this is going to be the best night ever."

15

The sound of glass breaking wakes me up but the flames have me jumping off the couch. I throw my blanket over the fire that is eating through the rug and then stomp on it. Smoke fills the room and the stench of the rug's melting synthetic fibers makes me gag. Once I'm sure the fire is out, I run to the door, throw it open, and try to see who's out there, but all I get is screeching tires and fading taillights. Mom and Lucinda barrel down the stairs and Aunt Lucinda starts screaming when she sees the big hole in the front window and the black smoke filling the room.

"Oh my God! What happened?" she shrieks.

"Owen, your foot," Mom says.

I look down and see blood pooling underneath my left foot. "It's fine. I just stepped on some glass."

She pulls me to the closest chair and pushes me to sit down. "Stay here. Let me get a towel and some water to clean you up and then check if you've got any shards stuck in there."

Mom's calmer than I expected but Aunt Lucinda is freaking out enough for all of us. She's on the phone with 911 trying to explain what happened while sobbing profusely.

"They're on the way," she says after she hangs up the phone. "Did you see anything, Owen?"

"No. I was asleep. Heard the glass break and then saw the fire."

Mom's back with a towel and a bottle of hydrogen peroxide. She pours a liberal amount over my foot then blots it away with the towel as I grind my teeth so I don't scream out. Damn that stings.

"You're getting that all over the rug, Maggie!" Aunt Lucinda screams.

Mom turns around and looks at her. "The middle of the rug is missing because it was on fire. It's a little late to worry about a stain."

There's really just one cut along the edge of my left foot and Mom has it cleaned and bandaged in no time. She gets up and moves to the closet where my clothes are stored and brings back a pair of slip-on shoes.

"Keep these on until we get this cleaned up," she says.

Aunt Lucinda paces the front hall and gives periodic updates as to how many minutes have passed since she called 911.

"I mean, we'd be dead by now if we had to wait on them to save us." She turns to Mom. "This is all your fault. This wouldn't have happened if y'all weren't staying here. No one wants to rush over here to help us because it's you."

And as if on cue, the room fills with the flashing lights of the first responders. Aunt Lucinda rushes out to meet them but Mom and I wait inside. She tucks herself into the corner of the couch and pulls one of my pillows in her lap as if she's trying to hide behind it.

Within seconds, uniformed officers and firefighters file inside until there's barely any space left. Must be a slow night around town because it looks like every cop on duty answered this call.

A couple of the firemen examine the hole in the rug without actually touching it while one of the police officers approaches Mom, crouching down next to her so they are eye level. He's older than most of the other guys in the room, and since they're all looking to him, I'm assuming he's in charge of this shit show.

"I'm Officer Hadwin. Can you tell me what happened?" he asks. While every other person gives their full attention to Mom, Mom looks at me.

"I was upstairs. Owen was asleep on the couch. He can tell you exactly what happened," she says, nodding toward me.

Officer Hadwin stands, moving closer to my chair and repeats his question to me.

"Like Mom said, I was asleep. The glass broke. That's what woke me up and then I saw that the rug was on fire. Once I put it out, I opened the door to see who did this but they'd driven off." I look around the room again. "Is Detective Hill coming? This is his case, isn't it?"

"I called him on the way over. He'll be here shortly." Officer Hadwin moves to the center of the room and toes the charred edges of the rug.

One of the firemen says, "It looks like whoever did this used a glass bottle filled with some sort of accelerant. Probably had a rag or something stuffed in the top. Lit it and threw it in. You'd have to be pretty close to the window or have a helluva arm to chuck it in here from the yard, past the porch."

Officer Hadwin nods along while pulling on a pair of gloves. Once his hands are covered, he picks up a piece of broken glass and looks at it.

"Let's find as many pieces as you can and test them for prints," he says.

Another cop walks in from outside. "There's something out here you should see," he says to Officer Hadwin.

Hadwin follows him out and of course we're all right behind him, me the last in line since I have a slight limp. It's hard to see anything because it's so dark outside.

Aunt Lucinda, not being able to stand the suspense any longer, pushes through the crowd. "Well, what is it?"

The cop takes his flashlight out of his belt and shines it on the grass in the front yard. The words *burn in hell* are written in orange spray paint across the entire lawn and *house of thieves* is painted across the front of the house.

Mom shrieks and throws her hand over her mouth while Aunt Lucinda lets out a string of curses I didn't know she was capable of.

"My house! My yard! It's all ruined!" Aunt Lucinda screams, pointing at Mom. "Because of you! If you have any of that money, give it back!"

Mom crumbles and I catch her just before she hits the ground. She looks at me, tears pouring out of her eyes, and says, "If I could give all the money back, I would. I promise I would."

I brush her hair out of her face. "I know, Mom."

Headlights sweep across the front yard and everyone tenses up. But it's just Detective Hill barreling up the driveway. He stomps across the yard and it looks like he crawled out of bed, grabbing the nearest pair of jeans and a wrinkled T-shirt.

Officer Hadwin catches him up while Detective Hill inspects the yard, the spray paint, the window, and finally turns his attention to the crowd watching him.

"Carl," Detective Hill says to the officer, "send some guys to check with the neighbors, see if they saw anything or if they have any exterior cameras that may have picked up who did this." The officer pulls a few of the uniforms to go with him. Detective Hill turns to one of the cops. "Bag the rug and let's figure out what was used to start the fire."

Officer Hadwin nods. "We've collected some glass fragments from what we believe is the container used to break through the window and start the fire. We're hoping to pull a print or two off of them."

"Probably a dead end but let's go over everything with a fine-tooth comb and maybe we'll get lucky," Detective Hill says, then runs his hand through his hair, messing it up even more. "And get the location secured."

By the time the rug is removed, the window is boarded up, and everyone clears the room, it's almost four in the morning. I wonder if anyone would have gone to this effort had Detective Hill not shown up.

Aunt Lucinda takes one long last look around the room and silently trudges up the stairs. A minute later we hear her door slam shut.

Detective Hill is across the room, talking on his phone. I only catch bits and pieces of what he's saying but it sounds like he's catching someone up on what went down here, then offers reassurances that the location is secure and cops will be posted outside around the clock.

He ends the call and moves closer to where we're sitting on the couch. We're the only ones left in the room.

Detective Hill sits in a chair by the couch and says, "I'll post an officer on the street. And I'll let you know what we turn up. Let me know if you think of anything that might help."

"Are we in danger? Is my son in danger?" Mom asks him.

He runs a hand through his hair. "I am worried because the violence seems to be escalating. It's probably in direct result of the latest news that just came out. No one knew for sure if there was any money left until now, so speculation that you have some or know where it is was bound to increase. Plus we know he had help, but we can't figure out who it was. Good chance that he split town without giving his partner his cut."

Mom turns to me. "I want you to go back to Sutton's. I'll call

William Cooper right now and tell him you'll be there tomorrow."

I stand up. "No way. If you're staying here, I'm staying here. I'm not leaving you."

We're in a standoff and it doesn't look like either of us is budging. Detective Hill holds his hand up.

"Maggie, while I'm concerned about what happened here tonight, I think whoever is doing this is just lashing out. Hoping to scare you."

Mom's voice trembles when she says, "Someone wrote 'burn in hell' in the front yard and then threw a flaming bottle through the window!"

He's nodding. "I know. And we're on it. There will be a cop outside twenty-four/seven. No one is coming near this house without us knowing it."

Mom doesn't look convinced. "I still don't like it," she says quietly.

"I don't like it, either," he says. "Let me go see if they found anything out from the neighbors."

Mom shakes his hand, thanking him for coming, and I do the same.

"There's no way I can go back to sleep," Mom says once it's just the two of us. "Why don't you crawl in my bed upstairs and get some rest? I'll finish up down here."

"I doubt I can go back to sleep, either."

I help her move the chairs back so she can clean up the glass particles from the broken window that landed underneath them. Mom sweeps while I hold the dustpan.

"Someone out there thinks we're sitting on all that money. Or we know where it is," I say. "Someone must really hate us."

Her broom stops moving for just a second so she can wipe away another tear. "Go upstairs and get some sleep. You can check in late for school."

. . .

By the time I get up and drag my ass to school, it's lunchtime. There's a sticky note waiting on the table I've been sharing all week with Pippa:

> I waited around. Decided to see how things
> are going with the auditions for the play.

I'm disappointed. Lunch with Pippa—as short as it is—has become the high point of my day. By the time I woke up, there wasn't much point in coming to school since the day was mostly over, but I thought I could make it here by lunch. It sucks to think she waited here for me and wondered why I didn't show, although there's no way she hasn't heard about what happened at Aunt Lucinda's. By the stares and whispers, *everyone* knows what happened.

I head out of the cafeteria toward the auditorium but before I pull the door open, I stop myself. What am I doing here? Am I going to lurk around the back of the room, watch her from a distance in the hopes she'll come over and spend five minutes with me?

I'm pathetic.

Before I completely humiliate myself, I turn around and walk back to the parking lot. After everything that happened this morning, it's probably better to keep her as far away from me and this mess as possible.

Noah—Summer of 1999

Maggie drags me through her friend Annie's house. It doesn't take long to realize no matter your income level, most of these parties are basically the same. Either the parents aren't home or they don't care what's going on, music is playing, some girls are dancing, and every person is trying to get drunk or high as fast as possible.

I was knee-deep in this scene back home and it almost never ended well. I refuse to make that mistake here when I feel like my life is finally coming together so I turn down every drink and joint that's offered to me.

"Hey, this is Noah, Noah this is Missy, Ella, and Sidney."

I nod to the girls and they nod back, giggling and whispering to each other.

Missy leans closer to Maggie and says, "Warning you that Nate's here. And he's pretty wasted."

"Nate is always wasted. That's not surprising." There's a bite in her voice I haven't heard before.

I lean closer to her and ask, "Is Nate the ex?"

She nods and scans the room.

Sidney says, "Let's go hang out by the pool. It's too crowded in here."

There are people everywhere. Most are like Maggie who just graduated but a good number are people who are back home after their first year of college, looking for something to do in this small town. I know this because they're the ones complaining loudly about *how lame it is to be back* while decked out in their college fraternity or sorority T-shirt.

Maggie grabs a beer and offers one to me, but I decline and say, "I'm driving."

Our small group finds a spot on the back patio and the other girls launch into talk of upcoming moves to college, last-minute beach trips, and how ready they are to meet boys that don't live here.

I have absolutely nothing to add to the conversation. Maggie links her fingers through mine and squeezes my hand gently.

"So you're the reason we haven't seen Maggie all summer?" Missy asks.

I shrug and Maggie leans in closer to me.

"So, Noah, what's it like working for Gus? I hear he completely lost his shit when his wife died. Went absolutely crazy," Sidney says.

My shoulders tense up and Maggie squeezes my hand again. "He's not crazy. Just completely devastated," I say.

"Aww," Missy says. "I think it's so sad."

"Well, Daddy said some of them tried to go out there to see him and he ran them all off. Told them all not to ever come back," Ella adds.

What kills me is that no one knows the real Gus—all they see is this crazy guy, not the grief-stricken husband who lost the love of his life, too soon.

"It's been tough on him," I say quietly. "Abby was a really special person."

They all nod like they understand, but none of them do except Maggie.

"Well, look who finally decided to show her face!" A guy drops down on the arm of Maggie's chair and pulls her in close to his side. I don't need three guesses to figure out this is probably Nate, the ex-boyfriend.

Maggie untangles herself from him and pushes him off of her chair and he falls to the ground, too drunk to catch himself.

"What's that for?" he says when he finally makes it to his feet.

"You know what that's for," she says. "I told you not to come near me again after last time."

Last time? I tense, but she grabs my arm, keeping me in place.

"It's not worth it," she whispers to me.

"What's he talking about, 'last time'?" I ask her, but she shakes me off.

"I'm going to find a bathroom," Maggie says and hops up from her chair. I watch to make sure Nate doesn't follow her but he seems distracted by something on the other side of the patio.

Her friend Sidney leans in close. "A few weeks ago, we were at this charity thing at the country club, a tennis tournament raising money for one of the staff who was diagnosed with cancer. Maggie got paired with Nate. Her parents were there, his parents were there, and all of them were eating it up, so glad to see the two of them hanging out together. Nate was making it worse . . . putting his arm around her, calling her cute little names, basically making it look like things between them were all good."

Sidney keeps talking. "Anyway, Maggie kept pushing him away, telling him she wasn't interested in getting back together. But it was hard with both of their parents egging him on. When the match was over, everyone was supposed to go to the dining room for a big dinner and Maggie's parents pretty much forced her to go and sit at the table with Nate and his parents. I think he was pretty touchy-feely under the table. Maggie finally had enough and dumped her water in his lap."

As murderous as I feel hearing about this jackass touching Maggie without her permission, I can't help but smile when I hear that.

"Well, Maggie's parents didn't think that was funny. At all. And pretty much told her in front of everyone in the room that she had humiliated them."

Every muscle in my body tenses. "She humiliated them? Her dad should have kicked Nate's ass."

"Well, he didn't. He told her she had to sit back down and finish dinner but she ran out of there crying. It was horrible."

I press my hands into the seat of my chair, forcing myself to calm down and not do something I will regret.

"You know, I think that was the same night we were all supposed to meet you for the first time. She told us she met this really cute boy and was going to bring him to hang out."

The night she was late and showed up crying. The night she wouldn't talk about what happened.

I keep looking back but don't see Maggie. It's been a while since she went to the bathroom and the hairs on the back of my neck are standing up straight.

But just as I get up to go find her, I see her. She's across the room talking to another girl, Nate is nowhere to be found, so I relax and sit back down.

Missy leans close and asks, "Do you know that guy, Robert, who's been showing up at our parties lately?"

I nod. "Yeah, he's Abby's cousin. Came in town for her funeral and won't leave. Why?"

She shrugs. "I don't know. He seems nice enough, but there's something about him. He kind of gives me the creeps."

I laugh. I freaking love hearing this. He always makes me feel like he's in with this crowd, but maybe that's not quite right.

"What's he doing that's so creepy?" I ask.

Her lip curls. "He's so nosy. Every time I've ever talked to him, I feel like I'm being interviewed. It's weird."

"Yeah, that doesn't surprise me. He seems really concerned with what everyone else is doing. And he especially loves telling me about it."

Missy laughs. "How much longer is he staying?"

"Hopefully not too much longer. I'm ready for them to go." It's getting old being the buffer between Abby's family and Gus.

Maggie makes her way back and drops down in my lap.

Scanning the room for signs of Nate every few minutes, I feel like I'm on high alert. The way he acted to Maggie at the country club a couple of weeks ago bothers me all night. We stay a little longer but when we get close to her curfew, Maggie pulls me in the house and out of the front door. We're almost down the driveway when I throw her the keys to the car.

"I'm going to run back in to use the bathroom really quick."

She nods and I sprint back into the house.

It doesn't take me long to find Nate. He's in the kitchen talking to a group of guys.

"Hey, man. Got a minute?" I ask.

He looks me up and down then says, "What the hell do you want?"

"Fair warning, if you bother Maggie again, you'll be dealing with me and I don't give a shit about who you are or who your daddy is or how much money you have."

Nate laughs and his friends behind him join in. "She's just slumming with you to get back at me." He stumbles closer to me. "Her parents are worried about her. She's cut herself off from her friends. They know she's hiding things from them. They barely recognize her."

It's like he knows exactly what to say to bring me to my knees.

He's drunk and cocky, getting close, his friends egging him on. "I told her sister not to worry. She'll be off at school soon and she's just rebelling against them this summer." And now he's in my face, whispering, "But hey, you should know . . . even if it's just for a little while . . . you're getting the best piece of ass in town."

He's not surprised when I flinch at his words and his hands fly up to defend himself like he knows it was only a matter of time before I hit him. But living on the streets as long as I did taught me the best way to win is doing the unexpected. Even though I've bulked up since I've been at Gus's, I was usually the smaller one, so I had to learn to be quick and use my brain. Most of the fights I won were done before I threw the first punch.

I smile at him and he takes a step back.

"I'm going to give you three chances," I say in a loud voice to make sure everyone in the room hears me. "And I suggest you knock me out because if I'm still standing, you're going to regret it."

His eyes get big. "What?"

"Three shots." I slide my hands in my pockets. "You better make them good."

His friends are getting rowdy behind him, encouraging him to hit me. I can see the beads of sweat that have popped out on his forehead. He doesn't know me—doesn't know what I'm capable of—and right now he's probably regretting letting his drunk mouth get him into this. Nate has probably been in a fight or two but it's not like the fights I've been in. I learned how to take a beating years ago, so I'm not scared of this asshole.

"I'm not waiting all night," I say.

"What's going on?" Maggie says from somewhere behind me.

Damn. I was hoping she wouldn't witness this. "Nate had some shit to say. And I'm going to beat his ass for it. But he gets three free hits first. Otherwise it wouldn't be fair." I hate this side of me is coming out and I hate Maggie is going to get a look at who I really am, but there's no way I'm letting him off the hook after what he said about her.

Nate cocks his arm back and swings at me but I shift slightly to the right and he misses, almost falling over from the momentum.

His friends are howling with laughter and more people have crowded into the kitchen.

"Two more," I say in a singsong voice.

He's really pissed now and rushes me. Again, I twist away just before he makes contact and he slams into the wall behind me. He's drunk and reckless and this is way too easy.

His friends have turned on him. Instead of cheering him on, they're heckling him.

"Last chance, Nate. Better make it good."

He comes at me screaming, arms flailing, and I crouch down ready to absorb whatever he throws at me. He gets one lick in, but doesn't do any damage, then he's stumbling back.

Nate is scared and he should be. I could break his nose with one punch. And that's exactly what I'm planning to do until I hear Maggie behind me.

"Noah, don't. You're better than that. You're better than him."

So instead of hitting him, my hand goes around his throat and I back him up against the wall he just plowed into. I lift him up slightly and his hands claw at mine. I've cut off his airway and he's flipping out. I lean in close and whisper, "Talk about her like that again and I'll tear you apart. Are we clear?"

He can't nod or speak so I'm just going to have to believe he understands. I let go of him suddenly and he falls to the ground and pukes. Then he leans forward and pukes some more.

His sickness has more to do with how drunk he was than anything I did to him but I'll take it. He gets up and stumbles away. I can tell he's embarrassed and to most guys that's worse than an ass whipping.

Maggie pulls me out of the kitchen, through the front yard, and out to the car.

We spend the last little bit of our time together riding around and talking. She's not happy about what happened in the kitchen but I can tell she wasn't upset at seeing Nate put in his place. Ten minutes before eleven, I leave her at her front door after a very PG-rated kiss good night.

I pull Abby's car into the garage and am just about to walk to my place when I see Robert jog down the front porch steps.

"What's up?" I ask.

"How was your date?" he asks.

There's a hint of anger in his question that I don't get. "It was good. What'd you do tonight?"

"I was at that party. And here I thought we were getting to be friends, but I guess you're just ready for me to leave."

Shit. He heard me talking to Maggie's friend.

"Look, man, I'm sorry I said that. . . ."

He holds up a hand. "Whatever. I'd worry more about what Nate's going to do to get back at you for humiliating him like that."

"He said some shit about Maggie that I couldn't let go." Truthfully, I should have just left with her and not gone back inside but I couldn't get over that he's been harassing her and not even her parents were doing anything to stop him.

"I get it. And you won that fight without barely touching him, but don't think he won't remember that. Just be prepared for him to do something to get you back. He's got a lot more friends than you do."

I watch Robert walk back inside and I feel bad about what I said about him earlier. All he's ever been is nice to me and that was a dick move on my part to talk about him like that. With my head down and my hands in my pockets, I head into the darkness for the long walk home.

16

I haven't been home from Gus's ten minutes when the front doorbell rings.

"I've got it!" Aunt Lucinda launches herself from the kitchen and practically skids across the foyer to answer the door. Mom told me she's been driving her crazy all day, spending half of it scrubbing the spray paint off the front of the house and scalping the grass to remove the words from the yard and the other half staring out of the front window like she's waiting for the next attack.

"Owen, it's for you," she says in a disappointed voice.

I'm filthy from a long day of shaking trees and want nothing more than to jump in the shower and find somewhere to lie low while Mom thinks I'm at the dance.

"Tell whoever it is I'm not here," I say.

"You know I can hear you," Pippa says as she walks in the room.

Damn, she looks hot. She's in a short black dress and her hair is curled and she's wearing more makeup than normal but not so much that she doesn't still look like herself. She takes in how dirty I am, and my arms full of clean clothes Mom borrowed from Aunt Lucinda's friend. It's a suit her grandson wore once and I'm supposed to be wearing it for my date tonight. The one she thinks I'm going on with Pippa.

"I was just about to clean up," I say, still trying to figure out why she's here, dressed like that. I know we're telling Mom we're going to the dance together but she's really going with Seth Sullivan.

I can tell she's nervous because she's clasping her hands in front of her so tightly that her knuckles are turning white. "I'm here to call in my favor."

"Favor?"

"Yeah, the one you promised me. I'm calling it in." She glances around the room and notices the scorched wood floor and the piece of plywood where the window used to be. "Are you okay? I heard about what happened last night."

"We're fine." Changing the subject, I ask, "What do you need?"

"A date for the dance."

She could have asked me for anything else and I'd have been less shocked. I glance around the room, mainly seeing if Aunt Lucinda is listening at the door, and whisper, "I thought you were going with Seth?"

She shrugs. "You didn't go to the game last night, but he got injured at the end. He thought he was going to be okay but he woke up this morning and his knee is super swollen. They just got back from the hospital and he tore his ACL. He can't walk on it right now much less dance, so I'm out of a date." Pippa does a small turn in the middle of the room. "But I have this dress and these shoes and Mom paid someone to fix my hair and makeup and I really don't want to miss tonight."

"You know no one will come near us if you're with me."

She smiles. "I know, but you're the only guy I know well enough to ask that doesn't already have a date."

I can't help but laugh. "So I'm the last resort?"

"Pretty much. And you owe me. And now we're not lying to your mom. That part was really bothering me."

"So what's the plan for the evening?" I ask, shifting the clothes in my arms, hoping they're not getting too wrinkled or dirty now that it looks like I'll need them.

"I guess we'll get something to eat? Then head to the dance?"

I nod. "Give me twenty minutes to get ready." I'm heading upstairs while Mom's heading down.

"I put a little money in your coat pocket for dinner," she says when she stops on the step ahead of me.

"It's okay, Mom. I have a little bit from working. You need to keep it."

She squeezes my arm and gives me a bright smile. "No, it's okay. Elise paid me half up front so I could buy the groceries I needed. I'm so glad you're going to the dance."

Mom's gig is tomorrow night. Mrs. Sullivan has a huge group coming over to watch the LSU game in their media room and I know everyone there will be blown away with Mom's food. And hopefully it will lead to other jobs for her and then we could get our own apartment.

I move up to the next step and give her a hug. "Thanks, Mom. I really appreciate it." I'm glad things worked out like they did tonight because there's no way I could take a dime from her then lie about where I'm going.

She hugs me back, squeezing me tightly, then pats my arm. "It's not much. Have fun tonight." I head up while she heads down, and just before I close the bathroom door, I hear her say, "Oh, Pippa! Don't you look beautiful!"

• • •

"Maybe they think I put a hit out on Seth so he couldn't take you tonight and you'd be forced to go with me," I say, just before taking a big bite of spaghetti. We're at one of her favorite places, Geno's, eating some of the best Italian food I've ever had. There are several other tables full of people from our school, all dressed up for the dance and staring at us.

Pippa laughs. "I don't get why they're still staring. I mean, we've been sitting together at lunch for a week now. It's not like this is new."

"The guys are staring because you're the prettiest girl in the room and the girls are staring because they know it, too."

She throws her roll at me, hitting me in the forehead.

"What?" I ask.

"Be serious," she says.

She thinks I'm screwing with her but I'm dead serious.

"So where's the dance?" I ask.

"The school gym."

"I guess there will be balloon arches and a cheesy photo backdrop. They couldn't at least spring for that big room at the Holiday Inn?"

"Owen, your snobbery is showing. This isn't your fancy New Orleans boarding school." She smiles when she says it but she's effectively put me in my place.

"You're right. I sound like an ass."

"It's okay, you can't help it."

This makes me laugh so hard that all the people that had stopped looking at us stare at us again.

Once dinner is over, we head to the dance, and the gym is full. Half the people are dancing while the other half are sitting on the bleachers that line the far wall. We take a selfie in front of the balloon arch because how could we resist.

We move across the room and I see David sitting with a group at one of the tables. I told Pippa about our truce at the sporting goods store, so when she notices who I'm looking at, she says, "We should go say hi."

We walk up to their table and David seems surprised to see me.

"Hey, man," I say to him.

He nods back. "You try out those new shoes yet?" he asks.

I shake my head. "Not yet. I really need to get some shooting practice in before the season starts."

He glances around the table and I know most of the guys sitting with him are on the lacrosse team, too. When he looks back at me he says, "We play a pickup game on Sundays in the field behind school. Eleven o'clock. You should join us."

I hope the shock I feel doesn't show on my face. "I will. Thanks." The fact he's inviting me to join them makes me feel better than I thought it would.

We say good-bye to their table and move away with no real destination in mind.

"Look at you, making friends," Pippa teases.

My hand finds hers and I thread our fingers together. "David's cool."

A slow song starts playing and I pull Pippa to the edge of the dance floor, then tug her close. She hesitates just a second, then presses up against me. All night we've been tiptoeing around that imaginary friend line and now we're getting dangerously close to crossing it.

I'm all for it.

Her hands slide up around my neck while mine are anchored at her hips, keeping her close. She ducks her head so the top of it lands softly against my shoulder. I hope it stays there through the rest of the song.

"What were you really going to do tonight? Because I know you had something planned and it wasn't coming to this dance." I stiffen slightly but she doesn't miss it. She raises her head and looks at me. "I've always known when you lie to me."

"But you don't know when I tell the truth?"

Her forehead scrunches up. "What do you mean?"

"Earlier. When I said you were the prettiest girl in the room. I was telling the truth and you blew me off like I was screwing with you."

I can tell I've caught her off guard because she just stares at me, her mouth slightly open, and I decide Surprised Pippa is one of my favorite Pippas.

She's about to say something else but gets distracted when she spots a group of her friends heading in our direction.

We pull apart and stand side by side but I slide my hand in hers so we're still connected. Thankfully, she is okay with that.

"Hey," she says in her most upbeat voice.

A few hellos bounce back at us and a couple give us a half-wave sort of thing but that's it.

"So what's going on?" she asks.

A girl I recognize from the bonfire says, "We're trying to decide how long we're staying before we head to Drew's party."

"I'm ready to go now," some guy says. "This dance sucks."

Most of the group throw similar statements back and forth and the general consensus is that even though the dance only started twenty minutes ago, no one wants to stay.

"You coming, Pippa?" the girl who spoke earlier asks.

It's clear the invitation is only for her. I lean in close and whisper, "If you want to go with them, I understand."

I don't want her to go but I also don't want to her to stay with me if that's not what she wants.

Pippa doesn't hesitate. "Y'all go ahead. We're going to hang out here a little longer."

I can't help it; I pull her close, anchoring her to my side. She turns to me after her friends leave, her hands sliding up around my neck again, so we can resume dancing. "Your first high school dance in a gym isn't complete until we've taken pics against that cheesy backdrop, had a cup of warm punch that unfortunately isn't spiked, and gotten busted by one of the chaperones on the dance floor for slightly inappropriate behavior."

"Well, we better start crossing things off the list," I say. "There's no one else I want to be slightly inappropriate with."

With my hands on her hips, I pull her close until we're touching from top to bottom. I'm teetering on the edge, ready to barrel across that imaginary friend line and move us into completely new and different territory, but something holds me back.

Fear.

Fear of ruining what we have. Fear she'll regret it. Fear that I can't handle losing anything else.

So we sway to the music and—for now—I'm content with the feel of her body next to mine.

Noah—Summer of 1999

"Smile for one more," Maggie says, then lifts her small camera to her face, but before she can take another picture of me, I tug the camera away from her, pointing it in her direction, and snap one of her. The Polaroid picture shoots out of the bottom and I grab it before it hits the ground.

Shaking it to make it develop faster, I know it will be the best one of her yet.

It's late afternoon. It's hot out, the air feels like a wet blanket, and it's hard to drag in a deep breath. It won't be long before it's dark and the mosquitoes run us inside, but for now, we're on an old quilt at the base of this giant pecan tree in front of my little house near the river, glad for the shade it offers. The roots are so big and old that they've pushed out of the ground, forming a semicircle that makes it seem like the tree is hugging you.

It's our favorite spot.

The picture comes into focus and I was right. The setting sun lights up her hair and she's smiling at me like she does just before she kisses me. It's my favorite smile. I tuck it in my pocket, knowing it's one I'll keep forever.

Maggie leans into me and we rest against the base of the tree.

"What are you thinking about?" Maggie asks.

"I'm thinking about the preacher who used to live in this house. The one who preached to these trees like they were people."

She snuggles in close. "This was probably his favorite tree. It's the biggest, prettiest one of the whole bunch."

"I feel like that preacher had the right idea. This place feels like the safest spot. Like I could tell these trees anything and I know my secrets would be safe."

She shifts around until her head is in my lap and she's looking up at the tree limbs above her. "Oh, I love that. Let's tell it a secret, let our words soak through the bark. And we'll know forever that a piece of us is buried inside this tree. Our tree."

My fingers run through her hair until I have it fanned out around her. "What secret do you want to tell it?"

She reaches her hand out to touch the tree, her eyes still locked on the branches overhead. "Tree, it's Maggie. My secret is that I'm in love with this boy. He's kind and sweet and cute. He's strong and I feel safe with him. But he doesn't know how awesome he is. And I'm afraid when I go off to college the distance will tear us apart and that makes me sad."

Her words gut me. Humble me. She tears her gaze away from the limbs and leaves and looks at me.

"Your turn," she says.

I smile at her and reach behind me, placing my hand behind my head so it rests on the trunk. But instead of staring at the branches above, I stare at Maggie.

"Tree, it's Noah. My secret is I'm scared. Scared to death. Scared I'm not good enough for the girl I love. Scared I'm not good enough for her family. Scared that one day soon she'll realize she can do so much better than me."

She sits up and faces me, her long hair falling in waves behind her. "Don't be scared." She leans in, kisses me. I shift her around until she's in my lap. Her hands push through my hair and mine dig into her waist, pulling her closer and closer.

I never want to leave this spot. Forever, I want us wrapped in the safety of this tree. This tree that now holds all of our secrets.

17

"*Thank you again* for doing this," I say I as follow her to her car.

"This is the worst idea ever," she mumbles. "And I'm dumb for going along with you."

My fingers land on her wrist, stopping her, and she spins around. "You don't have to go." And once I touch her, I can't stop. My fingers wrap around her wrist and I pull her close. I want to lean down and kiss her and by the look on her face, I think she wants the same thing. But the same reason that kept me from taking that next step last night stops me this morning.

She squeezes my arm. "I promised I would. But I still don't understand why it's so important for you to go to this auction." She pulls away from me and disappears inside her car. I slide into the passenger seat. Her hand is on the key in the ignition but she hasn't cranked the car yet. "Tell me the truth. Why do you want to go?"

We stare at each other for what feels like an eternity. I really don't want to keep anything from her. Not anymore.

"I want Mom to have one thing. Just one thing that was hers. They took everything from her and it kills me," I whisper.

"Won't you have to put up a credit card or something to show you can pay for it first?" she asks.

I shrug and she narrows her eyes at me.

"You're just going to take something, aren't you? Steal it?"

"It's hard to steal something that's already yours," I answer back.

Pippa tilts her head to the side. "It's not yours anymore, O."

I shake my head. "No. Some of those things were not paid for by Dad. Some of those things my mom got from her parents. They shouldn't have taken that stuff from her."

"Then let me buy it for you. I'm not going to take you there if you plan on stealing something. I won't be a part of that."

"I have some money saved up from working for Gus. I can pay you back."

The drive to my old house is short and the gate to the subdivision is wide open, since it's obvious the steady stream of cars that pull through the gate is going to the auction. People from the neighborhood don't even bother with cars, they come riding up in their golf carts or on foot. We park along the street a half mile away from the house, the closest spot we could find.

"This is going to be a nightmare," I mumble when Pippa shuts off the engine.

"You can stay here. Tell me what you want me to get. I'll go bid on it," she offers.

"No, I want to go."

We walk side by side down the street and every eye is on me. People don't even try to whisper so I hear every comment about how tacky or wrong or disgraceful it is that I'm here.

Pippa grabs my hand, linking her fingers with mine, and I've never felt so grateful for a show of support before.

"If we're doing this—head up. Be strong. Let it all roll off."

I'm not sure if she's saying that for my benefit or hers, but I straighten up and look ahead, ignoring everyone we pass.

There's a huge tent in the front yard with chairs lined up underneath it. Most every one of them is full. At the end of the driveway, there's a check-in table with a booklet showcasing everything up for auction.

Pippa steps up to the table, still clutching my hand, and asks, "How do I sign up to bid on things?"

The company running the auction is out of Alexandria so thankfully the woman at the table doesn't recognize me, but everyone near us does. All of their expressions are the same: eyes big, jaw dropped, mouth open.

"You'll need to fill out this form and put a credit card on file. We'll give you a paddle with your bid number on it. The big items will be auctioned under the tent, then it will move inside and go room by room," she says, handing me a piece of paper. "Here's the schedule."

Pippa lets go of my hand long enough to fill out the form and hand the woman a credit card. The woman swipes the card then hands it back to Pippa with the numbered paddle.

"Enjoy the auction," she says with a big smile.

"I'm sure we will," Pippa mumbles back. She grabs my hand and pulls me away from the table to stand on the side of the driveway, away from most of the crowd.

"Do you think they'll stare at me the whole time?" I ask.

"Yep," she answers and she browses through the book. "Do you know what you want to get her?"

I've clicked through the items on the site a hundred times by now. "Yeah, there's a bracelet under Women's Jewelry. In the fourth group down. My grandfather gave it to my mom. It's a silver bracelet, nothing special, but she loves it. And it shouldn't go for too much money."

Pippa bites her lip. "It may if anyone gets wind you want it. What time are they auctioning it?" She pulls the schedule out of my hand. "They'll be in your parents' room at two. We should leave and come back for that. No reason to wait here the whole time."

I watch the action going on under the tent in the front yard. "What time do they auction the house?" I ask Pippa.

She glances at the paper again. "Eleven a.m."

So that's what the crowd is gathered for. Pippa starts to move down the driveway toward her car, but I pull her back. "I want to watch this."

She glances to the tent and checks the book again. "O, this is a terrible idea. We should leave now and come back later. We're only here for the bracelet, remember."

"I just want to see who bids on it. And then we'll go."

I circle around the tent to the other side and we end up more in the neighbor's yard than ours. People are still looking and pointing but it seems to be less and less as the upcoming auction is getting started. Under the tent, first up is the house, then the cars, the ski boat and Jet Skis, then some of the bigger pieces of furniture, all of the art, and ending with Mom's really expensive jewelry.

It's hard not to get distracted by the conversations going on around us. Not only are people pulling apart every little thing, but there is wild speculation about what *could* be inside the house. Words like *secret vaults* and *wall safes* are being batted around. Do people really think there are secrets buried somewhere in that house?

Is that possible?

The auctioneer greets everyone and explains the rules of the auction. Only those with a blue paddle can bid on the house and other big-ticket items since you had to be pre-approved. Obviously, that's code for "you can't bid on it if you can't prove you can pay for it."

There seems to be a handful of people with the blue paddles, but most of the crowd is just here for the show.

The auctioneer stands at the podium and his voice booms across the yard. "This home is only seven years old but its beauty is timeless. It's twelve thousand square feet; ten thousand are heated and cooled. Five bedrooms, five bathrooms, gourmet kitchen, theater room, home gym, his and hers offices, and every other amenity you can dream of. The backyard boasts a swimming pool, hot tub, outdoor kitchen, pool house, and a view of the ninth hole of the golf course. The bidding will start at one million."

I knew this house was ridiculous when we bought it but I'm embarrassed when it's spelled out like that.

The auctioneer starts the bidding but no one raises their paddle. Probably because no one in this town has that kind of money after what Dad did to them.

"Come on, folks, this house is a steal at a million. It was appraised for almost double that!" He looks like he's getting desperate. What will happen if no one bids?

He ends up dropping the price in small chunks while begging someone to bid. He gets to an even eight hundred thousand dollars and one blue paddle goes up. It goes once, then twice, and then sold to the blue paddle with the number 132 on it.

One bid.

I can't see who it is from here so I move up a little to get a better look just as he stands and approaches the auctioneer.

"Holy shit."

"What? Who is that?"

"It's my friend Jack's dad."

"Why did he buy your house?" Pippa asks.

That's a really good question. And now all of that crazy talk earlier doesn't sound so crazy. Is it possible Mr. Cooper was the one helping Dad and Dad screwed him over and now he thinks there's some hidden vault inside the house? In all the time my family was friends with the Coopers, Mr. Cooper never came to Lake Cane, and now I've seen him here twice in one week. And both of those places had a connection to Dad.

I walk toward the tent while Pippa pulls on the back of my shirt, trying to stop me.

I'm a few feet from him when he finally notices me. He smiles and extends his hand. "Owen, didn't expect to see you here."

I force my hand into his when it's the last thing I want to do.

"Well, we're both surprised then. I didn't expect to see you here either," I say, then pull my hand back.

No way he's missing the hard tone in my voice.

He's about to say something else when I interrupt. "Why did you buy my house?"

There's a crowd watching but I'm used to it by now. There's always a crowd watching me except when I'm at Gus's.

Mr. Cooper puts a hand on my shoulder and guides me to an empty corner of the tent. "This is just business, Owen. I knew this house would go for less than it was worth. And I knew there aren't many people who could afford it. So I'll sit on it awhile, until the town bounces back, and make a little money on it. And your father's victims get some much-needed restitution."

The auctioneer is back, announcing the next item up for bid— Mom's car.

"Well, there's plenty more good deals to be had here. Don't let me stop you." Grabbing Pippa's hand, I pull her away from him toward the house.

"Are we leaving now? Please tell me we're leaving now," she says.

"I want to walk through once before we go, then we'll come back closer to two," I answer.

We wait in line to enter the house. It's unbelievable how many people are here but somehow the crowd helps us blend in. We finally get inside and it's surreal being back. The last time I walked through this door was on my way out as I left for senior year at Sutton's.

Everything is still in its same place but now there's a bid tag hanging from it and there are room monitors watching everyone who walks through making sure no one tries to sneak out with anything.

Pippa and I go with the flow of the crowd and head upstairs. I know my room will be the hardest one to see like this so I'm glad I'm getting it over with early on.

"Is this your room?" Pippa asks when we step inside.

"It was," I answer. It feels foreign now even though everything is recognizable. You can get my bed for only a couple hundred bucks and each lamp for less than half of that. Even the drapes are for sale. Several people stop walking long enough to take pictures before moving along.

This sucks.

"I can't believe you kept this," she whispers.

I turn to see what she's looking at and spot the wooden sword on a table with a bunch of other random things that are being sold together since none of the items are worth much on their own. It's scarred and still has some of the pink paint from a bet gone wrong.

"Yeah. That was the sword I used to proclaim myself King of Dogwood Drive. Of course I kept it."

She moves closer to the table and picks the sword up and points it at me, just like she did when we were little.

"Miss, no touching the items," the room monitor says, and Pippa twirls the sword in her hand a couple of times before returning it to the table.

"You totally cheated on that challenge that made you the King of Dogwood Drive. If you would have finished the obstacle course like you were supposed to, I would've won and been named Empress of Dogwood Drive."

I laugh because I did totally cheat. She was so much faster than me and I couldn't stand it. "Do you still have yours?"

"Not sure. Been a while since I've seen it," she answers.

Her dad took us to Dallas when we were little to eat at that medieval-themed restaurant and he let us each pick a souvenir. It wasn't a surprise when we both wanted a wooden sword. And that began the never-ending battle to decide who would rule our street.

But as I see that sword lying on the table with all of the other things that only mean something to me, even that memory sours.

"Let's go back downstairs," Pippa says. She wants out of here as much as I do.

We take the stairs at the back of the house that will drop us into the kitchen. There are mostly women in here picking through Mom's pots and pans.

"I always wanted a big gumbo pot like this," some woman says. "But who would pay four hundred dollars for one pot?"

"Well, you oughta bid on it. I bet it doesn't go for that high," her friend says.

Every time I was home, there was always something good cooking in one of these pots and it's hard not to think about how much

Mom needs them now if she's going to get her catering business off the ground.

"This sucks so bad," I whisper to Pippa.

"I told you not to come," she answers back.

"C'mon, let's head to Mom's room and find that bracelet." Pippa follows me as I weave through the crowd to my parents' room. There are security guards next to a folding table where Mom's jewelry is laid out. All of the really good stuff is outside in the opening auction but the rest is in here. Some of the nicer pieces have their own bid number while other pieces are grouped together in lots.

I bury my hands in my pockets so no one will think I'm taking anything—but also maybe to stop myself from doing exactly that.

"Is that it?" Pippa asks.

In the center of the table is the thin silver bracelet I remember Mom wearing all the time.

I nod and then she pulls my arm. "Okay, so we've seen it. O, let's go. We'll be back in a few hours."

She guides me away from the table and I'm glad she does because I'm so tempted to grab everything I can manage and make a run for it.

"Let's leave through the family room," I say. "We can go out the back door and cut through the side yard."

"Good, I'm ready to get out of here," Pippa says.

But one last glance at Mom's things has me stopping short and Pippa plows into the back of me. "Ow," she says. "Why'd you stop?"

Backtracking, I pull us back to the table.

"What is it?" Pippa asks.

"That necklace. Look at what's engraved on the pendant." It's a rectangular piece of copper and since it's grouped with five other pieces under one item number it's not worth much.

Pippa moves closer to the table so she can check out the item. "'S 6 R 9 T 4.' What does that mean?"

"I don't know, but I've seen that combination of letters and numbers before." I pull out the picture of Mom from my wallet, the one that was once inside the Preacher Woods house. "See, same letters and numbers on the back of this."

Pippa looks from the picture to the necklace and back again. "This is weird."

"I know, and that's why I'm bidding on it along with the bracelet."

. . .

I need to clear my head and kill some time between now and when we head back to the house to make a bid on Mom's bracelet and the necklace, so I bring Pippa to the only place where I can get away from everything going on in town and at home—the orchard.

"Are you sure it's okay for me to be out here?" she asks for the fourth time.

"Yes. It's fine. I don't know why Gus has the reputation for eating nosy kids for breakfast but he's really a cool guy."

There's a white painter's drop cloth spread out in the yard and a couple of rocking chairs sitting on top of it. Gus is leaned over, painting the underside of one of the chairs, but stops and turns toward us when he hears his truck pull up.

"He looks younger than I thought he would, you know . . . for a hermit," Pippa whispers.

"Were you expecting a long gray beard, a hump on his back, and yellow teeth?" Laughing, I add, "And you don't need to whisper. He can't hear you from here."

"Oh, yeah, right."

"C'mon, let me give you the tour."

We get out of the truck and I wait for Pippa to come around to the driver's side before moving closer to Gus. He's watching us and despite my telling Pippa he'd be cool with her coming out here, I don't know that for sure.

"Who's this?" Gus asks when we get close.

"My friend Pippa. Pippa, this is Gus."

She gives him a small wave and he nods back at her.

"I thought I'd show her around, is that okay?" I ask.

Gus nods and I motion for Pippa to follow me inside the house.

"He doesn't say much, does he?" Pippa says once we're inside.

"No and I find that I like that."

Pippa stops in the middle of the foyer and spins around in a small circle, taking in all the space from the floor to the ceiling. "This place is beautiful."

"You should have seen it a couple of weeks ago. It was a disaster. And the smell. God, the smell. Gus found almost a dozen dead raccoons inside here."

She looks horrified. "And he lived in here when it was like that?"

I shake my head. "No, there's an apartment in the building next to the house. He's been living there for years, I think. No one ever comes here except the occasional delivery vehicles and a woman named Betty who brings him groceries and stuff. I don't think he ever steps foot off this place."

Pippa moves closer to the curved staircase, running her hand along the gleaming banister. "You don't think that's strange?"

"Hell yeah, it's strange." I pass through the doorway that leads to the back part of the house and Pippa follows. The floors are clean as are the windows but there's still no furniture and nothing on the walls.

"Everything out here is strange. Did you know my dad worked and lived here the summer he moved to town?"

The surprise on her face is answer enough.

"Yeah, wait until I show you where he lived."

We wander from room to room until we find ourselves back outside. Waving to Gus, we get back in the truck, following the worn path toward the Preacher Woods. I can tell Pippa is surprised when the house comes in sight.

"Wow," she says.

"Wait until you see inside."

She jumps out as soon as I throw the truck in park and rushes up the stairs, through the front door. I'm not far behind her. She stands in the center of the room and does a small circle.

"I like it," she says with a small smile on her face. "There's something about it, the . . ."

"The smell, the dust . . ." I add.

She shoves my arm. "No. It's quaint. Feels homey. I bet even more so after a good cleaning." And it's like once she said it, she starts doing it. Cleaning. There's a rag and small bucket under the little sink and she wipes down every surface she comes across. And I can't just watch her clean without helping, so I pick up the couch cushions, taking them outside so I can beat them against the porch railing.

Once I'm finished with all the cushions, I move to the blankets on the bed. I really should take them to Lucinda's and wash them but this will have to be good enough for now.

"What's this?" Pippa says from somewhere behind me.

I turn around and see her next to the small bookcase holding a map. The crease marks are so prominent that you can tell it was folded years ago and never opened up again until now. She spreads it out on the floor and I drop down beside her so I can get a good look at it.

"It looks like this orchard." I point to a square shape close to the front. "That's got to be the house. And this is the river that runs along the back of this property."

"What do all these numbers mean?"

I study the map. It seems that the orchard is broken up in sections, each of them numbered. And in each section, each row is also numbered. And then each tree has a number as well.

"Someone mapped out the orchard with coordinates. I bet you can find an exact tree with just a couple of numbers."

I glance at the bottom of the map and see the name *Leonard Trudeau* scrawled across the bottom.

Pippa looks at it like it's a puzzle. "Like this one right here," she says pointing to some random tree in the middle. "I bet I could say 4, 17, 3 and Gus would probably know the exact section, row, and tree I'm talking about."

Section, row and tree. 4, 17, 3. S 4 R 17 T 3.

Oh shit! That's what the numbers on the picture stand for. And on the pendant that's up for auction. I look at the map again, searching for the exact tree that apparently meant something to Mom and Dad.

I find it and I'm not surprised it's the one right outside the front of this house. Grabbing Pippa's hand, I pull her off the floor and through the front door.

"Where are you taking me?" Pippa says, laughing.

"Right here."

We're standing in front of a massive pecan tree. The roots are sticking out of the ground and the trunk is so wide I don't think Pippa and I could circle it and touch hands.

"Remember the pendant at the auction? And the picture of Mom? SRT 6, 9, 4?"

She looks at me and then the tree and I can see when she puts it together. "Yes! It's the coordinates for a tree in this orchard."

I put my hand on the tree in front of us. "This tree."

Pippa puts her hand on the trunk right next to mine.

"This tree must have meant something to her. I have to get that necklace back for her."

Noah—Summer of 1999

Pushing open the side door, I quietly make my way into the kitchen.

For the last week, I've been sneaking in here after everyone else has gone to bed to pilfer the things of Abby's that Gus wants since he's refused to step foot inside. It sucks to be the referee between these two warring factions.

All the things her parents mention taking with them as mementos to remember her by are things Gus refuses to part with so I sneak in to steal them so he can hide them somewhere in the barn.

I get where he's coming from but the guilt when I see her mom searching for them the next day is eating me up inside. I'm sure she suspects me but I play dumb every time she asks me where something has disappeared to.

"You're up late," a voice says, cutting through the darkness. A light flips on and I see Robert leaning against the door that leads from the kitchen to the laundry room.

"So are you," I answer back and make my way to the cabinet near the sink. I haven't really seen much of him since the night I came home from that party.

Tonight's mission has me looking for this small set of coffee cups that Gus and Abby bought on their honeymoon. They were in Mexico and she fell in love with them while they were walking through some outdoor market and had to have them. Gus told me the story about how they were inexpensive but she still wanted to bargain with the guy, hoping to get him to come down on the price. He said she was so proud that he knocked a little off the price that he didn't have the heart to tell her the same cups were in the next stall over for even cheaper.

I find the coffee cups and unroll a length of paper towels to wrap around them before putting them in my bag so they don't break when they bounce against each other.

Robert moves a little closer. "You know, Aunt Susan told me earlier that she wanted to take those home with her after Betty mentioned to her the other day that they were Abby's favorite."

"Yep," I say, placing the last one in the bag, then look at him. "I want to apologize again for the other night. I'm sorry I said what I said to Maggie's friend." I hold out my hand and he hesitates a second or so then reaches out to shake it.

"Are we good?" I ask.

He nods and gives me a small smile. "Yeah, we're good. I think we're both cracking from being under the strain of what's going on in this house."

"Yeah, I'm sure that's it."

"Well, don't run off. It's so damn boring around here at night. Uncle John and Aunt Susan go to bed before it's even dark and there's nothing to do around here. Stay. Have a drink with me."

I rarely drink anymore but it's been a long month and I want things to be cool between Robert and me.

He walks to the pantry and comes out with a dusty bottle of whiskey and two glasses. I pull the ice cube trays out of the freezer and meet him at the large island. Robert pours us both a drink while I drop a couple of cubes in each glass. He puts the bottle down and his hand grazes a decorative jar of seashells that sits next to the sink. It falls over, the glass breaks, and the shells slide across the counter.

"Shit," Robert mutters, then begins picking the large pieces of broken glass up. "Grab one of those big ziplock bags from the pantry so we can put those shells in something."

I fill the plastic bag full of shells while he cleans up the glass. "I hope that jar wasn't something Gus was going to ask you to steal next," he says.

I leave the bag of shells on the counter and drop down in one of the kitchen table chairs.

"He hasn't mentioned it, so I think you're safe."

Robert sits down across from me. I linger with the glass at my lips, thinking about that party at Annie's. "Did you hear what Nate said to me in the kitchen that night?"

Robert nods.

"Do you think that's true? That Maggie's parents are worried about her?" He always seems to know what's going on in town and he's the only person I know to ask.

Robert swirls his drink, the ice hitting the sides of the glass. "According to her sister, Lucinda, yeah. But Lucinda is pretty jealous of Maggie so maybe she was exaggerating."

He's trying to make me feel better.

"Want some advice?" he asks.

"Sure," I say in the most indifferent voice I can manage. Being more like Robert, without the creep vibe he gives off when he's nosing around for gossip, might help me have a future with Maggie. I'm here for whatever he has to say, but pride won't let me beg for it.

"A place like this can be tricky. All these people have known each other for generations. I'm from a town like this and once you get a certain reputation, there's no changing anyone's mind. Don't be the guy who picks a fight with the town's favorite son and who sneaks around with the town's favorite daughter."

He takes my silence as a cue to continue. "How much do you know about her? Or her family?"

I shrug. "Enough."

Robert lets out a laugh. "Enough. Okay. I'm just saying, I've seen her around. Her family's business is one of the few here that keeps this town running so they're like royalty around here. And her daddy is hell-bent on joining their family to Nate's since his family is one of the biggest land owners around."

I push my glass away and lean back in my chair. "You got all this from hanging out at a few parties in town and talking to her sister?"

Robert grins. "It's amazing what you can learn when you ask a few people the right questions. Like, for example, I've learned that Maggie's older sister is very nice and very talkative when she's given a little attention. And she knows everything about everyone. Lucinda also told me that Maggie and Nate do this all the time. Break up, get back together, break up, so you know, maybe don't get too invested."

I throw back the rest of my drink.

Too late for that.

I'm almost asleep when Maggie tiptoes in and climbs into bed.

"Hey, I can't stay long, but I was dying to see you," she says.

It's been a few days since I've seen her. She went out of town with her mom and sister and just got back this morning.

I roll over and pull her in close, feeling instantly better now that she's by my side.

"I missed you," I whisper in her hair.

She buries her face in my neck and mumbles, "I missed you, too."

Every day that went by that I didn't see her was the longest of my life. She asked me if I wanted to go with her to a party tonight but things with Gus are getting worse and I thought I should stick close to home. The big house isn't the only place he's avoiding now. He's now avoiding the entire rest of the world. He hasn't left that small apartment in days.

We lie there in silence for a while, so long that I think she's fallen asleep, but then I hear her whisper, "Don't be mad but I started the paperwork for you for financial aid at LSU. Just need you to fill in the parts I don't know to finish the application and then we can send it in. If you can take the ACT this fall, I think you can start school in January."

I can't help that my entire body tenses at her words. Me going off to college. With Maggie.

She takes my reaction wrong and tucks in closer. "Please don't be mad. I just hate the thought of going off without you. And you said you wanted to go to college. I heard you tell my dad that. That's what you want, right?"

I do want that. I want the degree, the MBA, everything. I know there's more to running a place like this than driving a tractor and if I'm ever going to get somewhere like this on my own, I'm going to need to know how to earn some serious cash.

Turning over so I can face her, I pull her in close. "Yes, and I'm not mad. Not at all. I want nothing more than to go with you."

My life has been so different from hers. College was something I never thought would happen for me. While she was enjoying high school, I was in constant trouble with the police. The first couple of times I was arrested, I got off with probation or spent a couple of days in county either because I got a lenient judge or because I was a minor, but the last arrest wasn't as pretty. I got a year since I had just turned eighteen. So instead of graduating from high school, I got my GED from behind bars. The judge who passed my sentence promised the next time I got in trouble he was locking me up and throwing away the key, so the day I got out is the day I got on that bus headed south.

And now Maggie's telling me there's a chance I can go off to college. With her.

"I think you'll qualify for enough aid to cover tuition but we need to figure out how to get you some money for living expenses. I'll be in the dorm but after freshman year, we can get a place together so I can help out. . . ."

I put a finger against her lips. "You've done more than enough for me. Let me figure out the rest. I have an idea or two of what I can do to get some money."

She relaxes against me and I feel like I'm flying inside. And then I remember the gift for her that I have on the table by the bed.

I sit up, still holding on to her so she doesn't fall off the narrow bed. "I made you something. It's kind of cheesy so don't laugh too hard when you see it."

She sits up, pushing her long hair out of her eyes. "What is it?" she says in an excited voice.

I hand her the small wrapped package and she's agonizingly slow opening it. Finally, she pulls it out.

"It's too dark in here. I can't see what it is," she says.

I reach past her and turn on the lamp. Light floods the area and she peers closer to the piece of metal.

"It's a pendant. I thought you could put it on a necklace," I say. "It's copper. And I engraved it myself."

The copper pendant is rectangular with a hole on one end so that it could be attached to a chain. I let it sit in an acid bath for two days to get the patina just right before I engraved it with the crude metal stamps I found in Gus's barn.

Maggie runs her finger across the front several times. "It's beautiful. But what do the letters and numbers mean?"

I take it from her and hold it in front of her. "S 6 R 9 T 4. It turns out Gus has a mapping system for this orchard. These three numbers— 6, 9, 4—lead to one particular tree. Section 6, Row 9, Tree 4 is our secret-keeping tree right outside this house."

She squeals and grabs the pendant from me. "Noah! I love this.

It's like the coordinates to our place. Our favorite place." She takes off the necklace that's around her neck, removing the gold cross from the chain, then threads it through the hole of the pendant I made. Once the necklace is back on, she says, "I'll never take it off."

She pulls me back down and kisses me. I can't help but feel hope for the future . . . hope I never thought I'd have. But underneath that, I know it won't be that easy. It's never that easy for me.

18

Pippa and I get back to the house ten minutes before the contents of my parents' bedroom are set to be auctioned. There are still a good number of people here but not near as many from this morning, which proves most people just showed up for the entertainment value of it.

We wander through the house, making our way to my parents' room, and it's unbelievable how different the place looks in such a short amount of time.

"This is awful," Pippa says.

"I guess once you win something, you take it away," I answer. It looks like someone moved out in the dead of the night, only taking the valuables and leaving everything else. God, this is almost unbearable. "C'mon, let's get to Mom's room."

There's a crowd in here, all sticking close to whatever it is they want.

"They're like vultures," I whisper to Pippa and she nods.

"There had to have been a better way to do this. I mean, this is . . . just awful."

Her hand reaches out for mine and I squeeze it tight. I shouldn't have asked her to come with me, but I know it would have been a disaster if I was here on my own.

A woman enters the room, her blue shirt indicating she works for the company handling things, and everyone gets quiet.

"Thanks so much for sticking with us. I know it's been a long day but this is the last room up for auction. As I've said before, all bidding is done by paddle and all bids are final so if you don't want it, don't raise it!"

This gets a laugh even though I bet these people have heard the same joke all day long.

She starts with the big stuff, the bed, the chest, the nightstands, and I feel like I'm going to come out of my skin. Pippa pulls me to the side of the room, sandwiching me between her and the wall. Her back is pressed against my chest and I snake my arms around her waist and drop my forehead to her shoulder.

"Okay, now come closer. We're going to bid on Mrs. Foster's jewelry. Each piece is listed in your book. We'll start at twenty-five dollars for lot 321, which includes this beautiful turquoise beaded necklace."

Each lot goes until we're finally at the one with the necklace I've been waiting for.

"Okay, folks, this is lot 340, which includes an unusual piece. It's . . . umm, it's a copper pendant with hand-stamped letters and numbers. The chain is a, um, a silver chain we believe. There are also a lovely pair of silver earrings and an initial ring with the letter M."

Pippa leans in just before the bidding starts. "Do you think she wants that necklace? I mean, your dad . . . left. Maybe it doesn't hold the same meaning it once did?"

This has been the thought I've pushed far back in my brain. But I can't get over that the necklace stands for the place they met. A place that has become very important to me.

"We'll get the bracelet, too, so if you're right, she still has something I know she really wants."

She nods and we turn our attention back to the woman in the blue shirt.

"We'll start at twenty dollars for this unique grouping."

Pippa waits a second, then slowly raises her paddle. This is the moment we've been waiting for—will other people bid on it just because they know I want it?

"We have twenty. Do I hear twenty-five?" The woman looks around the room while most everyone is watching us.

"Ah! Twenty-five to the gentleman in the back."

I spin around to see who is bidding and it's a man in a dark suit. Someone I don't know and have never seen before.

"Who is that?" I whisper to Pippa.

She stands on her tiptoes to get a better look then shrugs. "I have no idea."

Pippa raises her paddle again, bringing the bid to thirty dollars. And almost immediately the man counters with thirty-five.

Pippa and the stranger go back and forth until the bid is over a hundred dollars, definitely more than I can afford.

"Want me to keep going?" she asks.

The woman in blue calls out $120. "Going once."

"O, do I bid?"

I watch the man in the back. He's completely unflustered and I bet he'd take this as high as he needed to win. But why?

"A hundred and twenty. Going twice."

"O!" Pippa says.

"Let it go," I answer just as the woman screams "Sold!"

We watch the rest of the auction and the only other item the man in the back bids on and wins is the silver bracelet.

The room clears while he makes his way to the front to claim his winnings.

I move in his direction but Pippa pulls on the back of my shirt, stopping me. "What are you going to do?"

"Talk to him."

He's signing off on his purchases when I approach him.

"Excuse me," I say. "This was my mother's jewelry. Is there any chance I can purchase the copper pendant and silver bracelet you outbid me on?"

He turns toward me and says, "I'm sorry. I'm not the actual bidder. I was hired to procure certain items and that pendant and bracelet were on the list."

Someone hired him to bid on these things? I look at the item booklet he set down on the desk so he could sign off on his purchases and see everything marked that he must have been told to buy. I grab it before he can stop me.

"Wait a second . . ." he says, but I'm already skimming through the book. He bought most of my mother's favorite things, like the painting she bought when she took me to California and that ugly vase she made when she went through a pottery phase. And the jewelry.

"Who hired you?" I ask.

He barely blinks when he says, "I'm not at liberty to say."

I throw the book down on the desk and step closer to him, preparing to force him to tell me when I feel Pippa slam into my back. Her arms lock around me then pull me backward.

She doesn't say anything and doesn't let me go. I could probably free myself if I tried, but then what? Start a fight with this guy because he's doing what he was paid to do?

The man collects his things and leaves quickly. A woman who seems familiar but I can't recall her name watches me from across the room, then stops next to me on her way out.

"I shouldn't be surprised that you're here, acting like this, but I am. But then after what your father did, I shouldn't expect for you to be any better. I guess the apple doesn't fall far from the tree."

I can feel Pippa tense up behind me.

Looking at the woman, I say, "I'm sorry if my dad stole anything from you. My grandfather gave my mother a silver bracelet when she was younger and I was only hoping to get it back for her. Neither of us have any desire to own the things Dad bought with stolen money."

The woman is shocked and by the quiet gasp behind me, Pippa is, too.

Pippa leans around me and addresses the woman. "Mrs. Trent, I know you don't believe someone is guilty of their family member's sins."

Mrs. Trent turns from us with a grunt and flees the room.

"With the way her son and husband act, she has no room to judge anyone else," Pippa mutters behind me.

The only other person left in the room is the woman in blue.

"Do I need to call security?" she asks.

"No," Pippa says, untangling herself from me. "We're done here."

Pippa pulls me from the room, through the door that leads outside. We don't stop until we're on the other side of the pool, tucked behind the pool house. No one is on this part of the golf course right now so thankfully, we're alone.

I lean against the back wall of the pool house and slide down until I'm on the ground, my head falling to my raised knees. I failed Mom today. Totally failed her. Pippa sits down next to me and I cover my head with my hands. I hate that she sees me like this. I hate that I'm falling apart in front of her.

Her hands wrap around me and she pulls me close.

I shift, my arms going around her waist, and I drag her to my lap and bury my head against her neck, while her fingers slide through my hair.

If it wasn't for Pippa, I feel like I would shatter into a million pieces. Sitting here, with her wrapped around me, fills some of those empty spaces inside.

"Things are so screwed up. I feel like I'm about to come out of my skin. And as pissed off as I am about everything that has happened, it's nothing compared to how bad I want to kiss you right now," I whisper against her, my words drifting across her soft skin.

She doesn't say anything but shifts slightly. Her hands are on either side of my face, pulling me closer to her. Our mouths are inches apart and I can see she wants this as badly as I do. We've been dancing around this and when her soft lips crush against mine, I'm lost in her. My hands grip the back of her shirt, drawing her even closer, as I deepen the kiss.

Kissing Pippa is better than I ever thought it would be.

She's the first to pull away but only after we've kissed long enough that we're both short of breath.

"I've wanted to kiss you, too. I was afraid it might be weird. But it's not. Not at all," she says. Her hands are still wrapped around my neck, her fingers sifting through my hair. "I thought I lost you when you moved. And when you came back, you were someone else, someone I didn't recognize. But that's not right, either. You're different, but so am I. And I'm happy you're back."

I smile and kiss her again, letting her words rush through me. I don't know where this is going but all I know is I like it. I want to be with her like this. I want us to be friends plus something more.

There are a lot of things I'm unsure about, but being with Pippa isn't one of them.

• • •

Mom's at the kitchen table when I finally get home. "Hey," she says when she sees me. I can tell by her voice something is wrong.

"Hey." Nodding to the pans and white bakery boxes stacked in front of her, I ask, "Is this for Mrs. Sullivan's party?"

"Yeah, she just called and wants me to deliver everything."

And that's it. She doesn't want to leave the house. She doesn't want to show up there and possibly run into her old friends.

"Want me to deliver it for you?" I ask.

Relief floods her features. "Would you?"

"Of course." I grab the stack of containers closest to me while she picks up a few of the white bakery boxes.

"Did you work today?" she asks as she follows me out to Gus's truck.

Balancing everything against the side of the truck, I free a hand so I can get the door open. "Pippa and I went to the auction."

She groans behind me. "Why would you go there?"

I get everything inside before I answer, "I wanted to get you something. One thing that was yours."

She secures the boxes on the floorboard then runs a hand across my back. "Oh, Owen, I don't need anything from that house. That life is gone and I'm okay with it. I mean, not okay with what he did, but I'm okay. We're okay."

We sit in silence a moment and then she asks, "How was it?"

I let out a quiet laugh. "Like vultures circling over a dead carcass."

She covers her mouth and laughs, too. "That bad?"

"It was horrible. And guess who bought the house?"

"Do I want to know?"

"Jack Cooper's dad! I mean, isn't that weird? He's only been here like once. And then he's going to drop almost a million on our house?"

I follow Mom back in the house to get the second load. "Well, I'm sure he has his reasons. And at least it sold. I was worried no one would buy it."

I wait until we're back in the kitchen so I can see her face and gauge if she's telling me the truth and ask, "You're not mad you lost the house and all our things?"

She takes a deep breath and turns to me. "That house was never really our home. You never lived in that house full-time. It's just a building. And one that was always too big without you there. I'm mad at what he did. I'm mad he stole from all those people. I'm not mad we lost that house."

We finish loading the last of the food and she gives me an invoice and a set of heating and serving directions to present to Mrs. Sullivan along with her address since they moved after the divorce.

Their house is a few streets over from our old house on the golf course. I thought it would be a while before I was forced to come back here, but here I am. My old street is empty now that the auction is over and I have mixed feelings about seeing it again. One of the best memories I have from that house—when things changed with Pippa—was only made after it wasn't mine anymore.

There are only a few cars in the driveway when I get to the Sullivans' so hopefully I won't run into too many people. I park and carry as many of the containers as I can through the open garage door. I'd rather not use the front door if I can help it.

Using my elbow, I ring the bell and I'm surprised when Seth opens the door. His left leg is encased in a huge metal brace and he's leaning against the door for support.

"I'm delivering food for your mom's party."

He nods and hops back, then I move past him, carrying the containers inside.

"Go through the doorway on the left and you'll see the kitchen," he says.

Mrs. Sullivan is at the sink and she directs me where to put the food. "Everything smells wonderful, Owen," she says.

Seth drops down in a chair next to the table and watches me. The crutches fall to the ground next to him and I notice his right hand is covered in a bandage.

He holds his hand up. "Tried to catch myself when my knee gave out. Fractured my wrist. So even if the knee is okay, I'm done for the season."

"Man, that sucks. Sorry to hear it."

He nods and I go back to the truck for the rest of the food. Once I get everything inside, I hand Mrs. Sullivan the bill and she runs to her small home office to get me a check. Seth is still in the chair, looking surly. I'm not sure if it's because he's in pain or if it's because I'm in his kitchen.

"How was the dance?" he asks.

Ah, so he's pissed I took his place.

"It was good," I answer. I wonder how much he heard. Just that I was there with her or maybe how close we were on the dance floor or how once I started touching her I couldn't stop.

Ignoring him, I glance around the kitchen. The room is covered in pictures and knickknacks and other crap people junk up space with. Rather than have to look at or speak to Seth, I study the pictures on the wall, but stop when I get to one that makes my stomach drop.

It's Mom with Elise Sullivan and Elise's sister, Sheila Blackwell. They are on a beach somewhere, looks like maybe the Caymans, and they are tanned and smiling and probably half-tipsy since they are holding some huge drink with little umbrellas sticking out of the top.

"Here you go, Owen," Mrs. Sullivan says and I hear her breath hitch when she notices I'm staring at the picture. "I was really hoping your mom would bring everything by and I could talk her into staying awhile."

I give her a smile and pocket the money. "We really appreciate you giving her your business."

She walks me to the back door then follows me out to the truck. I can tell she wants to say more so I stop and turn to face her.

"There are quite a few of us who know your mother had no idea what was happening. And there are some of us who believe your dad is innocent. There has to be another answer to what happened to all that money."

I'm floored. She's the only person who has ever mentioned "dad" and "innocent" in the same sentence.

"You really don't think he did it?" I ask. "Mom said most of her friends, like Mrs. Blackwell, won't speak to her anymore because they think she was in on it."

She shrugs. "I don't believe that he would willingly leave you and your mom. He loved you both. And I can't believe he'd make you two face this alone. That's the part I can't understand. Your dad had a way of going after what he wanted and he made enemies along the way, but I just can't believe he'd take off without you and Maggie. Deep down, Sheila believes that, too."

No one knows about the note he sent me. The meeting he wants to have in just a few days. Once I found out he'd disappeared, the note he sent me at school took on a different meaning. I thought he wanted to prove to me somehow that he didn't do what he's accused of. But being here, listening to everyone else, has hardened me toward him.

But what if my initial reaction to his letter was right?

My silence must be making Mrs. Sullivan uncomfortable because she's fidgeting with her necklace and looking back toward her house.

"Well, if you or your mom need anything, all you have to do is let me know. And I'm making it my personal mission to get your mom back to the land of the living. Tell her I'll be by on Monday to discuss food for the Thanksgiving party I throw for the employees at the store."

"Yes, ma'am," I answer. "I know that means a lot to her."

Mrs. Sullivan heads back inside while I jump into the truck, my mind racing to understand what really happened.

Noah—Summer of 1999

There's a knock on the door and Gus lets out a groan then says, "Good Lord, what could they want now?"

We know it has to be either Abby's parents or Robert because no one else has been out here since the funeral except Betty and Maggie and both of them just left a few hours ago.

I get up from the small table and pull the door open. It's Robert.

"Hey," he says. "Hope I'm not bothering you."

I look at Gus but he seems unfazed by Robert's visit or his question. Pulling the door open wider, I invite Robert inside.

He sits down in the chair by the door and I go back to my spot at the small table.

"What's going on, Robert?" I say when I realize Gus plans to ignore him.

"Uncle John and Aunt Susan are packing."

This gets Gus's attention. "They're leaving?"

Robert nods his head. "Yes. Tomorrow morning."

Gus nods too and goes back to ignoring him.

It's quiet for a few minutes and I know there's more to this visit than Robert wanting to let us know Abby's parents' plans.

"The thing is," he finally says, "I'd rather not go with them. I only have a few weeks before I go back to school and the thought of spending it with them is enough to make me come beg you to let me stay here until school starts."

Gus and I both look at him. I can't say I blame him. Abby's parents are miserable and I get why she didn't have anything to do with them once she married Gus.

Sensing the need to make his case stronger, Robert offers, "I'll work here, doing whatever you need. I don't expect to stay for free. And it won't be long. Four weeks."

Gus lets out a heavy sigh and looks at me, silently asking me what to do. It's strange to see how our roles have reversed from when I first showed up here.

I hesitate a moment. "It's only four weeks," I say. "I wouldn't want to go back with them, either."

This gets a smile out of him. The first one I've seen in a while.

"Four weeks. Not a day more," Gus says.

Robert looks visibly relieved. "Thanks. I won't be in the way. Promise."

He leaves the room quickly, probably worried Gus will change his mind. I remember having that same feeling when he gave me the job at the beginning of the summer.

"What's he gonna do around here?" Gus asks.

"I'll find something to keep him busy."

The next morning, Abby's parents are finally leaving. Gus refuses to see them off. Instead he stands at the window in the small apartment and mumbles *Good riddance*, then turns his attention back to *Jeopardy!*

Abby's parents gave no fight or argument when Robert told them he was staying, so I'm guessing they felt the same way about him as he did about them. I did notice Abby's mom load more bags in the trunk of their car than she came with, so I'm assuming her mission to leave with something of Abby's was successful.

Robert and I stand next to each other and watch them pull out of the driveway. "I feel like jumping for joy or having a beer or some other form of celebration at the sight of that car pulling away from here forever," he says.

"We'll celebrate by cleaning up the back section of the orchard," I say, then walk to the barn. I keep Robert busy getting the tractor out of the stall and fueled up while I go up to check on Gus. He's in the chair in front of the TV in the exact same spot I left him in.

"They're gone. It's safe to go back in the big house now."

He doesn't respond but I know he heard me. Betty is in the small kitchen, shaking her head, while she prepares our meals for the day.

I walk in between him and the TV and he doesn't even flinch.

"He's getting worse," I whisper to Betty.

She's putting together some sandwiches that will be waiting in the fridge for us later. "I know. Abby warned us it would be bad but I don't know what to do with him."

"Y'all can quit talking about me like I'm not here, that's where y'all can start. And don't forget I can fire you both if you keep trying to tell me what to do," Gus yells from his chair but never looks at us.

Betty rolls her eyes. "Fire me and good luck finding someone else to run to the grocery store for you and cook for you and care for you. I could have another job lined up tomorrow."

"She's only been gone three weeks," he says quietly. "Three weeks. But it feels like forever. How am I going to go years without her when three weeks feels like forever?"

His words wreck me. I can't imagine what he's going through or what it feels like to know the rest of your life will be spent without the one person you love the most.

Betty wipes her hands on a towel and moves closer to him, pulling a chair up close, and whispers in his ear. She may be praying with him or giving him words of encouragement or cursing God for him but it seems to pull him back from the edge he was teetering on.

I tiptoe out of the room, deciding I'm helping him more by keeping the place together, but the truth is, I have no idea what to say to him or how to make things better.

Excerpt from the diary of Leonard Trudeau:

Step three—Harvesting the pecans

Now that all of the pecans are on the ground, it is only a matter of picking them up and cleaning them off. But be careful during the cleaning process since it is easy for a few rotten ones to sneak their way through.

19

With the auction over and the possibility of seeing Dad in a few days, I'm feeling restless. My new school in Lake Cane takes the entire week off for Thanksgiving so I'm up early on Monday morning to get a run in before I head to Gus's.

As I crisscross through the neighborhood, my mind wanders to yesterday.

Yesterday was a good day.

I spent the morning playing lacrosse with David and the other guys from the team, and as good as my team at Sutton's is, this one may be better. This could be the year they take state and I'd be lying if the idea of being a part of that team didn't excite me, which is the main reason I'm out this early for a run. There's no way I won't be in the best possible condition when the season starts.

But as good as the morning was, it couldn't compare to the afternoon with Pippa. We went to a movie, hung out at her house for a while—thank God her parents were happy to see me—then finished the night with Mom's shrimp and grits.

It felt incredible to reach over and hold her hand, to lean in close knowing she'd kiss me back, to fall asleep with my phone against my ear because we weren't done talking for the day.

Yesterday was actually better than good. It was damn near perfect. For the first time since I came home, there wasn't anywhere else I'd rather be.

Once I'm back from my run, I head to the kitchen and stop short when I see Mrs. Sullivan at the table with Mom. True to her word, she's here to go over the food she wants for her office Thanksgiving party.

I nod to both of them then stick my mouth under the faucet instead of dirtying a glass.

"Owen!" Mom yells, then thrusts a glass at me.

But I'm already finished so she puts it back in the cabinet.

The house phone rings and Mom motions for me to get it.

"Hello," I answer.

Silence on the other end and I'm just about to hang up when I finally hear, "I know you know where he is. This isn't over."

The caller is hiding behind one of those voice-changing machines. I glance at Mom and her forehead crinkles as she looks at me, trying to figure out who I'm talking to. I point to her and mouth *telemarketer* and she rolls her eyes.

I turn my back to her and say quietly into the phone, "I'm not scared of you. You're nothing but a sorry-ass fucker that gets off on harassing a woman. You're right it's not over because I haven't kicked your ass yet. And I will kick your ass. Anytime you want to get off the phone and come over like a man, I'll be ready. So until you're ready to man up—don't fucking call her again."

I slam the phone down and Mom and Mrs. Sullivan jump in their seats.

"Sorry, I didn't like what they were selling."

Mom laughs it off but I can tell she thinks there was more to that call than what I've given her. Mrs. Sullivan just looks confused.

"I need you to come to my house and handle those calls for me as well, Owen," she says. Then she turns to Mom. "At least a telemarketer is better than those threatening phone calls you've been getting. I do hope that's stopped, Maggie."

Mom nods. "Yes. Haven't gotten one in a while."

I get to the small den I call a bedroom and pull out my cell to call Detective Hill.

"What's going on?" he asks.

"We just got a call. See if you can trace it."

I hear him peck away on his computer. "What did they say?"

" 'I know you know where he is. This isn't over.' "

"Anything else?"

"No. I had a few words for him and then hung up."

"Yeah, I bet you did," Detective Hill says on the other end.

I grab my boots and clothes and head toward the front door. "Did any of the neighbors have any cameras that picked up what happened the other night?" I ask.

"No. Half of those cameras don't work and the other half aren't pointed where they need to be. Waste of time."

Damn. "Do you have someone close by?"

"Yeah. Parked in a blue sedan across the street."

I step out on the front porch and scan the street until I see him. "Okay. I'm headed to work. Call me if something happens here."

• • •

"What's the plan for today?" I ask Gus when I get to the orchard.

"We're harvesting today. I'm going to put you on this tractor," he says, pointing to the one closest to us. "Start up front. You'll circle each tree, pulling the harvester behind you so it can pick up all of the pecans. When you finish with the first tree, move on to the next one. Watch the hopper and when it's full, you'll dump the pecans into the cleaner."

I turn and look at another piece of machinery not far away.

Gus motions for me to follow him as he demonstrates what the cleaner does. He turns it on and it's loud, like a blower.

"Raise the hopper up until it's level with this," he says, pointing to a large bin on one end. "Then dump the pecans. They'll go through the blower, which blows out anything that doesn't belong—leaves, sticks, bad nuts."

"How does it do that?" I ask.

"Anything lighter than the weight I set or bigger than the size I set gets rejected."

He opens the little gate and the pecans in the bin start moving through the process. And sure enough, leaves and sticks are blown straight out of the top and fall in a pile next to the machine.

"Once it goes through the blower, what's left runs along a conveyor belt. One of us will stand here and pull out the bad-looking pecans and any other trash that got through the blower."

It doesn't take long until the conveyor belt is full. Gus grabs anything that doesn't belong faster than I can focus on what's going by me.

"At the end of the belt is a Super Sack. All good pecans should fall in there."

The Super Sacks are huge white plastic bags. "When the sack is full, use the spear on the front of the tractor to move it under the big covered shed behind the barn."

"Is this something you and I can handle on our own?" I ask. It looks like it would be easy for things to get out of control. And my head is spinning over all of the steps. I'm barely capable of backing a trailer out of the barn without jackknifing it. This part seems way more than I can handle.

"We can take it slow. If it gets to be too much, I can always ask Betty's grandsons to come by and help."

I've yet to see Betty but I know she's Gus's link to the outside world.

"For today, you run the harvester and I'll work the cleaner."

I look at tree after tree after tree down the line and it seems like this job will never end. Jumping on the tractor, I crank it and get to work. I pick up pecans under four trees until the hopper is full. Driving back toward the barn, I back up to the cleaner and move the pecans from one machine to the other.

This is the first time I've gotten something right on the first try and it feels incredible.

I'm about to head back out into the orchard for another round when I see Pippa coming down the driveway. The smile that breaks out across my face is ridiculous but I don't care.

Turning off the tractor, I jog to meet her where she parks in the front circle drive. Gus is coming out of the main house and gets to her at the same time I do.

Pippa gets out with a brown sack in one hand and a stack of mail in the other.

"Hey, I hope it's okay I came by. I was bored and thought y'all might want some lunch." She shakes the brown bag. "I brought BBQ sandwiches."

"I'm starving and that smells delicious," I say.

"That's really nice of you," Gus adds.

She hands the stack of mail to Gus. "The mailman came by right as I pulled in. Thought I'd save you a trip to the road."

Gus takes the mail and thumbs through it quickly, then stops when he gets to a large white envelope. He tears it open and his entire demeanor changes. His eyes are racing across the pages and deep lines form across his forehead.

"Is everything okay?" I ask.

He ignores me and I look at Pippa as if she has the answer for what's come over him.

Finally, Gus says, "Uh, yeah. Fine. Everything's fine. But this is something I need to take care of so let's call it a day."

I check my watch and it's barely noon. "You sure?" I ask.

He's distracted. "Yeah, we'll start again tomorrow morning." And then he's gone, disappearing up the stairs to his small apartment.

"That was weird," Pippa says.

It is weird but I'm not going to let it spoil the fact that she's here and I don't have to work today. I pull her in close and surprise her with a kiss. She laughs against my lips then wraps her arms around my neck.

"Feel like having a picnic at the Preacher Woods house?" I ask.

"Lead the way."

Noah—Summer of 1999

"All right, boss," Robert says. "What torture did you have in mind for today?"

Even though he says it with a smile, I can hear the sarcasm in his voice. Robert was a big talker when he was begging Gus to let him stay, but now that I'm putting him to work every morning, his tune has changed.

"We're going to clean up the small cemetery where they buried Abby. Headstone won't be here for a while but I'm hoping to get Gus out here to visit her so it needs to look nice. Grab those flats of flowers and put them in the back of the golf cart with the other equipment."

He does what I ask even though he's moving so slow I could've done the task three times over already.

We ride to the back part of the orchard in silence and once there we unload the flowers and all the tools we'll need to work the area.

The Trudeau family cemetery sits on a small hill in an open spot surrounded by some native pecan trees. From the small hill, you can see the narrow river that runs along the border of Gus's property. The graves are enclosed in an ornate iron fence that comes about waist high, tall enough to keep any unwanted animals out but not much more than that. A quick count shows seven headstones so Abby's will make eight, but there's plenty of space for others who may come along.

Although if Gus doesn't snap out of it, he very well may be the last of his line.

I grab the Weedeater out of the back and hand it to Robert. "Use this to trim the grass inside the fenced-in area."

He stares at it a moment, clearly not happy about today's work, but eventually carries it inside the cemetery and cranks it up. I pull out the blower and follow behind him.

Once the grass is cut and the clippings blown away, Robert asks, "Okay, what now?"

I'm trying not to get frustrated. It's clear by the equipment we brought what needs to be done.

"Grab the bucket, that gallon jug of water, the brush, and some soap, and get to work cleaning off the headstones."

I pull out the flat of annuals and a small spade and start planting.

"He's not going to come out here so I don't know why we're doing all of this."

I glance at the mound of earth where I know Abby is and say, "Even if he doesn't, we're still going to keep this place looking nice."

"So I guess this was the original Trudeau. Says his name is Leonard." Robert is perched in front of his headstone, scrubbing at the face of it with the soapy brush.

"Yeah, that's what Gus said," I answer.

"Gus never leaves so he doesn't have a regular job. He just putters around this orchard. And he's got all this land and that big beautiful house. That truck and Abby's SUV. Wonder where he gets the money?" Robert asks. "I mean, he's not that much older than us and he's already living the life of leisure."

I don't take the bait. It's not like that question has never crossed my mind but it's not something I want to speculate about with Robert.

I stay quiet, moving from headstone to headstone, planting the flowers Abby loved.

My silence doesn't seem to bother him.

"I envy you. Gus already looks at you like you're his brother. Hell, he doesn't have any family left, you're crazy not to use that to your advantage. I mean, between him and Maggie's family, you could be king of this little pissant town."

"You shouldn't say shit like that," I tell him but there's a little part of me that soaks up those words, lets them tumble around my brain, wishing that it was that easy to become someone else. Someone who mattered. Someone who people looked up to and admired.

Robert keeps talking like he didn't hear what I said. "But you gotta get out there. Spend time with her family. Get to know other people in town."

"You make it sound easy," I say. "But it's never easy for people like me. People look at you and the way you dress and the way you talk and you're halfway there."

Robert stops scrubbing and looks at me. "Everyone sees what I want them to see. Everyone thinks what I want them to think about me."

I get back to planting and he gets back to scrubbing.

"You can't become a hermit like Gus. I get he's heartbroken but he's too young to be hiding out here like his life is over."

He's right. I'm going to have to work on getting him back into town with the living.

Something Robert says floats through my mind. "When we were having that drink the other night, you mentioned Lucinda likes to talk. Has she mentioned what her family thinks about me?"

Robert smiles at me but it's a smile that says he's got me, and I hate he knows how much I care about what they think.

"She says Nate's their first choice for Maggie. I told you that already. You're going to have to bring something to the table other than your dirty boots. I'm telling you, Gus could change the way this town sees you. But you have to get him back among the living first."

"I don't want to use him like that," I mumble.

"Then you're dumber than I thought. The only way to get ahead in this life is to use everything you can to your advantage."

I take the empty plastic containers the flowers came in and put them back in the golf cart.

"Well, I guess I need to watch my back around you, then," I say, joking around.

"I would if I were you," he answers back. He's smiling and laughing but I can't help but think there's some truth there.

20

It takes nine calls before Jack answers his phone. Even though running into his dad all over town has freaked me out, I don't hesitate calling him. There's no one I trust more.

"What the hell, O?" Jack says. I imagine him sitting up in the bed, hair sticking up and T-shirt on inside out. "Why are you calling me so early?"

I'm perched on the front steps of Aunt Lucinda's house dressed for a run. The sun isn't up yet but it's close. "I need to talk to someone."

"Give me a second," he says. I hear him put the phone down and then he's back a couple of minutes later.

"I had to piss first," he says when he gets back on the phone.

"Well, I appreciate you not taking the phone in the bathroom with you. I'm really surprised I haven't heard your new roommate screaming at you to shut up and go back to sleep."

"Dad's convinced I can talk you into coming back so he told Winston to leave it open."

Some rooms have three guys bunking in them so it's a miracle that Dr. Winston hasn't moved someone in there already. It would suck to know I'd been replaced even though I turned down the chance to come back.

"That's pretty sweet."

"Yeah, I've been catching hell from everyone on this floor since I got this room to myself."

"When are you headed home for Thanksgiving?"

"As soon as I get up and moving. But you didn't call at the ass crack of dawn to ask about my holiday plans. What's going on?"

I lean back against the porch column and stare at the brightening sky. "I think Dad wants me to meet him."

"Seriously? How do you know? Did he call you? Holy shit, O, what are you going to do?"

"I got a letter from him right before I left Sutton's. He was telling me about some restaurant he discovered and how good the burgers are. Mentioned there was a Wednesday-night special and that we should go when I'm home for break."

I can tell by Jack's silence that he thinks I'm reaching. "He tells you about some burger he ate. Is that all?" he asks.

"He never wrote to me before. Literally, this is the only piece of mail I've gotten from him that wasn't a card my mom bought and forced him to sign before dropping it in the mail."

"What do you think he wants? He's gotta want something to pull this James Bond secret message bullshit. What if he wants you to run off with him?"

"I wouldn't run off with him. He probably does just want to say bye or something like that. Or maybe tell me where he stashed money for Mom and me. I don't know. But I am going to try to convince him to turn himself in."

Jack lets a laugh. "He won't. He ran. That says everything you need to know about him."

Even though the words are true, they're harsh, and I bite back the desire to defend him. Whether he deserves it or not, he's still my dad.

"You don't think he'll be there, do you?" I ask.

I hear muffled sounds like he's rolling over in the bed. "Who knows? That's some cryptic shit so maybe he will be. Or maybe it was just a damn good burger. I guess there's only one way to find out."

"I'll call you and let you know how it goes," I say as I push off the steps and jog down the front walk.

"If you get in a bind, give me a call," Jack says. "And the offer still stands to come back."

. . .

I can't concentrate. Today is the day. The day I discover if I read Dad's note correctly. The day that maybe Dad has an explanation for what's going on or some plan to make things better. Or it's the day I forget about him and move on.

One way or another, my life will be different tomorrow.

At least I have a full day ahead of me at Gus's to keep me busy. I'm working the cleaner while Gus moved to the south edge of the orchard with the harvester. There are a line of big white Super Sacks waiting to be cleaned and I'm managing them one at a time. When I line another bag up with the tractor, I notice a white work vehicle parked in front of the big house. Parking the tractor, I cut off the man before he makes it to the front door.

"Hey, can I help you?" I call out.

The man spins around, clipboard in his hand, and says, "Yes, hello! We made it a couple of days earlier than I thought we would! Trying to get as much done before the holiday as we can."

He's an older black guy and seems really enthusiastic about his job. I look back at his truck and see a younger white guy still sitting in the passenger seat.

"Oh, okay. Are you here to fix something?" I ask, glancing at the house.

"Um, no. We're here for the installation," he says, pointing back at his work truck, where the words *Southern Granite* are written across the side in a bright blue. He holds his hand out and says, "I'm Jimmy."

I shake his hand and say, "Owen. Do you need me to let you in?" I ask, gesturing toward the house.

The guy looks at the house and then back to me, confusion on his face. "No, I know my way to the back so I'll just head there. I will need someone to sign off on the delivery and installation. Can you do that?"

I nod, more confused than ever, and the guy says, "Want to ride or follow me back there?"

"I'll follow," I answer since I have no idea where "back there" is. I jump on the golf cart parked near the barn and follow him toward the house in the Preacher Woods. Is Gus fixing up something in there? Maybe the small kitchen is getting an update?

I'd be lying if I didn't have dreams of moving in there just to get out of Aunt Lucinda's house, but I can't leave Mom alone with her.

Instead of turning left to head to the old house, we go right. Maybe he's confused. But it doesn't take long to figure out where the destination is.

The truck pulls up along the side of the small family cemetery and it feels like my stomach is bottoming out. What could he possibly need to install back here?

This time, both guys get out of the truck and open the back, revealing a big rectangle covered in Bubble Wrap. Jimmy pulls a heavy-duty dolly out of the back of the truck while the white guy jumps inside and starts undoing the straps anchoring it to the floor of the vehicle.

It's pushed to the platform at the back of the truck then mechanically lowered until it's on the ground. Jimmy and the other guy get it on the dolly and wheel it inside the fenced-in area that outlines the small cemetery.

It takes a while to get it lined up just right, then off the dolly. Jimmy starts unwrapping the Bubble Wrap.

Layer after layer comes off until there's a pile of plastic that's being blown against the short iron fence. It would be scattered across the entire orchard if that barrier wasn't in place.

"Before we attach it permanently, I'm going to need you to sign off that everything on the headstone reads correctly," Jimmy says.

He and the other guy are standing in front of it so I haven't gotten a good look at it yet.

"Okay," I say moving closer. "I'm not sure I can do that since . . ."

And then I'm frozen.

I read the words five times before my brain processes what it says.

"Is something not right?" Jimmy asks, worry in his voice as he looks from me to the headstone. "Did we spell his name wrong?"

And there next to Abby Trudeau's grave, in front of a rounded mound of earth, is the brand-new headstone for Gus Trudeau, husband and friend, who died five months ago.

Noah—Summer of 1999

It's only a couple of weeks before Maggie leaves for school and I feel desperate. Even though we've made plans for me to join her in January, there's a lot I need to figure out before then. Like money.

Another issue I have to figure out before I leave—what to do about Gus.

He never gets off the couch, barely showers, eats nothing but junk food, drinks beer throughout the day, and watches lots of bad day-time TV.

The smell from that upstairs apartment filters down the stairs and out of the barn.

"Gus," I say when I walk inside the apartment. "It's time to get up. You've been on that couch for weeks. Betty's threatening to quit if she comes back and you're still in those clothes."

He takes a swig of the beer, looks at me over the bottle, and then his attention goes back to whatever courtroom drama is playing out there.

"Seriously, I'm about to pull your ass off that couch."

"And then I'll fire your ass," he mumbles back.

That's it. I grab both of his ankles and yank as hard as I can. He flies off the couch and hits the ground.

"She would be so pissed if she saw you right now! In fact, she's probably stomping around up there looking down on your stinky ass!"

Gus roars and then comes at me. It's not long before we're rolling around the floor. Neither of us throws a punch and I'm not sure what either of us is trying to accomplish but at least he's moving. And showing some sort of emotion.

He finally pulls away from me and leans against the wall, dragging in deep breaths.

I get up and walk to the door. "Want to fire me? Fire me. I'd rather get kicked out of here than watch you fall even farther down this hole you're in."

"You don't understand," he says.

I throw my hands in the air. "You're right! I have no idea what you're going through. But I promised Abby not to let you go too far over the edge and I'll be damned if I go back on my word to her."

He's surprised by my words. "What did you say?"

I drop down in the chair, all of the fight draining right out of me. "The last conversation I had with her was about you. She said you wouldn't handle it well. And she asked me to promise her not to let you go so far over the edge that you can't find your way back."

He drops his head in his hands.

"And so I promised her. Don't make me break it. That's the last thing I said to her."

Gus is quiet and I'm praying my words are sinking in because if he keeps this up, he won't last the year.

Finally, he stands up and says, "I'm going to get a shower. When I'm done, you can show me what you've been doing around here the last couple of weeks."

He walks into the bathroom and I feel like a weight has lifted off my chest.

Robert is waiting for me at the bottom of the stairs.

"I was worried there for a minute. Sounded like one of you were going to come crashing through the ceiling."

I straighten my shirt and move past him. "It's all good."

He follows behind me while I walk from the barn to the big house. "I've been doing a little research," he says.

"Oh, yeah?"

"Yeah. Trying to figure out where all Gus's money comes from. I mean, a twenty-eight-year-old guy who has never held a job? And lives on a place like this? Got to be a ton of money coming in here from somewhere."

I feel like every conversation I have with Robert since Abby's parents left, he's baiting me. And it takes everything for me not to take a bite. Because money is what I need.

But the thing about Robert is he doesn't wait for me to ask, he just goes on and tells me.

"So I figured out where it comes from," he says.

I stop and spin around to look at him. "I won't let you take advantage of him," I say.

He holds his hands up. "Who's saying that? All I'm saying is I figured out a mystery. Gus owns thousands and thousands of acres of land. And every one of those acres is leased to an oil and gas company. A big one out of Houston. Can you imagine the damn checks he gets every month?"

I turn away and finish the short distance to the house. Today, we're cleaning out the front beds, getting rid of the summer flowers that have died in the unending heat and replanting them with flowers that will take us through the fall.

We stop in front of the flower bed that wraps around the front porch.

"You're going to need some gloves and a small shovel. Also go get a wheelbarrow from the barn," I tell him.

Robert puts a hand on my shoulder. "Aren't you listening? Gus doesn't have any other family. It will be a miracle if he ever leaves this place and remarries so he probably won't have any kids. Who's going to get all of this once he's gone?"

"Quit saying shit like that. He's not even thirty. There's still time for him to have a life."

"I'm just saying. I plan on staying close. I mean, I am related to Abby. So maybe I'll be in line to get some of this," he says with his arms spread wide. "Or maybe you will," he adds. "Although I'll make it hard for you to cut me out. After all, I'm Abby's cousin. And you're just some guy who showed up looking for a job."

More and more I'm wishing he left with Abby's parents.

And since all I need to make things work with Maggie is money, more and more I'm wishing he didn't put these ideas in my head.

But one thing I know for sure is Robert is looking to cash in and there's no way I'm letting him take advantage of Gus. "When are you heading back to school?" I ask.

"Ready to be rid of me?" he asks.

We're both thinking about that night a few weeks ago when he overheard me say I was.

I turn and face him, squaring my shoulders. "I'm just not sure this is where you belong."

He raises one eyebrow. "But you do?"

I shrug and we stare at each other.

Robert picks up the shovel and shoves it in the ground, uprooting the old, dead plants. "I guess we'll see," he says.

Another thing I know for sure? It's past time for Robert to go.

21

I can't move. Or speak.

Jimmy looks at the tombstone and then looks at the paper in his hand, trying to find the problem.

"It's spelled right," I finally manage to say.

I drop down next to Leonard Trudeau's grave and watch them permanently attach a tombstone that has Gus's name on it to a concrete footing that was under a thin layer of dirt. It should take longer than it does but within ten minutes, Jimmy and his helper are loading up and driving out of the orchard.

Looking at the tombstone I feel my eyes tear up, but it's not possible to mourn a man I didn't know. Because the man I thought of as Gus is obviously not Gus.

Something inside snaps and I jump up and race to the golf cart. Who is the guy I've spent almost every day with?

It has to be someone who knows this place, knows the history—someone who knew Gus when Gus was still alive.

But how would he get away with this?

He never goes to town. No one ever comes here . . . except Betty. But I've never seen Betty. Only heard about her.

And all of those people that worked on the house were from Alexandria. No one local.

Mr. Blackwell's words come back to me: *Some guy from Dad's past is back in town.* And then the conversation with Mrs. Sullivan: *Your dad had a way of going after what he wanted and he made enemies along the way.*

Is that who's been here, acting like Gus? The guy from Dad's past? Maybe an enemy of his who is set on destroying him?

Mr. Blackwell said he overheard that conversation back in the middle of summer . . . around the same time Gus's tombstone said he passed away and the same time someone moved in here and pretended to be Gus. That can't be a coincidence.

I've got to get out of here. I need to talk to Mom.

Thankfully, when I pull up at the house, Gus isn't around. I head to the truck, not thinking about anything other than getting out of here, but stop.

Whoever is acting like Gus is way on the other side in section three, completely oblivious to what I've discovered, or that the tombstone has been delivered and installed days earlier than he expected, but his ignorance won't last forever. This is my only chance.

I race up the stairs to the small apartment and push open the door, thankful it's unlocked. If he's the one threatening Mom, I don't want him to know he's been found out yet.

It looks just like it did last time I was here so I move to the desk against the far wall and dig through the papers on top. Most of them are invoices for the work that's been done to the house. I need to call Detective Hill and tell him there's an imposter living here, spending the real Gus's money.

I look at every piece of paper and find nothing but the bills.

Who is this guy? There's not a shred of information here on anyone but Gus and this house.

Moving to the drawers, I dig through each and every one. In the bottom drawer, I pull out a thick manila folder. Dropping it on the top of the desk, I open it and scan through what's inside.

It's pages and pages of information on Dad's business . . . blueprints, inventory, employees, financial reports. There are copies of the EPA complaints and list after list of wells Louisiana Frac worked on, the landowners who owned the wells, everything.

Then I run across a letter from William Cooper on his company's letterhead. It's handwritten and short, consisting of only a few lines:

Received the plans you sent. Everything looks good. Hopefully, it won't be long until the Feds show up. It'll be an open and shut case. And then we can move forward.

I gather up everything I can put my hands on, anything that shows this guy isn't who he says he is, and that there's a really good chance he set Dad up . . . along with help from Mr. Cooper . . . and shove it into a plastic bag. Then I take a quick look at the surface of the desk, hoping everything looks like it did when I walked in.

I'm halfway to the truck when I see Gus pull up on the tractor.

Not Gus.

He hops off and walks toward me just like the world isn't falling apart right now.

"Did you get finished?" he asks.

I shake my head and force myself not to look at the bag in my hand. I have to act normal so I can get out of here. "I'm going to have to call it a day. I'm not feeling well. There's something going around at school and I'm scared I got it."

His face shows concern and I want to punch him. If he was concerned about me, he wouldn't have lied to me.

"Oh, yeah, sure. Get on home then. I came back to tell you we were shutting it down early today," he says.

I take a deep breath and concentrate on not running full out to the truck. He stands in the yard and watches me pull away, giving me one last wave before I'm out of sight.

Noah—Summer of 1999

"Where are we going?" I ask Maggie. We're in Abby's car again and I just picked Maggie up. It's the first time I've left the orchard since that night with Nate. It's been a rough couple of days and I'm glad to be getting away. Thankfully only her sister was home so I didn't have to sit through another awkward conversation with her dad or worry her mom was mentally cleaning up behind me.

"A movie. There's a new one out that looks really cute. And I'm dying for a huge box of popcorn."

I'm about to try to talk her into the scary one I saw advertised just as I notice the cop behind me. Before I can check my speed, he throws his lights and sirens on.

"Shit," I say.

Maggie tenses in the seat next to me. "What's wrong?" she asks.

"I have no idea."

I pull over and we're quiet while we wait for the officer to approach the car. I roll down the window.

"License, registration, and insurance," he says behind mirrored glasses.

"Yes, sir," I answer, then dig out my wallet for my license while Maggie goes through the glove box for the other forms he's requested.

We hand everything over and he takes them back to the patrol car.

"Why do you think he pulled us over?" she asks.

I shrug. "I don't know. I wasn't speeding. Maybe there's a taillight out or something."

It takes him forever to come back to the car but when he does I know this is more than a normal traffic stop.

His hand rests on the gun in his holster and I brace myself for what's coming. "I'm going to need you both to exit the vehicle and put your hands on the hood of the car."

"What!" Maggie says loudly from the passenger seat. I can tell she's about to argue with him so I turn to her and say, "Let's just do what he says."

We both get out of the car and I notice there are two more patrol cars pulled up behind his. This is not good.

I put my hands on the hood and look across the car at Maggie doing the same thing. We're on the main drag in town and I know probably every person passing by notices her.

By the look on her face, she knows this, too.

An officer from one of the other patrol cars gets out with his K9 dog and I'm stunned. Why would they need a drug dog at this stop?

The officer lets the dog loose in the car and it goes nuts almost immediately. I drop my head on the hood.

"What does that mean?" Maggie asks.

I mumble, "He found something in the car."

"What did he find?" she asks.

I look up, searching her face, and she's totally clueless. I'd forgotten what different worlds we come from.

"Drugs."

"Drugs!" she yells. "Why would that dog find drugs in the car?"

The officer who pulled us over comes close to me and jerks me up, pulling both of my arms behind me. "You have the right to remain silent. . . ."

"Wait! Wait! What are you doing?" Maggie screams from the other side of the car just as the officer slaps the cuffs around my wrists.

"Anything you say can and will be used against you in a court of law. . . ."

I'm fucking freaking out on the inside but trying to remain calm on the outside for Maggie. "Maggie, it's okay. There's been a mistake. Don't worry." But then I notice the other cop moving toward her, cuffs dangling from his fingers. "Wait, what are you doing?" I ask him across the hood.

The cop behind me continues with the Miranda warning while I watch the other cop pull Maggie's arms behind her, thankfully more gently than mine were.

But Maggie doesn't remain calm. She panics and starts fighting him, screaming, "Why are you doing this? We haven't done anything wrong!"

I turn and look at the cop behind me, taking in his name on his badge, and say, "Officer Hill, could you please tell us what we're being arrested for?"

Another cop walks up holding a large bag in a gloved hand and my stomach bottoms out. "Son, we found this under the passenger seat. We've got you both on possession and with the large amount, we've got you on intent to distribute as well."

I can feel the color drain from my face. Maggie looks wild. Her hair has come loose from her ponytail and the officer is having to physically restrain her.

"That's not ours. I swear to God that is not ours," I say.

Officer Hill pulls me to his waiting patrol car and says, "That's what they all say."

I've been waiting alone in a small white room for a long time. My left wrist is still cuffed but the other end is attached to a metal loop in the center of the table. The last time I saw Maggie she was being shoved into one of the other patrol cars, screaming my name while tears streamed down her face.

I feel like I could vomit.

Finally, two guys, both in button-down shirts and khakis, come in the room and I sit up straight. This isn't the first time I've been in this situation.

They both sit down in front of me and we stare at each other for a long minute.

"I'm Detective Gaines and this is Detective Broward. So, you understand the K9 found a substantial amount of drugs in the car you were operating?"

"Yes, sir." I've also learned from experience not to say a damn word more than necessary even though protests of innocence are bursting to come out. Why were drugs in Abby's car? I've been waiting for the moment Nate tries to get me back for humiliating him and I can't help but think this is it.

"And the car you were operating is registered to Abby Trudeau, who is deceased?" Detective Gaines asks.

"Yes, sir."

They both wait a moment, hoping for more from me but they won't get it.

"Do you have permission to drive Mrs. Trudeau's vehicle?"

"Yes, sir." God, I hope Gus backs me on this. He let me drive it without hesitation the first time I took it out but I didn't ask this time. I just assumed he'd be okay with it.

The two men look at one another and then to me. Detective Gaines says, "Okay, well, we're trying to contact Mr. Trudeau but we aren't having much luck."

Silence. But inside I'm freaking out at what they will tell Gus and if Gus will defend me or believe what they claim.

"The passenger in the vehicle is a Margaret Ann Everett?" It seems all questions will be asked by Detective Gaines while Detective Broward just stares at me.

"Yes, sir."

"And what is your relationship to Miss Everett?"

"Friend."

"Just a friend?"

"Yes, sir."

Silence.

"Want to tell us what was in the bag the K9 found?"

"I have no idea what was in that bag since it's not mine," I say. Both men strike an overly surprised expression but mine remains the same.

"Oh! It's not yours?" Detective Broward asks.

"No, sir."

Again they look at each other. "So it must be Miss Everett's?"

This gets a reaction out of me. "No! She has nothing to do with this. Nothing at all."

Detective Broward leans forward with a smug expression now that he's found my weak spot. "So you say the drugs aren't yours. And you say the drugs aren't hers. And the owner of the car is deceased. So, Noah, tell me . . . what are we supposed to believe?"

Silence. It's not my job to tell them what to believe. The best I can do is say as little as possible.

Detective Broward says, "I wonder how Miss Everett is going to fare in lockup? We don't have a big facility here and no place to separate men from women. I sure hope she's going to be okay."

I grit my teeth, absolutely refusing to give in to this. I know he can say whatever he wants no matter if it's truthful or not.

Detective Gaines leans forward now so both are as close to me as they can get with the table between us. "You know, we really don't need an answer from you. The drugs were found in your possession. It's a slam dunk. You can stay silent on this matter for the rest of your life but it won't change the outcome for you. Especially since we pulled your record. You're no stranger to trouble, are you, Noah?"

Fuck. I drop my head to the table. I'm so screwed.

"Now, the only thing up for debate is if Miss Everett was in on it with you or just an innocent bystander who was in the wrong car, at the wrong time, with the wrong boy."

I've been set up. There's no other explanation. Someone, probably Nate, wants me gone and now I'm gone.

There's nothing left for me to say except, "I want a lawyer."

22

I screech to a halt in front of Aunt Lucinda's house, barely putting the truck in park before jumping out of the driver's seat.

Mom's in the kitchen and it looks like she just got off a call.

"Owen, what's going on?" she asks when she sees my expression.

"Some guys delivered a headstone and I went with them to take it to that small cemetery and when they unwrapped it, it had Gus's name on it. So I don't know if the real Gus is dead or what but the guy living there isn't the real Gus."

"Hold on, hold on," she says. "You're not making any sense."

"Then listen to what I'm saying!" I shout but then feel instantly bad when I see her flinch. In a calmer voice I say, "The guy I've been working for, the guy living in that house, is not Gus Trudeau. I don't know who he is but I think he has something to do with Dad. I found pages and pages in his desk about Louisiana Frac and the people that work there and financial records."

Aunt Lucinda comes into the kitchen and I can tell she's heard every word. "What's going on?" she asks.

I don't want to talk about this with her so I look at Mom and say, "Come with me. Let's go somewhere we can talk."

Aunt Lucinda holds her hands out as if that's all it would take to stop us from leaving. "Might as well talk here. Anything affecting you is bound to affect me!"

I can't do this with her here. Can't say the things I need to say. We need to get out of this house. I turn back to Mom and say, "I need you to come with me. Right now."

The look on my face must convince her because she gets up from the table and grabs her phone and purse. "Okay, let's go."

"Wait . . . where are you going?" Aunt Lucinda says as she follows us out. I ignore her and latch on to Mom's arm, propelling her out of the house faster than she would have gone on her own.

We're in the truck when she finally says, "You're scaring me. Where are we going?"

I glance at the clock on the dash. It's already four thirty. With all that happened today, I almost forgot about the meeting with Dad. "There's a restaurant not far from here."

Putting the truck in drive, we pull away from the curb and head to the next town over. He may have only wanted to see me but he's getting us both, for better or worse.

And maybe what I have in the manila folder will be all he needs to set everything straight.

I drive in circles for about ten minutes. I know Mom is confused by the way she watches out of the window then looks at me like I've lost it, but I know Detective Hill has someone watching the house and I need to make sure we're not being followed.

Traffic is light and it takes no time to get there. I rode out this way a few days ago just to make sure I wouldn't have any trouble finding it.

The parking lot is about halfway full, mostly work trucks with drilling company logos on the doors.

"All of that just to come here?" she asks.

I haven't told her who I'm expecting just in case I'm wrong. There's no reason for us both to be disappointed.

"Let's go get a table," I say.

We find an empty booth against the back wall and wait. It's just now five so hopefully there's no chance we missed him.

The only thing I worry about now is if he won't come in if he sees Mom at the table with me. The background music plays old country, which seems to fit the crowd, and I tense up every time the door opens.

"Owen, please tell me what happened at Gus's this afternoon. I'm worried about you."

A waitress shows up at the table, pad and pen poised to take my order. "Afternoon, sweetie, what can I get you?"

I glance at the plastic menu. She's not going to like us sitting here, taking up space, without ordering anything, but I feel like I could puke. "Mom, what do you want?"

She looks like she's not well, either. "Uh, how about a glass of sweet tea. And maybe just a BLT sandwich."

"Same," I say and the waitress moves away from the table.

"Owen, talk to me," she pleads.

"Gus isn't Gus."

Mom runs a hand through her hair. "You keep saying that. What does that mean?"

I tell her again but slower and in more detail about what happened this afternoon. She falls back against the booth and looks shocked. "Gus is dead?"

Her eyes fill with tears and I hand her a few napkins from the dispenser.

"I guess. I mean, why else would someone put a tombstone with his name and date he died in the graveyard?"

Mom covers her face and I glance around the room. People at the tables near us have stopped talking and are watching what's going down at our table.

She wipes her face and pulls herself together. "Then who have you been working for?" she asks.

I throw my hands up. "I don't know. That's why I'm freaking out."

Mom keeps wiping at her eyes and the rough napkin has irritated her skin, making it look bright red.

"And there's something else, but please don't get mad."

She looks at me. "What is it?" she whispers. We're both wondering how much more she can take.

"I heard from Dad."

She's instantly pissed. "What!" she yells, and now everyone in the room is looking at us.

Mom notices we're causing a scene and leans closer to me and says in a quiet, but sharp, voice, "You better spill it. And I mean everything."

Since the letter has been burned into my memory, I recite it for her.

"I got a note the day before you showed up at Sutton's. It said, 'Hope things are going well at school. Just checking in on you. Thanksgiving break is coming up so you'll be home soon. Found a new place right outside of town called Frank's. Best burger around. They run a special on Wednesday nights. Maybe when you're in town during your break, we can check it out. It would be a great place to have dinner with your dad.'"

She scans the room, looking like she's ready to pounce on him the second he shows his face. But he's still not here.

"Why wouldn't you tell me this earlier?" she asks. I can tell I'm in deep shit with her.

"I'm sorry. I didn't know what to do. And you were hiding things, too. About the threats."

Her head drops in her hands and she lets out a strangled-sounding moan.

How did we get here? Like this?

I watch the door, then look at her, and back and forth.

The waitress stops at our table, depositing our drinks. "Food will be out shortly," she says before walking away.

Mom and I wait.

And wait.

The food comes and we both pick at it, neither of us having any appetite.

"He's not coming, Owen. He took the money and is long gone," she says when the waitress clears our mostly full plates.

"But he said it would be a great place for us to eat together. He mentioned Thanksgiving break specifically. And the special on Wednesdays. Why would he write that if he didn't plan on being here?"

She puts her hand over mine and sadness radiates off of her. "Let's get out of here and go talk to Detective Hill. Tell him what you found out this afternoon and then you and I are going to have a long-overdue conversation."

Mom is digging in her purse for money to pay the check when I see him.

"Oh shit," I mumble.

She looks up and says, "Language, Owen."

"It's him," I whisper.

Mom sits up and scans the front door, but I'm looking at the side door near the bathrooms.

"Where?" she squeaks.

"Look to your right," I say and I hear all of the air leave her lungs when she sees who I'm talking about. Her hands shake and all the color drains from her face.

"Do you know who that is?" I ask, because the man claiming to be Gus just walked in and it looks like Mom recognizes him.

Her hand flies to her mouth and she lets out a strangled sound.

Fake Gus notices us and he looks as shocked as Mom does.

I look between the two of them as he moves slowly toward the table, but they only have eyes for each other. He's a few feet away when I ask, "Mom, I don't understand. Who is he?"

"The note said this was a great place to have dinner with your dad," she says, almost to herself like she's working out a puzzle. "Owen, this is Noah Bennett."

Noah—Summer of 1999

The court-appointed lawyer sits across from me in the same small white room, my arm still cuffed to the center of the table.

"What do they have on me other than finding the drugs in the car I was driving?" I ask him.

Mr. Mitchell flips through some papers in front of him. "It doesn't look good, Noah. They pulled you over because there was an anonymous tip with that make, model, and plate of that car saying there's a new guy in town, trying to sell drugs to the kids here."

"Who would do that? I don't do drugs. Or sell them." This is a setup. It has to be.

He holds up a copy of one of my prior arrests that clearly disagrees with my earlier statement.

"Well, I don't do them or sell them anymore."

He shuffles through some other papers. "And then the bag with the drugs has your prints all over it."

My jaw drops open. "There's no way. No fucking way. I never touched that bag. I had no idea it was there."

I've been set up. But how did Nate do it?

"The real nail in the coffin here is your prior convictions," my lawyer says.

I knew it was only a matter of time before my past caught up with me. I'm not proud of it. I promised myself I wouldn't ever do anything that could land me in jail again.

And yet here I am.

It turns out that detective was right. I could scream from the top of my lungs that I'm innocent or stay silent until I die but I will go to jail for this.

"You've got two options at this point, Noah," Mr. Mitchell says. "First, admit to possession with intent to distribute and they'll let Maggie walk out of here immediately. That's straight from Detective Broward's mouth. They know her family and she's never been in trouble so they're willing to accept she was in the wrong place at the wrong time."

He doesn't add *with the wrong boy* but we're both thinking it.

"What's my other option?"

"We take our chances in the system. Take this case to trial. But I'll warn you, both you and Maggie will get booked into jail and you'll both be charged with possession with intent. The evidence against you is strong so I can't give you any guarantee this will end well for either of you."

This is no choice. The case against me *is* strong—looks like someone made sure of that—and with a public defender who believes this is a loser case, and no money to hire anyone better, I can't take Maggie down with me.

"I'll take the first option with one condition."

"Noah, you don't have to decide—"

"I'm not letting her get dragged through this with me."

Mr. Mitchell looks unsure but there's no way I'm getting out of this. Whoever built this trap didn't leave anything to chance—drugs, in my possession, in a bag with my fingerprints, with my priors.

"My one condition—I want a few minutes with Maggie. To say good-bye."

He looks resigned when he says, "I'll see what I can do." Mr. Mitchell leaves me alone and I drop my head on the table. These last two months were too good to be true. No way it could last. Not with my luck.

An hour later, a soft knock on the door has me lifting my head and turning toward it.

The sight of Maggie causes all of the air to leave my lungs and I struggle to catch my breath.

She hesitates just a second or so, then throws herself at me.

I bury my face in her neck, breathing her in.

"Why is this happening?" she asks in a quiet voice. "What is going on? They're telling me that your fingerprints are all over that bag they found in the car? And that you've been arrested for drugs before. And car theft. And that you spent time in jail."

Yeah, these are the things I never wanted her to know about me.

I lean back and look at her. Tears race down her cheeks and her bottom lip trembles.

"Is it true?" she asks.

I take a deep breath and say, "My neighborhood was rough. I ran with the wrong crowd and was arrested more than once. Everything they told you is true."

The way she's looking at me is killing me. So I try to explain what it was like even though she'll never understand. "Sometimes we stole things so we could put food on the table. Sometimes we fought to stay alive. Sometimes we smoked pot or drank too much because losing yourself in that high was better than being present in real life. Sometimes we did those things because we didn't know any other way to be. Those aren't excuses . . . just how things were. Before I came here, I didn't know it could be like this. Safe. Peaceful."

My eyes never leave hers while I speak. I know I should have told her all of this weeks ago.

"But the drugs in the car aren't yours. I know they aren't. You may have done those things in your past, but you're not like that now. I know you."

I didn't think I could love her any more than I already did. When faced with the ugliness of my past, she still believes in me.

"They told me you're taking a deal. That you're saying the drugs were yours so I can walk away from this, but I'm not letting you. I'll talk to my dad. We'll get the best lawyer in town. Or in the state. You are not going to jail for something you didn't do. I won't let you."

She barely took a breath while all of that spilled out of her. I know her and she won't let this go. And I know her dad won't lift a finger to help me. This will destroy her relationship with her parents. She won't get to go off to college in a few weeks like she was planning on. Maybe if Gus was in a better place . . . but he doesn't need this any more than Maggie does. And once he hears about my past, there's no way he'll stick his neck—or his pocketbook—out for me.

There's only one thing to do.

I have to lie to her.

"The drugs in the car today were mine."

Her hands drop from my shoulders. "No, I don't believe you."

"They were. I thought I could make some quick money so I could go off to school with you in January. For my living expenses."

She wraps her arms around her stomach. "I don't believe you," she says again but this time with less conviction.

"I told you that I always find a way to screw things up."

She gets off my lap and moves across the room. Her eyes scan my face, looking for signs this is a sick joke. It is a sick joke—just not the one she's thinking it is.

"You and I come from two very different places," I say. "You need to go off to school. You need to live a life that doesn't include someone like me."

She just stares at me and it takes everything in me to keep going.

"But I want you to know this was the best summer of my life. You are the best person I know and I'm sorry I couldn't be the guy you needed me to be."

She crumbles and races to the door, banging against it so she can flee this room and get away from me.

A guard opens the door and I think she'll fly right out of here but she stops in the doorway. She looks at me one last time and says, "It was the best summer of my life, too."

And then she's gone.

I'm lying on the narrow bunk in my cell when I hear shouting from somewhere on the other side of the cinder block wall. A guard shuffles in, his hair sticking up all over the place, and unlocks my door.

"Gus Trudeau is here to see you. I've been instructed to bring you to him," the guard says.

I don't think this tiny police department sees much action so no one really knows how to handle today's events.

I follow him down the hall, back into the room I spent so many hours in earlier. Gus is waiting at the table.

He points to the guard and yells, "Get out and shut the door behind you."

And the guard does exactly what he says.

I drop down in the seat across from him but he's still standing, staring down at me. "What in the hell have you done?"

I have to look away. "They found drugs in the car. . . ."

"That's not what I'm talking about. Why in the hell did you take a deal and sign your life away before talking to me?"

He finally sits down and we stare at each other from across the table.

I'm floored. "You don't think I did it?" I ask. I would have never guessed a few months ago how important the answer to this question was.

"No. I don't."

"Did you hear about my past? The other problems I've had with the law?" There's no way he knows everything about me or he wouldn't be sitting here. He'd leave me to rot in that cell.

"Yes," he says. "But I don't believe you would put drugs in Abby's car. And I don't think you would have them anywhere near Maggie Everett. I don't think you're the same guy who got in all that trouble before."

I hang my head and I hear Gus let out a loud breath. "Why didn't you wait for me to get here?"

I look back at him. "Whoever did this to me . . . framed me . . . covered every angle. *My prints* are on the bag! How would that even be possible? There's no way out of this for me and there's no way I was going to let them drag Maggie down with me. Not even for one minute."

"This isn't right. Nothing about this is right."

I haven't cried yet, I couldn't in front of Maggie, and I wasn't going to give the satisfaction to the cops for them to see me fall apart, but I can't hold it back anymore in front of Gus.

"I'm scared," I whisper.

Gus puts his hand over mine. "You may have already set your course, but let me see what I can do to make it a bit smoother sailing."

Gus managed the impossible. I don't know if he sold his soul to the devil or gave over his fortune, but instead of going to a regular state prison, I was sent to a federal facility in Florida that caters more to white-collar crimes.

I've been here almost a month now. The days are long and the nights are longer. If I try hard enough, sometimes at night, once lights are out and everything is quiet, I imagine I'm back in the Preacher Woods with Maggie, sitting under our tree, whispering our secrets.

But morning always comes and with it the harsh reality of where I am and that I'll be here for a long time.

I'm in the small library, working through some math problems for the algebra class I'm taking. One of the perks of this place is the program to help people like me have half a chance once we get out. Right now I'm taking basic college classes but I'm working my way toward a business degree. But I'm not going to stop with just an undergraduate degree. I won't stop until I have my MBA—just like I told Maggie's dad I would.

Just thinking her name makes my skin feel too tight for my body. She tried to call me when I first got here but I refused each call. Then the letters started coming in but I sent them back unopened. There's no way for us to work. Once I know one thing about her, I'll want to know everything, and that will make my time harder here. She should be off at school now, hopefully enjoying her classes and the freedom that she would get being away from her parents. I need her to forget about me and move on with her life.

I speak to Gus every Sunday night on the phone and we exchange letters regularly but I never ask about her and he doesn't offer any information. One day I'll ask Gus to tell me everything he knows, but not yet. I can't handle it yet.

I was afraid of what would happen to Gus once I was gone, and felt even worse that I couldn't keep my word to Abby about looking out for him, but him trying to figure out how to get me out of here early seems to give him purpose. I'm pretty sure he's written a letter to everyone in the states of Louisiana and Florida and probably the federal government as well.

A guard, one of the cooler ones here, sticks his head inside the small library and says, "Noah, you have a call." He pauses a second, then adds, "It's Gus, not the girl."

I walk to the bank of phones and pick up the one the guard indicates is for me.

"Hey, Gus, what's going on?" I ask. It's not our normal time to talk so I'm worried about why he's calling.

"Noah, I've been debating whether or not to call you but I finally decided this was something you needed to know. It's about Maggie."

"What is it? Is she okay?" My heart feels like it's going to thump right out of my chest.

"She got married last night. Small ceremony at her parents' house."

"Married!" I shout into the phone. She's supposed to be off at school, not walking down the aisle.

"She came to see me just before the ceremony. She's pregnant."

Gripping the phone tighter, I lean against the wall and slide down until I'm crouched on the floor. "Is it mine?" We always used protection but I know sometimes accidents still happen.

"Yeah."

"Oh my God. She kept trying to call me. To write me. To tell me."

My mind is spinning. Maggie is pregnant. With my baby. But she's married now.

"Who? Who did she marry?"

He takes a deep breath and says, "Robert."

I explode off the floor. "Robert! She married Robert?" I start to pace but get yanked back by the cord of the phone. The guard is eyeing me from across the room, trying to determine if I'm going to be a problem.

"After you left, she kept coming here. To check on me I guess. This is what I've pieced together after talking to her and to Robert. Robert said he would find her curled up on the couch in the Preacher Woods house, crying."

This is killing me. Hearing this is killing me.

"She was coming out here every day, spending hours sitting in that house. I guess she and Robert became friends. She found out she was pregnant and was terrified of telling her parents. Terrified of what they would do. Robert offered to tell them it was his and to marry her. I know it's 1999 but around here it might as well be 1955."

I feel sick. "She tried to tell me. She called me and wrote me letters and I ignored her. I thought I was doing the right thing."

"Don't be too hard on yourself. It's what I would have done, too," Gus says.

He's quiet on the other line for a moment. "In January, they're going to move to Baton Rouge so Robert can finish school. Not sure if she'll take any classes or not since the baby is due in the spring. After he finishes, they'll come back here and Robert plans to work for her dad."

I slam my fist into the wall and pain radiates down my arm. I cut myself off from her so she could go to school. Have a normal life.

And then I remember what Robert said to me when we were cleaning up the family cemetery—with Gus behind me and Maggie at my side, I could be the king of that little pissant town. But it seems like he'll be the king now.

"It's still your child, Noah. No matter who she's married to," Gus says.

"I'm in jail for being a drug dealer. What kind of father is that?"

"We both know you shouldn't be there. Don't give up hope. I'm still working on things. I've talked to the officer who got the tip and pulled you over—Officer Hill. He's helping me out. Says this case hasn't felt right from the beginning."

I hear what he's saying but nothing breaks through the thought that Maggie's having my baby.

"Did she seem happy?" I ask.

"She seemed relieved to have a solution. A way to keep the baby, your baby, and raise it in a way where she could give it everything it needed."

"Make me a promise, Gus. Watch out for them . . . Maggie and the baby."

"We're going to get you out of there. And then you can come back here and watch out for them yourself."

I rub a hand across my face. "I wouldn't do that to them. They'll both be better off without someone like me in their life. They both deserve better than anything I could offer them."

23

Noah approaches the table and he looks from me to Mom and back again several times.

Our waitress walks past us and pats Noah on the shoulder. "You need a table, hon, or will you be sitting with them?" she asks.

His mouth opens but no words come out.

Mom looks like she's on the verge of losing it. She whispers, "He'll sit here." Then she looks at Noah and says, "Please sit here."

"Mom," I whisper. I just told her this is the guy who's been impersonating Gus and she invites him to sit down.

He grabs a nearby chair and puts it at the end of the booth and sits. He takes a deep breath and starts to say something but I stop him.

"I don't understand what's going on," I say, looking at Mom. "You know him?"

She nods and a tear slides down her cheek. "Tell him about the letter you got at school."

I look between her and the guy she called Noah and back at her. "I don't understand."

She reaches across the table and her hand covers mine. "I know, and

I'll explain everything, but tell Noah about the letter you got from . . . your dad."

I recite the letter once more and Noah's head drops back and he looks at the ceiling.

"Someone needs to tell me what's going on," I grit out.

Mom takes a deep breath and says, "I was eighteen when I got pregnant with you and I married your dad—Robert—shortly after I found out. But Robert isn't your biological father." She pauses a moment and adds, "Noah is."

I'm shaking my head in disbelief but she nods, letting me know it's the truth. I look at Noah and then back at her. "This can't be true. How can this be true? Why are you saying this?"

Mom turns to Noah and asks, "Did you know? Did Gus tell you?" she asks.

He nods. "He told me. Just after your wedding."

Mom's hands cover her face and she falls apart in the seat across from me.

Why would she ask him that? Why did she think there was a chance he didn't know?

I have so many questions firing in my head that I can't focus on what's happening. Everything is blurry and I feel sick. I turn and look at Noah again. "I know why *we're* here. My dad sent me a letter and led me to believe he would be here, too. But why are *you* here?"

"I got a letter. A couple of days ago . . . when Pippa showed up with lunch. I've been . . . looking into Louisiana Frac and what happened there." He looks at Mom, then me, and back to Mom. "I was told if I showed up here, I'd find what I was looking for."

I scan the room like I'm still expecting him to walk through the door.

Mom uncovers her face and crosses her arms in front of her, like she's trying to physically hold herself together. "It seems like Robert set this up. For whatever reason, he wanted the two of you to meet."

I look at Noah. "If you knew I was your son, why did you lie to me? You told me your name was Gus Trudeau."

He closes his eyes and his shoulders slump. Then he looks at me and says, "Owen, I'm sorry. I didn't know what to say to you when you showed up. No one knew I was back. Well, no one but Detective Hill." He rubs a hand over his face and takes another deep breath. "No one was expecting anyone but Gus to be out there. And then you showed up and my heart almost stopped," he says. "I've only known you through pictures and from a distance but to see you just steps away was more than I was prepared for. And once I met you, I didn't want to let you go. So I offered you the job. Anything to keep you coming back. I knew once you found out who I really was you would hate me, but I was starved for contact with you."

My stomach drops. Every emotion possible is coursing through me: rage, sadness, confusion, and I can't process it. I have questions about everything. Questions about where he's been, why he was a secret, questions about Gus and my dad.

Mom's head drops and she sobs. Big, heartbreaking sobs. His hand reaches out for her and she hesitates a second or so before putting her hand in his.

I don't understand any of this. I can't process any of this.

"I was . . . working on something . . . something that I needed to handle before I came looking for you and your mom," he says.

I slide out of the booth and almost fall on the floor. "I need to go. I can't be here right now."

Mom's head comes up and she cries out, "Owen," but I'm looking around the restaurant and the most painful moment in my life is happening in front of a roomful of strangers and it's more than I can handle.

"I need some time," I say.

Mom starts to get up. "Do you want me to come with you?"

I shake my head and she sits back down. "Can you give her a ride home?" I ask Noah.

"Of course," he answers.

I'm almost to the door when our waitress approaches me.

"Sweetie, I got something for you. Didn't realize it was you until your mama said your name just now. I was expecting you to be alone."

She hands me a brown envelope.

"What's this?" I ask.

She shrugs. "No idea, honey, but it was worth a hundred bucks for me to hold on to it for you. He said you'd be here tonight. I thought he was a damn fool but here you are."

I look back at Mom and Noah and their heads are bent and they're talking to each other.

Pushing through the door, I wait until I'm in the truck before I open the envelope. I'm not surprised when I see a letter from Dad.

O—

    I haven't done many things in my life I'm proud of but I like to think I had a part in raising you into the strong, independent man you are and I'm proud of that.

    Whether you ever believe it or not, I love you and I love your mom. I never meant to leave you the way I did. I never meant for things to get so out of control. My only hope is that you'll forgive me one day. I wish I could have been a better man for you both.

    —Dad

Noah—Spring of 2000

"Noah, you have some visitors."

The guard lets me into one of the meeting rooms and Gus and the officer who pulled me over are sitting at the table in the middle of the room.

Gus gets up when he sees me and comes around the side of the table, embracing me in a hug.

"How you holding up?" he asks.

"Okay," I answer. I don't think Gus has been back to town in Lake Cane once since he showed up at the police station to see me, but he's been here three times in the six months I've been in jail.

I look at Officer Hill across the table and try to settle the anger that's running through me. I know he's been helping Gus try to prove my innocence, but I can't get over he was the one who started all of this when he pulled me over.

"So it must be something big if Officer Hill decided to come with you."

Gus says, "It's Detective Hill now. He was promoted last month."

I nod at him. "Congratulations." I hope it at least sounded like I meant it.

Detective Hill nods and says, "We've been talking to the judge who accepted your guilty plea. We're trying to get him to throw out your plea and reopen the case. There are a couple of things in your favor. I think we all agree the anonymous tip we received was a little too perfect. While I was on duty, I got a call from the station telling me to be on the lookout for your car and that you were a suspected drug dealer. That's all they gave me. So when I spotted you, I pulled you over and found the drugs, and the rest you know."

"So what changed?"

Detective Hill glances at Gus then back to me. "After Gus called me for the tenth time to tell me how bad I screwed up by arresting you . . ."

"*Screwed up* wasn't the word I used," Gus says.

Detective Hill bobs his head and rolls his eyes. "Yes, I remember your exact words. Anyway, I pulled everything we had on your case. I didn't realize the tip stated who you were, what car you were driving, where you left from, where you were going, who was in the car, and what type of drugs you had in the car."

I'm trying to wrap my head around what he's saying. "So I'm guessing that's not common?"

Detective Hill shakes his head. "No. I've never seen a tip that specific."

A tiny seed of hope sprouts inside of me. "So the judge is considering reopening my case?"

Detective Hill frowns. "You still have two very big things against you. You signed a piece of paper saying you did what you were accused of."

I nod. "What the second thing?"

"The most damning piece of evidence was that plastic bag the drugs were in. Your prints were all over it. I'm the one who handled that bag and I'm the one who checked it into evidence. They took the prints off of it in front of me and ran it through the system. That's how your priors showed up. I can't explain that. Can you?"

I lean back in the chair. "No. I have no idea why my prints were there. I mean, I never touched that bag."

Gus finally joins the conversation. "It was one of those regular ziplock bags that everyone has in their kitchen. Do you remember handling one?"

And then a memory comes flooding back. That night at Gus's when Robert asked me to stay for a drink. The first time I had been around him since that night he overheard what I said to Maggie's friend about being ready for him to leave. He knocked over that jar of shells. Asked me to get a ziplock bag to put them in. I left the bag on the counter.

I tell them what I remember and Gus lets out a string of curses.

"But why would Robert set you up?" Detective Hill asks.

I shrug. "Toward the end of the summer, Robert and I weren't seeing eye to eye on a few things. I all but told him he needed to leave and not come back. I guess he was trying to get rid of me just like I was trying to get rid of him."

"I thought it was Robert. Knew in my gut it was Robert. I should have never let him and Abby's parents in the front door," Gus says.

"No, Gus. I should have waited to talk to you before taking the deal. But I was so scared for Maggie. Scared her life would be ruined just because she was with me. This is on me. I took the deal. I signed the paper saying I did it."

We sit at the table, each of us lost in our thoughts.

"So there's no way to prove that bag was the one I handled in your kitchen that night."

It's not a question. The one thing I wasn't wrong about was whoever set me up did a really good job.

"And so the guy who sent me here is now married to my girl and will raise my kid." I squeeze my eyes closed. "He stole my life."

24

The only place I could think to go was Pippa's house. She takes one look at me and pulls me to the backyard since her entire family is inside.

There's a giant hammock hanging between two big oak trees and we stop right next to it.

"Hop in," she says.

When we were young, we would spend hours in this hammock. My arm goes around her while her head rests on my chest. We fit together perfectly.

"What happened?" she asks.

Everything rushes out of me. She listens quietly, absorbing every word.

"Owen, I don't even know what to say," she says once I finish.

"I don't know what I'm supposed to think."

"Do you know why they kept it a secret? Or where he's been? Or what the papers you found on his desk mean? And I can't believe your dad basically led you to him."

All of her questions are the same questions that have been bouncing around in my head. Plus a couple dozen more.

"You should go talk to your mom."

"I can't. Not right now."

"Just think about what she's going through. That picture of her with that tree's coordinates and the necklace, those were all about her and Noah, not her and your dad. And all that stuff Noah told you when you thought he was Gus about how hard your dad fell for your mom . . . he was talking about himself. I mean, my God, Owen, this is so crazy."

"Tell me about it."

Pippa laces her fingers through mine. "You need to go talk to him. And your mom. At least hear what they have to say."

I squeeze her hand. "Will you come with me?"

"No. This is something that you need to do. But I'll be here when you're done." She moves to get out of the hammock and when I try to stop her, she says, "I'll be right back. I've got something for you."

She's gone a few minutes and when I see her, I can tell she's hiding something behind her back. Pippa stands in front of the hammock then swings her matching wooden sword around, stopping it right in front of me.

"I found mine," she says.

I sit up in the hammock and she touches the tip to my left shoulder, then my right.

"Sir Owen Foster, I name you the Emperor of Dogwood Drive."

My hands go to her waist and I pull her on top of me. She laughs and the sword falls to the ground. I kiss her slow and long, our hands moving over each other, our feet tangling together.

"Tell me about your day. Tell me something normal," I say while kissing her neck.

She squirms when I get to a sensitive spot. "My mom made me take a pie to Seth's. She said I needed to check on him and his leg. I got there right before he was leaving to go to his aunt and uncle's house for dinner."

Okay so maybe hearing this isn't what I had in mind.

"How'd that go?" I ask, tucking her head against my shoulder while my fingers play with the ends of her hair.

I feel her shrug. "Fine. Mad he's out for the playoffs."

"Yeah, a knee injury is hard to bounce back from."

"His hand is worse than his knee I think. I've never seen a burn that bad."

I pull away so I can look at her. "Burn? He told me he tried to catch himself when his knee gave out and fractured it."

Pippa's forehead scrunches up. "When I got there, he was in the kitchen rewrapping his hand. It was definitely a burn."

I lie back down next to her, moving her so she's halfway on top of me. "That's weird. I wonder why he would lie about that?"

We sway back and forth for a few minutes and then I'm sitting up again, bringing Pippa with me.

"What?" she asks.

"He got hurt the night of the game, right? The same night someone threw a flaming bottle through our front window."

Pippa's hand flies to cover her mouth. "No," she mumbles.

I pull my phone out of my back pocket and call Detective Hill. He answers on the first ring.

"Hey, I think I know who's been threatening us."

Noah—Spring of 2011

I sit in a chair facing a long table full of people who will decide my fate. Gus and Detective Chris Hill are sitting against the far wall and I know I wouldn't have half a chance of getting through this without either of them. Both of them drove down to speak on my behalf at my first parole hearing.

If they vote in my favor, I'll walk out of this building after almost eleven years here.

"We've gone through your file," says a man in the middle. "You've been a model inmate, you've gotten an undergraduate degree and an MBA through the program here."

I'm holding my breath, waiting for the *but . . .*

He continues, "It is our recommendation that you be released as we believe you are capable of being a contributing member of society and not a danger to yourself or anyone else."

Gus lets out a cheer from across the room. The relief is so great I feel like I might pass out.

It takes an hour or so to process my release, but Gus and Chris are waiting for me on the other side of the fence.

Gus pulls me in close and hugs me.

"This calls for a celebration," Chris says. "Steaks are on me."

Even though it's only four in the afternoon, we sit down at the nicest restaurant we can find in this small Florida town and we order damn near everything on the menu.

"What are you going to do now that you're out?" Chris asks.

I push my food around on my plate. "Owen will start school at

Sutton's in the fall so I think I'll go to New Orleans. I'd like to be close to him."

I was surprised when Gus told me Maggie pushed for Owen to go off to school. While it seems like Robert has been a good dad to him, I'm glad they won't be under the same roof anymore.

"You need to tell him who you are. You need to tell Maggie the truth," Gus says. It's the same thing Gus has said for the last couple of years.

"And I told you not until I can show her proof of my innocence," I say. "Or proof of what Robert is."

Gus's land has been leased for years with the same oil and gas company out of Houston and he's got a great relationship with the guy who runs the company, William Cooper. When Maggie told Gus she was looking around for a good school, Gus knew William's son was about to start at Sutton's, so he recommended it to Maggie. William made sure his son and Owen would be roommates.

William is also helping us get an inside look at Robert's business, Louisiana Frac, since they frack all the wells he drills in that area. I'm just waiting for the moment he makes a mistake, and I'll be there to catch him when he does.

"So I guess if I want to see you, I'll have to go to New Orleans," Gus mumbles.

"I'm giving you another reason to leave that orchard. And what would I do if I went back there? Live in that tiny apartment with you and watch your house rot?"

"Jail made you a smart-ass," he says.

"No, jail made me determined."

25

I called Mom's cell phone and she told me she was at the house in the Preacher Woods with Noah. When I pull up, they're sitting side by side on the top step of the old front porch.

Was it just a couple of hours ago that I found out the truth of who he really is?

"Shit. I don't know if I can do this," I say to myself.

I get out of the truck and stop a few feet from them. Before they have a chance to speak, I say, "Dad . . . Robert . . . left me a letter at that diner."

I dig it out of my back pocket and hand it to Mom. She reads it while Noah looks over her shoulder and I notice the copper pendant with the coordinates of the tree behind me hanging from a chain around her neck.

"You had someone bid on Mom's things at the auction," I say. It's not a question.

Noah frowns. "Yes, but I didn't know you planned to get this necklace back for her until it was all over. I'm sorry you didn't get to buy it. Detective Hill had mentioned several things your mom seemed upset to part with so I decided to get them back for her."

I wave him off like it's no big deal but I'm not sure how I feel about it. I was so pissed when that guy outbid me and I really wanted to be the one who got Mom something, but Noah beat me to it.

Mom folds the letter and hands it back to me. "I'm glad he was able to tell you good-bye."

I nod. "I want you . . . both of you . . . to tell me everything."

Noah stands up and motions for me to join him. "Come inside. We'll sit and tell you the whole story."

I follow them in and Mom and Noah sit on the couch while I take the small chair. There's a small space between them and they keep glancing at each other like they still can't believe they're in the same room together.

Mom fiddles with the necklace while Noah takes a deep breath and says, "I guess the best place to start is when I arrived here by bus at the beginning of the summer in 1999 . . ."

It takes a while to get caught up and I'm more confused than ever. Mainly because I get it. I get why he lied to Mom in the police station and why he ignored her calls and letters when she was trying to tell him she was pregnant. And then hearing her side about how scared she was and how old-fashioned her parents were. She knew they would try to force her to give me up or get rid of me if she was single. And she wasn't confident in her ability to take care of me on her own without any money or support from her parents. It's easy to forget that they were my age when all of this happened. But then Robert stepped in and she clung to that solution.

"Why didn't you contact me when you got out?" I ask Noah.

He runs his hands through his hair. It's been a long day for all of us and it's starting to show on his face. "It's not because I didn't want to. Things were hard when I got out, I'm not going to lie. I'd been in jail for a long time and I didn't know how to handle everything. I was angry at what happened. For losing you, your mom. Gus told me you were at Sutton's so I moved to New Orleans. Took me a while to find a job. Even though I had the education, no one wants to hire someone who's been in jail. Got an apartment, tried to rebuild my life in a place where I could be nearest to you even if you didn't know me. If your school had an event, I was there. I came to all of your lacrosse games," he says, then looks at Mom. "I saw you there, too, from a distance. And you both looked happy. I didn't want to come in and ruin that. At that time, I couldn't prove Robert was anything other than what everyone thought he was."

Mom's hand finds his and they're holding on to each other and it's hard for me to look at them like this. I can't wrap my head around it.

I get up from the chair and stand by the window, looking out into the darkness. "So what made you come back here when you did, especially since I was still at Sutton's?"

"William Cooper was hearing from some vendors that they were having trouble collecting from Robert. And then got wind of some of the environmental issues at some of the wells. So we started looking into his business. It didn't take long to figure out what he was up to and it wasn't good. It's not very noble but I've been waiting for a chance to prove who he really is for years. I came back so that I could figure out what was going on and how bad it was, but I was shocked when I got here to find Gus was sick. Really sick. He used to visit me all the time when I was in New Orleans, but I hadn't seen him for several months. He'd kept making excuses why he couldn't come down. I should've known something was going on."

I turn around and I can tell by Mom's expression that she's already heard this part, but it still upsets her hearing it.

"He refused to go to the doctor so I called one in from Alexandria. It was one helluva home visit but turns out it was too late to do anything for him even if I could get him to agree to treatments. He had cancer and it had spread all over."

I shouldn't feel the loss of someone I didn't know, but I do.

Noah wipes a hand across his face. "I moved into that small apartment with him and stayed there until he was gone, which was just a few weeks later. He didn't want a funeral or even a death notice to run in the paper. All he wanted was to be put in the ground, next to Abby, so that's what I did."

"When was this?" I ask.

"Gus passed away on June sixteenth. After he was gone, I was more determined than ever to find out what Robert was doing. I was still in contact with William and there were more and more signs that Robert wasn't just a bad businessman but probably a thief as well. I told him I wanted to wait until you left for school before we did anything."

Moving back to the chair, I say, "He knew you were back. Mr. Blackwell overheard him on the phone with someone and he was pissed you were back in town."

"I'm not surprised. Even back then, he was one step ahead of me."

Mom looks shell-shocked. Throughout all of this she always kept her composure, but this is obviously more than she can manage.

Noah gets back to where he left off. "So once you were back at school, we got to work. We gathered as much as we could on how he was running things and were just about ready to turn everything over to the Feds but he skipped town on us. He must have gotten wind of what was happening and left before he could be taken in."

"So he did steal all of that money." It's not a question but Noah answers it anyway.

"Yes. He did."

"Why has Mr. Cooper been in town so much lately? And why did he buy our house?"

"William is buying Louisiana Frac. It'll take some time but hopefully he can get it close to where it once was. He bought the house so he'll have somewhere to stay when he's in town but he'll hire someone to handle day-to-day operations."

Mom's head pops up. I guess this part is news to her.

Noah looks at her and says, "He'd have you back there if that's what you want. He didn't want to go public until we knew it was a sure thing. It's going to be tricky because he can't rehire everyone right away, but at least it's a start. Once the environmental stuff gets worked out he's hoping to bring more back. He's also hoping to expand the business to include other oil-field services."

I'm floored. And from Mom's expression, she is, too.

"What are you going to do now?" I ask him. "Are you staying here?"

"I might. If I do, I guess I'll finish cleaning those pecans and see if I can fetch a good price for them. Gus was good to me in every way possible so I'm thankful I can call this place home and have the means to relax and catch up on all the things I missed. And maybe if your mom wants to try her hand at being a caterer, I can get a job working for her." He looks at her. "Do you plan to stay here when this is all settled?"

"I'm not sure either," she answers in a quiet voice.

They stare at each other and I realize how weird this must be for them. If he hadn't been arrested, there's a good chance they would have gotten married since she was pregnant with me. They didn't leave each other by choice, but it's been almost eighteen years since they were together.

Noah gets up from the couch and grabs a stack of papers off the small counter near the sink. This must be something he brought with him since they weren't here earlier.

He hands them to Mom and says, "First, you need to look through these and decide what to do about it."

Her eyes get bigger and bigger as she scans through each page.

26

We ring the doorbell and it only takes a few minutes before it's answered.

"Maggie, I'm surprised to see you here," Peter Blackwell says when he opens the door. His eyes bounce from Mom to me and back again. I'm sure he's wondering why we're on his front porch this late.

"Hey, Peter. Can we come in a minute?" she asks.

"Sure, sure," he says. "Come on in."

He leads us to a room right off the foyer that looks like one of those home offices that never get used. Mr. Blackwell goes behind the desk while Mom and I sit in the two chairs in front of it.

Mr. Blackwell looks at me and says, "Owen, it's good to see you again so soon."

I nod and say, "You, too." I can't believe we're here. I can't believe we're doing this.

"Peter," Maggie says. "I know you're wondering why we're here."

His eyes are back on her. "Yeah, I have to admit this is unexpected."

Maggie takes a deep breath, then says, "I have some papers of Robert's. It looks like bank account information. Actually account info from several different banks in foreign countries. One of the accounts is in my name. But I don't know how to access it without the police finding out."

Shock is the only way to describe his expression. "So the rumors were true," he says, leaning forward on the desk. "You know where the money is."

Mom shrugs, unable to look him in the eye.

"I have to say, Maggie, this is surprising. I was one of the few who defended you but it seems like the joke is on me."

She shakes her head, staring at her hands in her lap. "I haven't always known. I just discovered these accounts recently."

"Let me get this straight. You found out where he stashed the cash and now you want it."

She shakes her head. "Not all of it. Just enough for Owen and me to start over somewhere else." She lets out a jagged breath. "I can't stay in this town. And things will get better here. I heard . . . someone . . . has plans to reopen Louisiana Frac. It won't always be so bad here. But it will be for us. I just want what's in that account with my name on it and I'll turn the rest of it in."

Mr. Blackwell leans back in his chair, his disgust for us evident. His forehead scrunches up and his eyes dart between the two of us. "So why are you here to see me?"

She hesitates a second or two then finally looks at him. "Because one of the other accounts is in your name."

"That son of a bitch," he mutters.

But before he can say anything else, Mom says, "He told me a few years ago to come to you if there was trouble. That if I ever found myself in need of anything, that you would always help me. That was the deal. I didn't understand what he meant back then but I do now. Well, I'm in trouble. I need you to help me. I need you to honor the deal."

Mr. Blackwell stands up, sending his chair flying behind him.

"If he wants me to honor the deal, he shouldn't have fucked me over the way he did! That son of a bitch could have never pulled it off on his own. He would have gone bankrupt years ago if it wasn't for me, but when he got scared, he skipped town with every last penny, leaving me with nothing. And now you're showing up here wanting me to help you?"

He's completely lost it. We hear a thumping noise coming from the hall and we all turn in that direction to see what it is.

"Is everything okay in here?"

Leaning on the crutches, hand and knee bandaged, is Seth Sullivan. He looks at me and I stare at him before dropping my gaze to the burned hand I know is hiding under that bandage. I'm not done with him yet.

"Everything's fine, Seth," he says. There's a knock on the front door and Mr. Blackwell motions for Seth to open it. He hobbles into the foyer and it's only a few seconds before Detective Hill and half a dozen uniformed officers fill the room. Noah is just a few steps behind them.

I dig my phone out of my pocket and disconnect the call that allowed Detective Hill to listen in from outside.

Detective Hill flips out his badge and says, "Peter Blackwell, you have the right to remain silent. . . ."

• • •

Peter Blackwell was stuffed into the back of a patrol car while screaming at his wife, Sheila, to get their lawyer to meet him at the police station. As Seth Sullivan stumbles between two uniformed officers to another waiting patrol car, I step close and say, "Looks like it's over now."

A few minutes later, we're standing in the driveway next to the truck, talking with Detective Hill, while the inside of the Blackwells' house is invaded with agents from every branch that were assigned to Dad's case.

"So who's going to tell Peter that Robert was the one who gave him up?" Noah asks.

The letter Noah got in the mail the other day was more than just a note saying to go to Frank's on Wednesday for the nightly special. There was a stack of papers included, the stack he shared with Mom. But it wasn't banking information like she told Mr. Blackwell. It was a list of business names, dummy corporations, and shell businesses that Robert created for the sole purpose of funneling money out of Louisiana Frac.

The list of names was long.

"I'll be happy to tell him," Detective Hill says. "But I'll have to give Owen some of the credit." He looks at me. "Not sure I would have put two and two together so fast if you hadn't called me about Seth's hand."

"I'll have to share that honor with Pippa because if it wasn't for her, I wouldn't have known Seth's hand was burned instead of fractured," I say.

Elise Sullivan's name had already come up in this investigation after that brick went through Mom's window. The brick was from the old bank building downtown that was torn down and Mrs. Sullivan was one of many who had purchased some of it, using it to build a small water feature in her backyard. Even though he knew Elise was Peter Blackwell's sister, there was no reason to suspect Elise since her business didn't seem to be impacted by Robert's theft while a few of the others on that list were.

But Seth's burned hand moved her up to a person of interest and had him checking every name on the list we got to see if any of them connected to her.

And he got a hit.

One of the fake business names was Cavaille Enterprises. Cavaille was Mr. Blackwell and Mrs. Sullivan's mother's maiden name.

Noah said Dad probably did that on purpose to make sure if he got caught, he wouldn't go down alone.

But that wasn't enough. A confession would help seal the deal and Mom stepped up to make that happen.

Mr. Blackwell wouldn't say another word once the police showed up, but Seth wasn't as quiet. He told the police he'd overheard his uncle yelling at Dad a few weeks before Dad disappeared that he was getting careless and that Mr. Blackwell wanted out, once he got his share of course. So after Dad disappeared, Seth confronted his uncle with what he heard. And since Mr. Blackwell has been taking care of Seth and his mom financially now that Mrs. Sullivan was divorced, Blackwell's money troubles became the Sullivans' money troubles, so he had no problem getting Seth to do his dirty work for him with the threats.

"Well, I better get inside. Looks like it's going to be a long night for us," Detective Hill says, then disappears into the house.

The three of us get in the truck and head back to the orchard.

• • •

I drop my phone in my back pocket and pace the length of the living room of the main house. Over the last week or so, Noah has moved a few things inside—mainly stuff for the kitchen—but this room is still empty. It's hard to believe how much has changed since I first entered this wreck of a house just a month ago.

Pippa was quiet while I caught her up on what went down tonight. Once I got it all out, she offered to come over even though it's closing in on midnight—which was huge since I know she's still a little scared of this place—or for me to come back to her house, but seeing her will have to wait until I figure out what Mom wants to do.

Leaning against the wall next to the opening that leads to the kitchen, I slide down until I'm sitting on the floor. I smell coffee and know they're sitting around the island in the next room but I can't bring myself to join them just yet. Tonight's events have left me drained. And my mind spinning. I need a little space from both of them right now.

Mom's soft voice floats out of the open doorway next to me. "Are you okay?" She's asking Noah, not me, since I'm sure she isn't aware that I'm parked out here, listening in. I pull my legs in close and rest my head on my knees.

"Owen . . . he's incredible. You did a good job raising him," Noah says.

My stomach feels like I'm on the downhill drop of a roller-coaster ride. I should get up . . . move away from the doorway . . . but I'm frozen. I'm in a strange place where I'm desperate to hear what he really thinks about me.

"There are so many things about him that remind me of you," she answers.

I do a mental inventory, thinking about him and wondering what parts of me are similar. Is it physical? Or maybe mannerisms?

"I'm surprised you didn't have any more kids," he says.

"I guess we're talking about this?" she asks.

And that's my mom. Always straight to the point.

"Yeah, I guess we are."

"We tried," she says. It's quiet inside for a minute or so then she says, "Ask me what you want to ask me."

I lean my head back against the wall knowing I shouldn't be listening in but doing it anyway. I don't think Noah is going to say anything but he finally asks, "Do you love him?"

I close my eyes and brace myself for her answer even though I don't know what I want it to be.

"I cared for him. He was there for me when I needed someone. I thought marrying him was the right thing to do. But I'm not sure I can get over the fact that I chose to be with the person who sent you to jail and kept you from us," she finishes in a soft voice.

The heels of my palms dig into my forehead as if that's all it will take to stop the thundering chaos rolling around inside my brain.

"I'm not sure I can get over the fact that I put you in the position that you had to make that choice," Noah says.

I can't take any more. I can't hear anything else. Jumping up, I turn the corner and interrupt their conversation.

"Mom, it's late. We should probably be going."

She nods, then turns back toward Noah. "Tomorrow is Thanksgiving. Do you have any plans?"

He shakes his head. "No. I don't."

"We have plenty since I don't think Elise will be showing up to pick up all the food she ordered." She looks at me, silently asking permission and I give her a small nod. "Maybe Owen and I can bring you some?"

The smile that breaks out across his face hits me in the gut. "The day I met you, you were bringing food to this house."

"I remember," is all she says.

"Only if you'll stay and eat with me," he answers, then looks at me. "Both of you."

We stare at each other for a few seconds before I finally nod and say, "I think we could do that."

27

We decided on an early dinner since we were all up late last night. I pull up in front of the big white house but instead of walking up the brick path to the front door, I move deeper into the orchard.

Even though we haven't had a traditional Thanksgiving dinner in years, since we were usually vacationing in places that didn't recognize this holiday, today is stranger than normal. I'm still trying to sort the pieces from yesterday in my head.

But knowing everything I do doesn't automatically change how I feel, and even though I agreed to this last night I don't think I can walk into that house . . . the same house that only weeks ago looked like it was being taken over by this orchard . . . and act like we're a big happy family.

"You okay?" Noah says from somewhere behind me.

I turn around and he's about ten feet away, watching me with concern on his face. Moments like this I wish I still knew him as Gus. Wish I could talk to him like I did before and not wonder what things would have been like if he hadn't gone to jail all those years ago.

I shrug and he nods.

We continue walking down the lane between two rows of trees. Neither of us speaks for a long time.

Finally, I say, "I feel guilty. I've had a good life. But having that life came at the expense of your freedom."

Noah stops and so do I. "That's all I ever wanted for you. Everything that happened—none of it is your fault. I made my own choices and the only thing I regret is missing out on all those years with you."

I swallow. It's still hard to think about all that time Noah was in jail while I was clueless of who he was.

"There's something I want to run by you before I mention it to your mom," he says. "I know neither of you is happy at your aunt's house."

That's an understatement.

I nod and we both turn and start back toward the house.

"What if I stay in the apartment in the barn and you and your mom move into the main house?" he says. "It'll give y'all a place to go. We can fix up the preacher's house to give you and your friends a spot to hang out. What do you think?"

"That would be . . . okay," I say. Truthfully, it will be weird, but I love it out here. And it would be nice not to live at Lucinda's.

"You think she'll go for it?" he asks and I can see he's a little worried if she'd actually agree to this.

"She'll be difficult at first but I think we can probably talk her into it. Especially after she spends today in your gigantic kitchen."

He laughs. "Maybe I can win her over with a new set of pots and pans."

"And one of those fancy mixers."

We're almost back to the house when I ask, "Why do you think Dad wanted us to meet? Was he even sure you knew I was your son?"

He's hard to read sometimes and this is one of them. "Your mom told him that Gus knew the truth and he was sure that Gus would have told me, so yeah, he knew I knew who you were. And the only thing I can think of is no matter what, he wanted you taken care of and he knew I could do that now. So I think he did it for you. And honestly, I've been racking my brain to figure out why he sent that list of names that led us to Blackwell and it wouldn't surprise me if he did that for you, too. It would be just like him to somehow be clued in on what's going on here and if he got wind of the threats, that was the quickest way to shut it down." Noah lets out a laugh. "It would also be just like him to stick it to Blackwell as a parting 'screw you,' but I'll guess we'll never know."

I hate to admit it but his second guess is probably the right one.

Noah looks over my shoulder and smiles. I turn around to see what's got his attention and spot a black Suburban pull in the driveway.

Jack jumps out of the passenger seat and I've never been happier to see my friend. He throws an arm around me the second he's close enough.

"What are you doing here?" I ask.

"Came to see you. Heard it's been a helluva of a few days," Jack says.

Noah moves to the other side of the vehicle and greets Mr. Cooper.

"Damn, I'm glad you're here," I say.

We follow Mr. Cooper and Noah up the front walk and into the house. "You may regret it because I'm not leaving here until I get you back. So you may want to sleep with one eye open."

I won't ruin his good time by telling him I'll take whatever he dishes out.

Noah holds the front door open for us and I'm the last to go through. I stop next to him and we study each other.

"This is hard for me," I say. "Separating what I know and what I feel. Even though I hate what he did, in my mind I still think of him as my dad. I wish I could just flip a switch but I can't."

Six months later . . .

"*The tassel goes* on the right side. Then you move it over to the left side after you get your diploma," Mom says as she straightens my cap while Noah takes pictures of us from every angle.

We're on the front porch waiting for Pippa to show up. Mom wanted to take some pictures of us here before we go to the school for the ceremony.

It's been a long and bumpy six months as we've tried to find our new normal, but finally we seem to have figured it out.

I'm not going to lie, it's hard growing up believing your life to be one thing only to find out it's not that at all. I wasn't the only one struggling, though. Mom and Noah have had some rough patches, too. They pretty much had to start at the beginning and get to know each other all over again.

But we're in a better place now and the overwhelming feelings that sucked out so much of me in the beginning—the anger, the sadness, the guilt—have faded. I'm not saying I don't have moments where they flood back through me, but it happens less and less these days.

We're all living in the main house together now and Mom and Noah are planning a small wedding under their tree. I'm really happy for them. If any two people deserve to be together, it's them. All they're waiting for is the paperwork to clear for Mom's divorce. She's claiming abandonment. It may be the greatest mystery this town has ever seen—where is Robert Foster? Since the police are no closer to finding him than they were when he first disappeared, no one believes he will come forward to dispute her claim.

Peter Blackwell didn't get so lucky. He took a plea deal for a shortened sentence. His house, and everything in it, was seized just like ours was along with any money they found, so the amount given back for restitution was a little higher when all was said and done. In exchange for testifying against his uncle, Seth Sullivan was given probation, and he and his mom moved away to somewhere in Texas, I think.

The town embraced the reopening of Louisiana Frac, and hopefully in the next few years it will be back to where it was, but Mom's catering business was a harder sell. At first, no one wanted to hire her, but people seem to be coming around. She's teaching Noah how to bake and he's terrible at it but it doesn't stop him from trying. My friend Ray is coming to stay the first week of summer and he's promised to give Noah some pointers.

Pippa finally arrives and she flies up the front porch steps, nearly knocking me over when she throws her arms around me. "We did it, O!"

I pull her in tight and lift her off the ground. This has been the best part of the last six months; the main reason I haven't completely fallen apart.

Since I miss New Orleans and Pippa has always dreamed of living there, we're headed to Tulane in the fall where I'll once again room with Jack.

I'm already plotting revenge for his latest prank, which involved him uploading a video to the school website of my humiliating moves at our eighth-grade dance with St. Ann's.

Noah takes more pictures of the two of us, then Pippa grabs the camera from him.

"Now let's get a family picture of you three," she says, pushing us together.

Noah looks at me, gauging how I feel about that. He was true to his word when he said he wouldn't push and even though I still deep down think of Robert as my dad, that part is getting smaller and smaller every day while my feelings for Noah get stronger and stronger.

I pull Mom to my side and then look at Noah. "You going to join us . . ." I ask. And then add the part I know he's been dying to hear. ". . . Dad?"

His smile is huge and his eyes look a little watery but he holds it together. "I'd love to," he says, moving to my side. He puts his arm around my shoulder and squeezes me tight.

The three us of us look at Pippa and smile for the camera.

Acknowledgments

I started writing The Lying Woods in the summer of 2015, and this book has truly been a labor of love. Some days I thought I would never be able to finish it and other days my fingers were flying across the keyboard. But certainly, this book would not be what it is without the love and support of so many. I always get a little sentimental with this part, so please bear with me!

Always, thank you to my agent, Sarah Davies, for believing in me and my work.

A huge shout-out to my editor, Laura Schreiber. Four books (and counting!) together! Thank you for pushing me to make each draft better than the last.

And to the entire team at Hyperion, thank you for making me feel like part of the family.

To my critique partners and dear friends, Elle Cosimano and Megan Miranda, thank you, thank you, thank you for everything.

Thank you to my friends who read messy first drafts and listened to every possible scenario I could think of for this book—Elizabeth Pippin, Aimee Ballard, Missy Huckabay, Lisa Stewart, Christy Poole, Pam Dethloff, and Lori Mays. Thank you to Stacee Evans for reading this when I needed a fresh set of eyes on it. And thank you, Stacee and Rachel Patrick, for the continued support on social media. I love y'all and I'm determined we will meet in real life soon! And a special thank-you to Nicole Cotter. I don't think I would have gotten the ending right without you.

A special shout-out to the winner of the St. Mark's "name a

character" auction: William Cooper Allen—thanks for letting me use your name!

To all my friends who answered questions about the oil and gas business, fraud, embezzlement, funerals, headstones, etc. . . . thank you! Any and all mistakes made and liberties taken are fully on me.

To my family, thank you for making me feel like a rock star.

To Miller, Ross, and Archer, thank you for being the best sons a mother could ask for. I'm so proud of all three of you. To my husband, Dean, thank you for being my biggest supporter. I couldn't do this without you.

In every one of my books, there is always a slice of my personal life included, and *The Lying Woods* is no exception. My husband has custom-harvested pecans in North Louisiana for years, and my favorite part is watching him shake trees. I loved being able to share this entire process and hope you think it is as cool as I do.